Unknown Soldier

Britt Pitre

DEVIANT PIXEL MEDIA

ATLANTA

Deviant Pixel Media
2316 Elmwood Cir SE
Atlanta, GA 30339

The text type was set in Adobe Garamond Pro
Book designed by Bryce Alarcone

Image Attributions
Cover: Composite of *Auf Vorposten in Ypern,* photographer unknown Public Domain, and *The Equatorial Jungle,* Henri Rousseau 1909 Public Domain

Back: *Passion Flowers with Three Hummingbirds,* Martin Johnson Heade circa 1875 Public Domain

Human Trade: *School Children Doing Exams Inside a Classroom,* 1940 Public Domain, provided by State Library of Queensland

Sleeper Cell: *"Shep", D-Day,* Victor Alfred Lundy 1944 Library of Congress No Known Restrictions on Publication

Butterflies: © Britt Pitre

Dead Pixels: www.pixabay.com sunset_369498, user ckirner Creative Commons Deed CC0 Public Domain

Living Dead: *The Chickahominy – Sumners Upper Bridge,* William McIlvaine 1862 Public Domain

Child of War: *Neugeborenes,* Egon Schiele 1910 Public Domain

Revenant: **U.S.** Army Photo Public Domain

The End: Composite of *A Castle Tower [Caernarvon Castle],* John Sell Cotman and *Trees Near the Greta River,* John Sell Cotman Public Domain

ISBN-10: 1-945273-00-3
ISBN-13: 978-1-945273-00-1

To Josh

HUMAN TRADE

001

December 2, 1954.

There were rumors that the Army was buying children.

And Charles was banking on it.

His son sat in the back seat of the family's haggard Buick, staring out of the window at nothing. Harriet, his wife, sobbed softly in the passenger seat. Charles tried not to drive too quickly – the timing of their arrival had to be perfect. But it was hard to ease off the pedal. He lit his third cigarette of the morning, took a long puff, and then let it dangle from his lips as he watched his headlights plow through the darkness ahead. After a quick glance at his watch, he slowed even more. It was still only six-thirty in the morning.

The first time Charles heard the rumor, he was at his favorite watering hole. He had chuckled and dismissed it. "Sounds like something they would do," he had said. But even that first time, there was something about the idea that slowly started to claw its way into the back of his brain.

He was a veteran himself, drafted at eighteen, serving at the tail end of World War Two in forty-four and forty-five. His son was conceived when Charles was twenty, prompting a quick marriage to Harriet in forty-six.

Things had been good at first – great even. They didn't want for anything, and most importantly, Charles didn't have to work. At the time, he lied and told Harriet that he received regular payments from the Army. But the truth was that he had a dirty little secret from the war that had set them up in those early years.

Charles was one of the fortunate soldiers who never saw any real action – a fact that perfectly suited his penchant for laziness. While others were closing in on Berlin in the spring of forty-five, he was frequenting cafés in a small town along the French border. The clientele was always the same, and things were always quiet, which is exactly why one particular stranger stuck out like a sore thumb – at least to Charles.

The stranger just appeared one afternoon, sitting at a corner table alone with a bowl of soup and a brandy. His back was partially turned to the rest of the café, and he seemed very absorbed by the activity of eating, never once glancing up at anyone. When he was done, he left cash on the table and walked out.

In the days that followed, Charles spotted the man again several times at the café. His demeanor was always the same, like he was trying to avoid eye contact. And the more Charles observed, the more he saw how deliberate the man's actions were. The stranger would never completely turn his back to everyone, but would certainly position himself in a way that didn't invite conversation.

When the man spoke to the waitresses, his French was thick and stilted – the accent of a foreigner. While Charles didn't speak French or German, he had heard other native Germans speaking French in the border town. In fact, it wasn't uncommon. But unlike all the others, this man clearly had something to hide.

Charles had watched intently one day as the stranger took out his wallet to pay. It was stuffed with money, mostly large notes, which only supported Charles' sneaking suspicion. As the man got up and left that day, Charles followed him, not about to miss an opportunity.

When he forced his way into the man's small apartment, gun drawn, the stranger's eyes widened. "No!" the man held his hands up and begged in broken English with an unmistakable German accent. "I give you money. Please."

Charles followed him warily up to his bedroom where the stranger unlocked a small briefcase and produced an incredible wad of cash – some French notes, some German. Charles scanned the bedroom, wondering what else the man was hiding.

Charles shoved the barrel of his pistol into the man's side and pointed at a locked chest at the foot of the bed. With shaky hands, the man fished a key out of his nightstand drawer, then went over and unlocked the chest. It was filled with clothes. Charles shoved him down on the bed and began tossing clothes on the floor, hoping to find something more interesting. And he did – only it didn't have any value.

Laid out very neatly at the bottom of the chest was a crisp, pressed SS uniform. For a moment, the man just stared at Charles as dust motes hung in the rays of the afternoon sun. Charles was never really sure why he did it, but he raised his gun and blew a hole right through the man's head. He grabbed the briefcase and never thought about it again.

Fearing discovery, Charles didn't dare spend a penny of it while he was still in Europe. But he most certainly did once he returned to the states. Back then, his Buick was new and shiny.

Now it just rattled along the road. Charles had never bothered to get a job and one brand new thing after another had slowly depleted his supply of stolen Nazi money. Gambling in the back room of the bar hadn't helped. Charles now found himself face to face with the want ads, and he didn't like it.

The second time he heard the rumor, he rolled the thought around in his head for a long time before dismissing it again. But the third time he heard it, from yet another source, he started to believe. He wanted to believe.

Charles began to casually ask about it, or to butt into conversations when he thought he heard anything even remotely related. The rumor was that the Army was going into local schools and administering some kind of assessment under the guise of a standardized test. Only the Army wasn't the Army – they were posing as a public agency. The parents of the kids who scored exceptionally well were supposedly paid visits and asked to sell their kids into service and keep quiet about it – only some of them obviously weren't.

At first, Charles couldn't get any further than the basic rumor. It was always something that had happened to a friend of a friend of a friend. When he would jokingly ask what he'd have to do to sell his own son, the response was always along the lines of having to wait until his son's school was 'visited.'

After so many dead ends, he really was starting to believe that it was just an urban legend. No one could name a single person to whom it had happened, or a school where the test had been administered, or even the name of the agency. That is until one day he spotted a well-dressed man sitting alone at the bar who stood out like a sore thumb – much in the same way that another stranger once had.

Charles had politely asked if it was okay to sit next to the man. It was obvious that he was the sort of guy who was two drinks in and 'didn't want to talk,' but was actually like a dam about to burst. Charles had spent his entire adult life in bars and could instantly recognize the type. It was the way the man sipped his drink and occasionally glanced over like he wanted to say something.

Charles finally broke the ice with small talk, and the other man seemed relieved. Discussion quickly shifted to family, and the man explained that his wife had recently passed away. Charles figured that must be it – he had uncovered the man's secret, and it wasn't what he was looking for.

He was just about to get up when a more interesting tidbit came along.

"Ever since the wife passed it's just been me and my boy," the man had said. "It's just… it's just not fair to him not to have someone at home while I'm at work. Fucking boss doesn't let me off until eight sometimes. It's just not fair to him." The man just kept shaking his head.

"Where is he now?" Charles asked the obvious question as he eyed his impromptu companion sipping his drink.

The man looked over at Charles and hesitated before responding. "He's at home." The words didn't sound genuine. Charles couldn't be sure, but it also seemed like the man was holding tears back.

Charles lit up a cigarette, timing his next move. He took a couple of drags, then leaned back on the bar stool. "I heard about something you might want to look into." The man glanced over at Charles. "How old is your boy?"

"Nine."

"Sounds about the right age," Charles took a well-timed puff. "I heard the Army is enlisting boys that age and paying."

The man's eyes got wide, and he slammed his mostly empty drink down, rattling the ice. "This is a test isn't it – to see if I'll talk?"

"What you're talking about?" Charles hid his own surprise.

"You're with the VPB, aren't you?" the man asked.

"What's the VPB?" Charles continued to feign ignorance.

"I don't know what you're talking about." The man stood up, threw some cash on the bar and left in a hurry. Not once did he look back at Charles.

It wasn't a lot to go on, but the acronym gave Charles a place to start. He scoured the phone book, looked at every single ad in the paper and asked everyone at the bar. The whole affair had become a conspiracy that he needed to unravel.

Finally he decided to call directory assistance and ask for the VPB. It took a little bit of searching, but finally the operator asked: "The Vocational Placement Board?"

"Yes," Charles hoped he was right.

There was a pause on the other end of the line, like the operator had made a mistake. "That's an unlisted number sir. Do you want me to connect you?"

Charles panicked and hung up. He wasn't prepared to speak directly to the source, but now he had enough information to continue his investigation. But he quickly found that the Vocational Placement Board was shrouded in mystery. With the exception of his conversation with the operator, it was like it didn't exist. He even spent an entire day going over deeds for commercial property – but apparently they rented or owned under a completely different name. He hoped that perhaps he would stumble across a building owned by the Army or Department of Defense, but the only ones he found were very clearly military installations. One day he called a nearby Army base from a pay phone and asked to be connected to the VPB. The person on the other end of the line denied ever hearing of it.

He was just about to give up again when more information came from an unexpected source. It was one in the afternoon on Halloween day when Harriet had phoned the local bar to ask him to pick up a very particular type of candy for the trick or treaters. He checked at two stores in the immediate vicinity, but they were all out, which necessitated a short drive into the city.

Inside another store, arms laden with the sensational candy of the year, Charles happened to walk past two housewives deep in conversation.

"No, when he passed the test at school, he had to go take another one," one wife said to the other. Charles skidded to a halt and pretended to browse.

"I'm still upset that Johnny didn't even pass the first one," a blonde shook her head. "His head's full of rocks, just like his father."

"At least you didn't spend the whole day in a waiting room just for them to tell you it was a waste of time." The first housewife gesticulated madly. "They told me not to be upset – only one in five hundred passes anyway."

"What's the test for anyway?" the blonde asked.

The other wife shrugged. "Beats the hell outta me. They just said that if he passed he would be placed on a career track."

"Are you talking about the Vocational Placement Board?" Charles finally asked.

The two wives nodded. "Did your son take the test too?"

"Yeah," Charles pretended to be confused. "But you know, I couldn't find the testing center."

It was all downhill from there. Not only did he get the location of the VPB, but the wives had commiserated with him, describing the initial testing process and the subsequent letter they had received in the mail that asked them to bring their sons in for further testing.

Through the month of November, Charles slowly began hatching a plan. Harriet thought that he was crazy. She had told him that the VPB was a figment of his imagination and also admonished him for even thinking of sending their son into the Army for money. But Charles wasn't terribly concerned – he knew that she didn't have much choice but to follow his lead.

He first located the building that the housewives had described, then drove past it on several occasions. It was totally nondescript and the lone sign at the front of the building only displayed the address. The first visit had been mid-afternoon and all seemed quiet, but the small parking lot was full. Charles drove past twice more around seven-thirty in the morning. Both times he watched as a dozen parents went inside with their sons.

Right after Thanksgiving, he started calling every school in a fifty mile radius to inquire about the strange test his son had recently taken. Some had no clue what he was talking about; others stated that it had been months since the test had been given. But finally he found one that had administered it in early November.

That was what had led up to him sitting in the car with his sobbing wife and a silent son who had no clue where his father was carting him off to on a school day. Charles wasn't sure if Harriet was crying because of the prospect of losing their son or if she truly thought that he had gone off the deep end and that her quietly unhappy marriage was spiraling downward.

To Charles, it didn't matter either way. He had grown accustomed to his daily trips to the bar and had no intention of getting a job. Surely his son could pass the test – he was on the honor roll and frequently corrected his own father. If anyone could pass, it was him.

Charles sighed deeply as the building finally came into view, and he pulled into the parking lot. He had rehearsed his plan a million times while pacing the kitchen floor, going through a whole pack of cigarettes at a time. They got out of the car and walked through the front door like they belonged there. As soon as Harriet saw that they were entering a very real building, the tears dried up, and she seemed more curious than anything.

The receptionist looked up and greeted them. A few childless parents already sat in the waiting area reading magazines. Charles leaned over the desk and spoke in a low voice, explaining that he had received a letter in the mail but had lost it after he jotted down the address in his planner. The receptionist politely asked for their son's name, and flipped through an appointment book.

"You sure you have the right day?" she asked.

"I think so," Charles nodded. "But like I said, I don't have the letter anymore." After more searching, the receptionist went to the back and returned with a man who looked important. He began to question Charles about the missing letter and his son, to which Charles responded very calmly, even explaining where his son went to school. After a lot of deliberation, the man finally told the receptionist to add the boy to the schedule.

"And your name sir?" the man asked.

"Charles Vincent," he said, confident that his plan was working.

"Okay, have a seat," the man smiled. "Someone will be out to get him soon."

Once their son was taken back, Charles and Harriet sat in silence, as did all of the other parents. They went through the motions as if their son were simply at a doctor's appointment. Harriet read a magazine while Charles tapped his foot impatiently.

After an hour went by, the important looking man returned to the waiting area. "Mr. Vincent, may I see you?"

Charles slowly stood up, wondering what the issue was. No other parents had been called back. After the man shut the door to the waiting room, Charles followed him down a drab hallway with tiled floors and wood paneling on the walls.

The man showed Charles into a private office and shut the door. Another man was inside, standing off to the side silently. It was impossible to fathom his expression from behind the sunglasses he wore.

"Mr. Vincent," the important man said just as he sat behind the desk. "How did you find us?"

"What do you mean?" Charles was genuinely surprised.

"We've questioned your son. Drop the act."

Charles' jaw dropped.

"We know where he really goes to school and that he never took the test. But you seem to know all about us. Care to explain?"

"I uh..." Charles thought for a second. He couldn't help but notice that the man in sunglasses had moved to block the door. Then he decided that the best option was to just tell the truth. All of it, except for the fact that he murdered a Nazi.

Charles did embellish the story a bit, garnishing his own investigative abilities and making his conversation with the housewives less happenstance. Then he begged for his son to be given a chance.

"So let me get this straight," the important man began, "you heard a rumor about us and wanted to sell your own son into service so badly that you researched us for months and then showed up here?"

Charles nodded. "Please, just give him a chance. He's a real smart boy." And after a moment passed – "I really need the money," he decided to throw in.

A Cheshire cat-like grin spread across the important man's face. "You know, twenty-eight is still young, not too old for service by a long shot. We have a very special place for men like yourself."

"Me?" Charles sat up, surprised.

The man nodded. "Your family will be well taken care of, and you will well compensated. Only thing is, I can't let you go back out there. You'd be leaving immediately for the base."

"You want me to leave my family for money?" Charles asked.

The man nodded.

"I can do that," Charles said quietly, staring down at the floor. "What's next?"

The man smiled again. He stood up and patted Charles on the back. "Just sign the papers."

***

The important looking man was happy that Charles had willingly accepted the proposition. At that point, he no longer had a choice anyway – but his acceptance of the deal just proved what kind of person he really was.

A man who would sell out his own family for money would kill for money too. But little did the important man know – Charles already had.

Sleeper Cell

002

Sometime near the present.

Inside of a perfect suburban home. Quaint. White picket fence. Fragmented dreams. Eyes moving back and forth under closed eyelids. R.E.M. sleep.

Orion lay in bed next to his wife, dreaming as he always did. In his mind, tight fitting military gear draped his lean body in camouflage. The heat of an oppressive, far off jungle was suffocating. He placed one foot in front of the other, slowly, deliberately, just as he had been trained. He followed orders as though they were hard wired into his brain. There were no questions, only routine.

He seemed to recall in some distant memory that he wasn't a normal rank and file soldier. There was something special about him and his training. Whatever it was tugged at the fringes of his mind, wanting to be remembered but remaining shrouded by the haze of his dreamscape.

In the dream, Orion's eyes darted side to side rapidly as he searched the path ahead. And in reality, eyes moved back and forth under closed eyelids. It was like this every night; he was forced to return to duty even though he had been discharged long ago. A recurring dream had become a personal hell. He had considered seeing a doctor about this.

Only the dream wasn't actually a recurring one. It was different every night, each one a continuation of the last. He was afraid to see a doctor. Not because of what might be wrong with him, but because he feared what might happen if the dreams stopped. War was a different reality, and once immersed, it was hard to return home. During his career, Orion had often had friends who were due for leave, or even done with their service. But they never went home. Just kept coming back. Until one day they died, then a part of them finally went home. It kept things simple.

Orion too had become a slave to that simplicity. One foot after the other, just as he was trained. Eyes darting back and forth. He craved his orders which granted him the ability to not have to think. When he was awake, it was easy to drift through the day, uncaring, knowing that everything would be decided for him as soon as fell asleep. There was a certain freedom in service, and he was frightened to have that taken away. So he never went to see a doctor.

Rivulets of sweat ran down his skin under the heavy gear, but he didn't dare remove anything even though it was always hot in the jungle of his dreams. The black carbon armor under his camo was there to save his life from flying bullets. Occasionally he had a fleeting thought of undressing, of feeling relatively cool air brush across his bare skin. And why not? It was a dream after all. No reason to fear flying bullets. But the armor was part of the routine, part of his orders. Part of his world. The one he needed.

As his feet obeyed his orders, moving forward through the underbrush, a sudden rush of adrenaline pierced the veil of blind routine – an instinctual response to an unseen threat. Something was about to happen, although Orion didn't yet know what. His knuckles grew white as he clutched his gun more tightly without even being aware of it.

Then there was a rustling in the underbrush, something racing towards him with unnatural speed. He looked down and saw the greenish form of a snake, but it was a blur in motion. Before he even knew what he was doing, he had already jumped back several feet and was drawing a machete from its sheath. The momentum caused him to fall, but his training kept his upper body on task. The machete sliced through the air.

In the real world, Orion fell out of bed. But he didn't wake. Nor did his wife.

Sparks flew as the machete made contact with the metallic scales of the snake. Orion bolted upright into a sitting position, preparing for a second strike. He quickly saw that he had already severed the snake's central control relay, its head barely clinging to the body. Beneath metal scales, a mess of tangled wires and steel lay exposed in the machete's wake. He had known it wasn't real the moment he'd heard it. It was too fast to be a living thing. The snake's mouth was frozen agape, prepared to strike. Sharpened metal fangs gleamed in the daylight.

Orion leaned down, taking a closer look at the eyes. Beneath their glass exterior, he could see two small lenses spinning, trying to focus. He lifted his machete and brought it down on the head again, sending it flying into a thick cluster of vines. He jumped up to his feet and surveyed the surrounding jungle, sensing unseen eyes watching him. He reached down and snatched his gun off of the ground.

In his bedroom, his body obeyed commands from the dream word, first moving into a standing position, then digging through a drawer in his nightstand until his hand closed over a pistol. All the while, pupils moved back and forth under closed eyelids.

The jungle seemed to close in all around him as he crept forward at a snail's pace, ever so careful not to make a sound. The enemy, wherever they were, had been watching him through glass eyes. He had to kill them first. He steadied his breathing, as he was trained, and remembered that it was only a dream.

The walls of a darkened hallway penned him in as he slowly made his way forward, eyes shut, oblivious to the real world. Dim light spilled through an open door at the end of the hallway. It came from inside of the kitchen where there were sounds of movement – something small.

Orion, gun at the ready, approached the open door of a dilapidated shanty in the distance. Wild vegetation had almost swallowed it whole, its dull brown walls barely visible through layer upon layer of leaves. The windows were broken, vines creeping inside. Orion was guessing that the snake's operator was inside. He thought about lobbing a grenade at the small structure from a distance. Otherwise, anyone on the inside would have complete advantage over him as he stepped through the only doorway.

But he knew that the grenade wasn't prudent. The silencer on his gun was better for hiding his position. Grenades were meant for killing clusters of men, not to be wasted on one or two in hiding. He stopped and listened, sure that he had just heard something come from inside.

There was more rustling from the kitchen, the clink of one glass against another. The dim light continued to spill out into the hallway, along with the quiet hum of an open refrigerator. A real one.

Orion paused right outside the door to the shanty. It hung open, the top hinge long broken. He strained to hear more signs of movement, but there were none. The hairs on the back of his neck prickled with a sixth sense that told him that there was definitely someone inside.

He had to go in. And the enemy would shoot at him the second he passed the threshold. The trick was to be smarter, to get the other soldier to pull the trigger with the gun aimed at the wrong spot. Then pray there weren't two.

A feeling a serenity washed over him. Perfect calm. In his dreams, this was just a game. No reason to stress or allow his heart rate to go up. No matter what, he'd wake up in his suburban home. Quaint. White picket fence.

He suddenly lunged forward, spinning in midair. There was indeed an enemy soldier sitting in the corner of the littered room, gun trained on the doorway. He was flush with the door, impossible to see from the outside without stepping in. As Orion predicted, he instantly took the shot. But Orion was already falling to the floor, dropping below the fatal trajectory of screaming steel. Before he even hit the ground, Orion had spun his barrel into position and took a shot.

The soldier's brains shot out of the back of his head, painting the surrounding walls and feeding the hungry vines that dipped into the room. Orion didn't see the impact because he was already scanning the rest of room for the next threat. But there were none. Just the one dead soldier in the corner, the heat of his spilt brain matter eclipsed by heat of the jungle.

Orion climbed to his feet as he surveyed his kill. Hit right between the eyes. There was that nagging memory again, that Orion was special. But before he could begin to piece it together, the thought had escaped him.

As he stood in the jungle in full gear, he also stood in a darkened kitchen in his underwear, a wisp of smoke rising from the barrel of a pistol that he held in his hand. A scream from the master bedroom echoed in the jungle. It was his wife.

Two worlds collapsed into one as he opened sleepy eyes to the sight of a falling glass of milk. It moved impossibly slow, a byproduct of senses made sluggish by the chemicals of sleep.

There was something else too – a tiny body also falling to the floor. Brains spattered inside the bright refrigerator. His wife screamed again as the glass of milk shattered on the floor, its contents intermingling with a pool of blood that was spreading across the clean white slate of the floor.

His ten year old daughter lay on the floor in a crumpled heap, one leg bent at an odd angle. Her hair was a tangled mess of blood, brains and shards of bone. He didn't bother to check to see if she was still alive; he knew she wasn't.

"Orion?" his wife called from the bedroom, her voice laced with primal fear. From where he stood in the kitchen, he turned his head and looked through the doorway into the empty hall. His wife's head emerged from the open bedroom door, and they stared at each other.

"Orion?" his wife asked again, this time in a whisper. He felt the pistol slip from his sweating hand and clatter on the kitchen floor. All he could do was stare at his wife as she exited the bedroom and crept down the hallway toward him.

He looked at the lifeless heap of flesh that used to be his daughter. Then his gaze slowly turned back to his wife who was now halfway to the kitchen. "Don't come in here," he said, his own voice foreign to his ears.

"What's wrong?" his wife asked, craning her neck to see into the kitchen.

A tear was forming in the corner of Orion's eye, and a knot in his throat made it difficult to talk. "Please…" the word escaped as a low hiss that hung in the air. "Don't come in here."

But she did anyway.

003

Dull gray light filtered through a mostly shuttered window. Orion sat alone in a stark white room that reeked of medical disinfectant. He wore a simple white cloth gown that was seared around the edges from over-drying. Everything was austere and devoid of color, so unlike the jungle of his dreams.

He still couldn't believe where he was, nor what had happened. In court he had asked for a death sentence. He had told everyone that nothing was wrong with him – he was a perfectly sane man who had killed his own daughter. But his lawyer had other plans. The doctors said it was PTSD from the war, among other things. Called him crazy. Drove him to the place where he now sat. White Sands Mental Health Institute. Even though he just wanted to die.

But that wasn't totally true. He felt like he should want to die, but he was actually just numb to everything. It didn't matter that he was in a nut house, or that his wife probably didn't love him anymore. All he had to do was go through the motions of living while he was awake. Anything to get back to the war.

The door creaked open, and a nurse entered. A tall woman, in her mid-thirties perhaps, with long black hair. She looked like she didn't belong there either. Her face was too beautiful, her hands too manicured as they wrapped around a clipboard. She crossed the room, her long legs visible below the hem of a short dress. Then a more unpleasant sight entered the room. Dr. Serapis.

Orion had met this man before. He was much older, his face a web of fine wrinkles. As the good doctor took a seat across from Orion, a fresh wave of disinfectant and mothballs assailed his nostrils.

"Good morning," Dr. Serapis smiled. He seemed overly enthusiastic about his work. It wasn't like forced bedside manner, but rather a dark curiosity. Orion imagined that the other man tried to seem like a normal doctor, but his bizarre interest was only thinly veiled. Especially to someone who wasn't crazy – like Orion.

"Did you sleep alright?" the doctor asked, waiting for a small nod from Orion. "More dreams?"

"Always," Orion said in a monotone voice. He didn't want to dedicate any more energy to this exercise in futility than he had to.

"That's exactly what your file says." Dr. Serapis shifted and sat back in his chair, then seemed to relax. But the motion was all wrong. It was like he was deliberately trying to look relaxed. To trick Orion into doing the same.

"Why don't you tell me about these dreams? Or would you consider them nightmares?"

"Depends on the night," Orion began. He considered just saying that he was bat shit crazy and asking for a healthy dose of sleeping pills. But he wasn't crazy. Maybe they would let him out if he could prove it. "Sometimes nothing happens, sometimes it's like I'm in hell."

"What are they about?" Curiosity burned behind the doctor's eyes. This was the small talk, the requisite questions. Not the ones he really wanted to ask.

"War," was Orion's simple answer. "The same war every night."

"You're a veteran, correct?" More small talk. The doctor must have known that from his file. Perhaps this was to see just how fucking crazy he was. Orion gave an almost imperceptible nod.

"Your dreams in and of themselves are not that uncommon among veterans, but what is strange is the way that they manifested." A concerned look fell over the doctor's face.

Orion just stared straight ahead at nothing in particular. He knew that his dreams were much more than what the doctor suspected, but all through the inquest he hadn't talked much about them. Nor had he during the psych evaluations. All of the doctors knew that he had dreams about the war, but didn't realize the scale of what they were dealing with. During the trial, Orion hadn't wanted to bring the dreams up since he thought that he just wanted to die.

The doctor must have mistaken his blank stare for something else. "You shouldn't blame yourself, you have a complex disorder."

That's what his lawyer kept telling him too. Orion just couldn't figure out why everyone else was so invested in him having a volatile mental state. He had considered the possibility that his wife was behind it all. As an executed killer, he was worthless. But as someone with a 'complex disorder,' he was probably worth a monthly payout from the government. He wanted to be bitter about that, but still couldn't bring himself to feel anything. And logically, what else was she supposed to do? She was still in the suburban house.

Quaint. White picket fence.

"We're going to start with something simple," the doctor's voice roused him from his reverie. Dr. Serapis scrawled something across a slip of paper and handed it the nurse. She held it up to her eyes and squinted. "That's three hundred CCs," the doctor said. She nodded and tucked the prescription into her front pocket, pulled at the edges of her skirt, then walked out of the room.

Dr. Serapis leveled his gaze back at Orion. "The medicine should inhibit the dream phase of your sleep."

For the first time in a long time, Orion felt something. A wave of panic. "What?"

"Theoretically it should prevent you from dreaming."

Orion's fingers clawed at the arms of his chair. "What would be the point of that?"

Dr. Serapis' lips curled into an ironic smile, a slight chuckle erupting from his throat. "Well the dreams are what caused it to happen, right?"

But I need the war, Orion wanted to say, but kept his mouth shut instead. Without the war, he had nothing. No Kid. No Wife – not one who loved him anyway. Nothing but the four white walls around him. And they would be suffocating without the open landscape of his dreams.

"But what will I do?" Orion dared to ask at least that.

Dr. Serapis looked at him as though he really were crazy. "You'll sleep," he thrust his hands out and shrugged. "And then we'll talk. You might get better."

Although he had considered the possibility earlier, Orion wasn't entirely sure that he wanted to 'get better.' Especially not if it meant no more war. If he went home, he would just sit in an empty house surrounded by four more suffocating walls. Even if his wife didn't hate him, she would still be terrified to sleep in the same house with him. And quite frankly, after what happened, Orion preferred being locked up at night.

"Any questions?" Dr. Serapis asked.

Orion shook his head, looking down at the white speckled linoleum floor. It was the most visually interesting thing in the room, and it seemed like soon, it might be the most interesting, period.

004

A restraint tightened over Orion's waist. He watched as a well manicured hand pulled another belt over his torso and wondered why the tall nurse with the long black hair was still working. She still looked fresh – not like she had been there for over twelve hours.

The restraints had become a nightly ritual, one that had taken Orion some time to adjust to. It had been enough to simply lock him up alone in jail, but at White Sands, they were apparently also concerned about him harming himself. He had to sleep on his back, but that wasn't the hard part. There was no tossing or turning, no adjusting his position. At least they gave him something that put him out quickly.

Only a single lamp illuminated the room, its light reflecting off the sheen of the nurse's impossibly black hair as she rolled an IV stand up to the bed. A bag filled with bright blue liquid, almost phosphorescent, swung to and fro from the metal frame.

Once again, Orion felt alarmed. This was new; they usually just gave him a couple of pills. And it was convenient that he was already strapped down when he discovered this new development.

"Your sleeping medicine is in the drip," the words rolled right off of the nurse's tongue as she attached a clear plastic vial of another liquid to the rubber tubing.

Orion clenched up. He wasn't afraid of needles, but he was terrified of the idea of dreamless sleep. They were putting him under, and he wasn't sure where he would go. His mind had to go somewhere, anywhere but where it actually was. The thought of absolute blackness until someone opened the door and unstrapped him wasn't comforting. He suddenly felt like he couldn't breathe. His room didn't have a single window. There were no stars. No moon. Nothing but the four white walls around him.

"Just relax," the nurse ran a smooth hand over the skin of his arm. He caught a whiff of something, some kind of lotion. It reminded him of something. But the bite of the needle entering his arm distracted him, and the thought was gone.

Bright blue liquid ran down the tube and into his arm. He could feel it, an icy chill creeping into his being. Something that didn't belong there.

The nurse smiled down at him. "It shouldn't take long." The words were supposed to be comforting, but they weren't. The smile faded from her face like a broken promise. Orion couldn't shake the feeling that he knew her from somewhere. Or that she knew something he didn't.

"What's your name?" he asked, his words slurring. She might have answered, but even if she did, Orion didn't hear her as he slipped into unconscious oblivion.

005

His mind wandered in darkness, only somewhat conscious that it was even there. He slowly became aware of sounds beyond the darkness. Birds. Insects. The sounds of a jungle teeming with life. Then a gunshot.

Orion opened his eyes to the war and breathed a silent sigh of relief. The medicine hadn't worked. But maybe he would lie and say that it had.

But thoughts of reality would have to wait – there were more immediate concerns to address. Orion was used to going to bed in one place, then waking up in the other. Coming to already on his feet in the middle of an operation was more than disorientating. It must have been the medicine. He could have been killed.

A certain silence hung in the air in the wake of the gunshot. Orion realized that his own gun was in his hands, and that a platoon mate flanked him. Orion had come to a dead stop, and the other soldier stared at him. Orion didn't know the soldier's name. It wasn't important, as long as they were on the same side.

The nameless soldier raised his chin, using the motion of his head to point forward. Orion gave a single nod, then faced forward again. They were in a dense thicket, facing a wall of vines that presumably gave way to a clearing beyond. Orion looked at the ground around him. It would be hard to move silently, but not impossible. One foot after the other. Just as he had been trained.

The vines were too thick. Orion could have cut a path through them with his machete, but that would have revealed their presence. Even though he hadn't been there when the gunshot went off, Orion could sense someone beyond the vines. He held up a hand and signaled to the left, towards a less dense exit from the thicket.

Orion and his nameless companion walked silently, killing machines ready to kill. When they finally found a way through the vines, Orion spotted their target. An enemy soldier, heavily camouflaged, lay on the ground in the distance manning a hidden machine gun battery that overlooked lower ground. His back was to them, and he was oblivious to their presence.

Orion held up his left hand again and signaled for his partner to move further down. He didn't have to look – Orion felt the other man moving behind him. They were two apex predators about to strike against a rank and file soldier – one who hadn't been trained as they had. Orion could have just raised his gun and took the shot, ending it right then and there, but that was what newbies did.

Orion and his partner couldn't risk discovery. The enemy soldier in sight could just be bait. If they didn't split up before Orion took the shot, it was possible they could both go down. Then there would be no one left to clean up.

The butt of his rifle felt reassuring against Orion's shoulder. It was a feeling that was more real than the nightly restraints being tightened over his body. Those were numbing. The gun was liberating. Orion aligned the theoretical trajectory of the bullet with the back of the enemy soldier's skull. He had no need for a scope.

He couldn't remember what the war was about, or who they were fighting. It wasn't important, as long as he could still recognize the enemy colors. The days blurred into one another, one long stream of lucid unconsciousness. There was another war somewhere else in the world – in a desert. But his war was the real one.

Orion lowered his gun, deciding that he needed to be ten yards closer. Over the present distance, gravity could yank the bullet too far down to hit the mark, and a head shot would turn into a paralyzing blow to the spine. He didn't need the yelling. Only impact and silence.

But as he crept forward slowly, he pictured himself walking down a dark hallway in a suburban home. How could he be sure that he wasn't repeating the past?

No – the nurse had strapped him down. He was lying in a bed in White Sands. There was no daughter to kill this time. But as he brought his gun back up to his shoulder, he found himself hesitating.

His platoon mate would be in position by now. He needed to take the shot. He tilted the gun barrel up and pictured the bullet flying through the back of the enemy soldier's head. Right through the middle, destroying the vital structures of the brain in both the left and right lobes, leaving behind a neat red hole.

Then, unbidden, was an image of a glass of milk falling in altered time next to an open refrigerator door. Another hole, not so neat, caused by a cheap civilian pistol. His daughter falling to the ground.

His finger was poised to pull the trigger, but he was frozen. Couldn't do it. His training failed. It was no longer just a routine, decisions already made for him. The world was turning upside down.

The enemy soldier shifted his position to look around casually. It wasn't because he had the same sixth sense that Orion had. It was because he was rank and file, poorly trained, and was purposely shirking his responsibility to watch the lower ground. But mistake or not, he spotted Orion and flinched, then started to twist his body around, pulling a rifle from the ground next to him.

Orion stared stupidly, his finger still poised over the trigger. It was just a dream. No need to dodge bullets there. But he didn't want to shoot a real one in real life. In a suburban home.

The enemy soldier's body jerked, his head snapping to the side before falling limply on the ground. Orion didn't bother to move. He already knew that his platoon mate had done what he couldn't. He sensed the other man coming up from the left even though he couldn't see him. Orion slowly let his gun drop to his side.

"What the fuck's wrong with you?" finally came the urgent whisper. Orion knew that he fucked up. Could have gotten himself killed – and his platoon mate. The one who's name didn't matter.

Orion turned to him with a vacant stare. "Bug in my eye," he lied. "Couldn't get a clear shot."

The other soldier just stared at him. Orion wasn't quite sure why he lied. It was just a dream.

006

"Are you always aware that you're dreaming?" Dr. Serapis asked.

"While I'm there, I remember everything from here," Orion said as he looked around the same room that he had been in the previous morning. He could still feel the pin prick of the IV in his arm, even though the tall nurse had been back that morning and given him a bandage. He had wanted to ask her about her bizarre work hours, how she always looked so fresh, but he could barely keep his eyes open in the wake of the phosphorescent drip.

"And you have complete control of your actions?" the doctor continued his line of inquisition.

This time Orion just nodded. He was busy staring at the shuttered window, wondering if they had found a way at White Sands to control the weather in order to keep it so damn gloomy all the time.

"Have you ever tried to change the dream?"

Orion's attention snapped back to Dr. Serapis. "What do you mean?"

"Since your dreams are lucid, it might be possible for you to consciously shape them," the doctor said. "Like if you imagined yourself in a different place, not at war. The jungle might disappear, and you could find yourself back at home. Have you ever tried that?"

Orion shook his head. "No, but... I don't think I could do that. I can control what I'm doing, but as far as the place..." Orion's eyes darted to the side, looking around the room again. "It's just like – I couldn't imagine my way out here."

"It feels that real?" Dr. Serapis leaned forward. "How long were you at war – in real life?"

A blank stare wiped the expression from Orion's face. "I… I don't remember." Orion searched for a thread – an inkling of a memory that was barely there. "I remember leaving to go to war, but I don't remember coming back." He usually didn't like to think very much during the numb journey from waking to sleep every day, but he felt as though he had just stumbled upon a profound thought.

Dr. Serapis leaned back. "Interesting."

A silence fell over the two men. Orion waited for some nugget of wisdom that might help to prod his thoughts out of hiding. But instead the doctor just sat there biting his lower lip. Orion remembered his training; Dr. Serapis was diverting some thought into a nervous habit. But what was it?

A fly buzzed nearby, circling around Orion's head unseen. It reminded him of the jungle, of the war, and for a split second he thought he could feel the stifling heat against his skin.

Finally Dr. Scrapis spoke. "I believe that your subconscious mind holds the truth." He leaned forward slightly, any hint of amusement gone from his usually jovial eyes. "Somewhere inside, you do remember coming home from the war. You just need to find it." He leaned back again, caressing his chin with wrinkled hands. "We'll cease the REM inhibitor altogether, let you dream freely so that may go on an adventure of discovery."

Dr. Serapis stood up, still deep in thought, seemingly oblivious to the fact that Orion was still sitting there. He began to walk towards the closed door, but just before his hand reached the knob, he turned back to Orion. "Remember, no one else in your dream knows that you are dreaming but you."

007

Orion stood with his back against the rough bark of a tree. Two platoon mates did the same, the three men forming a triangle in which their collective field of vision covered three hundred and sixty degrees. One of the men was the same soldier Orion had been with on the previous day – or night depending on how he considered it. Orion still didn't know his name, or the other man's for that matter. But he felt like he remembered them both from somewhere else.

He had never cared before that he didn't know their names. Due to perpetual stealth operations, they rarely talked and most certainly never used a radio. There was one at base camp, in case, but they were trained to die before giving their location away by breaking radio silence. Orion figured that it was there in the event that they discovered something that HQ absolutely had to know. Something that could impact the entire war, not just their expendable lives.

Now it was bugging him that he didn't know their names. They didn't even have handles. He seemed to remember something from training about anonymity. It was safer for everyone if no one knew real identities. And they just never bothered to make up fake ones. All they had to do was move silently and kill, one foot after the other.

Usually he found the dream comforting, a refuge from the harsh reality of White Sands. The four white walls. The gray light. The world where everyone thought he was crazy. But today, or tonight, he was ill at ease in the dream. Paranoia crept into his thoughts as he eyed his fellow soldiers. He knew them from somewhere, but where? And why did it matter? What was the truth that he was looking for?

Orion decided to try an experiment, per the doctor's orders. He closed his eyes and tried to imagine himself elsewhere. Instead of the rough bark of a tree, he imagined himself in a soft white bed in a quaint suburban home. It was another time, before he had killed his daughter, and his wife was also in the bed, propped up on an elbow, smiling down at him.

He opened his eyes, but the jungle was still all around him. A fly buzzed around his head, reminding him of the room at White Sands. For a moment, he could feel the stale conditioned air against his skin, the smell of medical disinfectant all about. He remembered the doctor's final words to him that morning and decided to try again.

His eyelids snapped shut, plunging him into darkness until his imagination could recreate the soft light of his former bedroom on a lazy afternoon. A wave of paranoia hit him again, his sixth sense kicking in.

When he opened his eyes, the same soldier who had confronted him the day before was standing inches from his face, a scowl warping his features.

"What the hell are you doing?" the soldier asked in a whisper so low that it sounded like a part of the wind.

Orion blinked.

"You're going to get us killed." He turned his head and surveyed the surrounding terrain, glancing briefly at the other soldier who stood a short distance away, watching them. Then he turned back to Orion. "Answer me. You're becoming a liability."

Orion started to consider his words carefully, but then decided to tempt fate. It was his dream after all. "I want to go home," he said.

The soldier's face became redder, if that was possible in the heat. "We all fucking want to go home. Get it together or you'll be heading back in a body bag." The soldier walked back over to his tree and glared in Orion's direction.

The threat was thinly veiled. They would just as soon kill Orion before allowing him to put their necks on the line. And there would be no questions, no investigation. Only a lie that he had been shot by the enemy.

Orion regretted all the thinking he was doing. The jungle was supposed to be a place where he could give in to orders and routine, just becoming another part of the sublime tableau of death. But now he had ruined it for himself. Something had to change.

So he took off running into the jungle.

008

Trees flew past his peripheral vision, leaves whipping to and fro in his wake. Orion was in a dead sprint, abandoning all pretense of stealth. He knew that his platoon mates were pursuing him, now just as deadly as the enemy. The only difference was that they knew exactly where he was – a fact that he need to quickly resolve.

Rays of sunlight hung in the moisture laden air, peeking through openings in the thick canopy overhead. They raked Orion's face as he flew by, like he was running past headlights on a dark highway.

As he ran, he tried to imagine himself at home again. Tried to will himself there. He recalled a promise that he had once made on a lazy afternoon. The scene was still fresh in his mind, like it had just happened the day before. His wife looked down at him, propped up on an elbow next to him in bed, a smile fading from her face.

"I don't want you to leave," she said.

"I'll be back," he responded.

She was silent for a moment, as if she couldn't fathom the magnitude of the dark visions that surely played in her mind. "What if something happens to you?" was all she managed to say.

Orion pulled her down on top of him, holding her tight. "I'll be back, I promise." He had never been afraid of the war, not even then.

As he raced through the jungle, he imagined himself running towards home and finding a way to see his wife again. If this was his dream, she would be waiting there for him, the smile still on her face, content that he had kept his promise. And his daughter would be there too.

But the jungle failed to melt away or disappear in a bright flash of light. The war was still all around him. Lactic acid burned Orion's calves, and his lungs heaved for oxygen. He figured that he had a significant lead on his fellows. It would have taken them a bit to react before giving chase, and Orion had more motivation to push himself.

He took a sudden dive into a thick patch of underbrush that was on a sharp incline, catching himself before he could roll downhill. Then he slowed his breathing and waited.

Almost immediately, the heavy footfalls of his companions were audible in the distance. Orion just hoped that the sound of their own running had masked the sound of his dive. The footfalls grew closer and closer, until the two men ran past Orion's hiding spot. Then they got farther and farther away as they continued to chase a ghost.

Orion allowed himself a sigh of relief, noticing for the first time that bugs were crawling all over his sweaty face. He was about to brush them away when he heard the others come a stop. As his heart raced, he debated springing back up and taking off again before he lost the advantage of his lead. If they had spotted him, they would already be silently making their way back to his position, and by the time he saw them, it would be too late. But if they hadn't, then he would be giving himself away for nothing.

As if in answer to his concerns, one of them spoke between harsh gasps for air. Their labored breathing made it impossible to keep quiet.

"Fuck," one of them said. Orion imagined them, scanning the underbrush and trees all around, unable to find him.

"I don't hear him anymore," the other said.

"Yeah, he's smarter than that." There was more silence, presumably as they strained to hear any sign of movement.

"We'll never find him out here."

"He was to sleep sometime."

***

Later that day, Orion watched the sunset from a perch high up in a tree. The spectacular golden rays cast a warm orange glow over the entire canopy. He imagined that as the sun was setting in his dream, it was rising in the real world. But the rays weren't as brilliant there, surely filling the rooms of White Sands with their usual grayish pallor.

He decided that he would spend the night up in the tree. It was the safest place since no one from the ground would be able to spot him without climbing above the general tree line. The thick canopy would even block thermal imaging devices. A helicopter or plane could spot him, but there were none that deep in enemy territory. And the enemy wasn't looking for him.

The gentle heat of dusk was making him groggy, and his eyelids drooped heavily. In all the time he had been at war, which was immeasurable, he had never taken the time to enjoy anything. Even though it was his escape from reality, his actions had always been dictated by survival. But the way he felt in that moment, he could have very well been in a rocking chair on his porch one late afternoon, perfectly at ease.

He was still in full gear, face painted black in preparation for night. He didn't know why he was concerned about what happened once he fell asleep. As far as he knew, he would simply disappear from the war and live out his daily life in the loony bin. There wouldn't be anyone to spot up in the trees – he would simply vanish.

In fact, he had never seen the jungle at night, not in his dreams anyway. He remembered the war – when he really was there – and there had been night time operations. But it all seemed so long ago, lost in the back of his mind as sleep slowly crept over his senses.

Then there was crackle. He jerked to attention, trying to figure out where the sound had come from. It was a familiar sound, but one that he hadn't heard in a long time.

It happened again, and he realized that it was coming from one of his own pockets. He unsnapped a steel release and fished out a small radio

– one that he had never used and was trained to avoid using. It was there, just in case, and now a transmission was coming over.

"Private, this is your commanding officer," a recognizable voice came through, filtered by the airwaves. It still struck Orion as funny how they omitted names, even then.

"If you're still alive out there, know that you have officially been declared AWOL and following protocol, we have orders for your arrest. Don't make us hunt you down."

Orion stared at the radio, wondering why they would break strict silence instead of just hunting him down. Then he realized that they probably wouldn't catch him, and they knew it. They were scared.

The soldiers of his outfit always traveled in groups, and groups of groups, each not far from the other. If one man was killed, they had orders to neutralize the enemy and retrieve the corpse of their fallen comrade. And if an entire group was killed, their companion groups had the same orders. This way, they were like a mystery of the jungle, striking out from the shadows. Enemy corpses would be found, but no trace of their invisible killers. The psychology of it wreaked havoc on their foes who didn't know if they were up against real soldiers or a primal force of nature. Rumors spread through enemy radio chatter, talk about mythical beings of the jungle. Vampires. Hairy beasts. Ghosts of the fallen who were jealous of the living.

Now that Orion was alone, there was a significant risk that he would be found and killed by the enemy, which would destroy the illusion. They were trying to scare him into returning to HQ on his own and surrendering, minimizing the collateral damage to their operation. Maybe they were hoping that one stray transmission would be interpreted as coming from the nearby front. Or at least that was the best Orion could figure. He surely wasn't important enough to break radio silence over.

009

A familiar dull gray light. The wizened face of Dr. Serapis staring at him through thick spectacles. Orion was anxious to get through his morning session and the rest of the day so he could get back to sleep. He vibrated with anticipation on the inside, ready to go somewhere else other than the four walls around him.

"But where are you going to go?" Dr. Serapis asked, as if reading his thoughts. Orion had just recounted his escape from the platoon.

"Home," Orion said with more than a hint of excitement in his voice.

Dr. Serapis seemed to consider his words, sitting back slightly and stroking his chin with thin fingers. "You do know what happened to your daughter, right?"

"But that never happened in my dream."

A scowl slowly spread over the doctor's face. "It's critical that we separate your dream world from reality. It was the crossing over of those worlds that caused your daughter's death in the first place."

Orion sat up in his chair and leveled his gaze right at Serapis. "You're not going to stop me from seeing my family again, even if it is just in my mind. What else do I have?" Orion threw his hands up, motioning around the room.

"We can cure you. You can leave here one day."

"For what?" Orion's face transformed into a mask of agony, and his voice cracked. "My wife will never love me again. My daughter..." he had to stop before the tears came.

Dr. Serapis stood up slowly like he was trying to escape a predator. "We'll have to start the REM inhibitor again. Double dose," he said to the nurse with the long black hair who stood quietly near the door. Then he looked back at Orion. "If that doesn't work, I'll order brain scans to determine the cause." Then he continued his slow retreat towards the exit.

"What if I don't want you to stop my dreams?"

Dr. Serapis paused at the door. "You have to stop living in that world. It's the only way to cure you." He turned and departed down the sterile hallway as the nurse approached to take Orion back to his windowless room.

010

Orion ran as fast as his legs could carry him even though he knew that the effort was futile. There was no way he could run halfway across the world back to his suburban home. But he didn't know what else to do. This could be his last chance.

The tall nurse had come to his windowless room at White Sands. There was even more bright blue liquid. Another pin prick. Orion had clenched up again, afraid there wouldn't even be a last chance if the sky blue liquid did its work. Consciousness faded to darkness – longer this time. But it was eventually pierced by the light of a familiar world.

As Orion continued to run with reckless abandon, he thought about lying to the doctor and saying that he hadn't dreamed. But the well manicured hands had attached sensors all over his forehead and temples. They would know.

Maybe this wasn't his last chance. After all, the bright blue liquid hadn't worked before. Orion figured that he easily had a couple more nights. Maybe the doctor wouldn't even be able to stop the dreams. Maybe there was a chance Orion could get home.

In the green blur of foliage, he tried to imagine himself elsewhere, anywhere closer to where he wanted to be. It didn't work.

He slowed his pace, coming to a stop. The running was pointless. He scanned the area until he found a patch of high ground bordered on one side by a steep rock wall. He climbed up, placed his back against a tree trunk and slumped down to a sitting position.

He began to rehash his conversations with the doctor, and he kept coming back to one thing in particular. Even though he had been back at home until a few months ago and had most certainly been there when he killed his daughter, he still couldn't remember going home after the war. It seemed as though there was a missing detail there. If only he could remember.

Instead, he recalled his first month at war, which was crystal clear in his mind. He remembered talking to his wife from base camp every day around lunch. It was always night back home, and he'd catch her right before bed. He made sure that he never missed a chance to talk to her, because he knew that he would soon be in the deep jungle. There would be no internet, no radio, and very little talking – most certainly not to his wife.

Orion closed his eyes, letting his consciousness drift. One particular conversation played back in his mind's eye, like it was happening again for the first time. He was laying on his stomach on the floor of a tent, laptop open, camera watching him. An image of his wife filled the screen, her face lit up only by the bluish light of a computer monitor.

"Please be careful," she told him.

"I made a promise, I'm not going to break it," Orion reassured her for the thousandth time.

His wife sighed deeply. "I know but," she started shaking her head.

"What?"

"I'm fine, I don't want to worry you," she said.

Orion smiled at her. "It's okay, I'm fine. You're the one who's worried."

His wife gave him a half smile that faded away before it was even there. "I keep having nightmares that something terrible happens to you. When I wake up and you're not in the bed, I don't know what's real."

"Sometimes I don't know what's real either."

Orion opened his eyes to the sounds of distant footsteps crushing foliage. It was the inexpert footsteps of the enemy. But what they lacked in skill they made up for in numbers. Orion cradled his gun in his palms, ready to rise to action.

He considered climbing a tree to gain a superior vantage point, but worried that the enemy soldiers were too close and might hear him if he tried. As far as he could tell, there were about a dozen of them. They moved parallel to him rather than towards him, so he decided to sit and wait.

Then gunshots erupted all around him. He lifted his weapon into position, ready to shoot, but there were no targets in sight. The firefight was happening elsewhere, the rat-tat-tat of assault rifles answered by the almost silent pings of high powered sniper rifles. Then there were screams.

But he shouldn't have been able to hear the sniper rifles – they were too close for comfort. And judging the proximity of the enemy, it was clear that they had somehow managed to surprise his former comrades. Something had gone horribly wrong. Just as suddenly as it began, the firefight was over, leaving an eerie silence behind. Then the foliage crunching footsteps hurried on their way, although there were less than before.

Orion stayed put with his back to the tree, even long after they were gone. If the bodies of his fallen comrades were to be recovered, now would be the time. And he was unlikely to hear those footsteps. He decided to wait a little longer before investigating. Fairly certain that he was secure in his hiding spot, Orion closed his eyes again.

Suddenly he was back in the tent at base camp, laptop open in front of him. It was another day. His wife was still having nightmares.

"At least you're dreaming about me," Orion said, a smirk on his face.

His wife instantly frowned. "That's not funny, I wish I wasn't."

"Let's make a deal," Orion looked down at his watch. "We have night operations later," he paused, doing the math in his head. "We'll both be asleep in four hours. Let's see each other tonight."

His wife laughed for the first time in a long time. "What?"

"Let's dream about each other. But no nightmares. And no kids." Orion raised an eyebrow.

His wife laughed again. "So… I'm supposed to do what exactly?"

"Just think really hard about me before you go to sleep."

A mischievous grin crossed his wife's face. "So this is like a date?"

Orion smiled at her, then glanced behind him as a bell rang somewhere in the camp, and other soldiers ran past the tent. He turned back to the screen. "I gotta run, but sweet dreams. I'll see you there." He terminated the feed, and the open window on the laptop screen went black.

And so did Orion's memory. He didn't remember what was for lunch that day, or what they did for training that night. That had been in the real world, not in his dreams where he never saw the night except for the dark insides of his eyelids – and even then, the glow of the sun penetrated through.

Orion opened his eyes and blinked.

011

Orion gingerly picked his way through the underbrush and tangled vines. One foot after the other, not making a sound. Curiosity had gotten the better of him, and he had finally left his hiding place. It had been long enough that if backup had been in the immediate vicinity of the firefight, they would have already come and gone. But it had not been so long that a more distant squad wasn't on its way, which was why he wanted to quickly assess the damage, take a body count of his true enemies, then disappear.

Fresh corpses were strewn all over the jungle floor, bursts of red decorating the leaves and vines all around like a macabre Christmas. It had been a sloppy fight. Tree bark was ripped away by bullets, leaves torn. Even long after the bodies were gone and gluttonous insects had lapped up all the blood, it would still be obvious what had happened there. No jungle spirits. No fantastic creatures. Just cold hard steel and death.

Orion didn't see any dead enemy soldiers, but he imagined that they were out there somewhere. Or perhaps their living counterparts had carried the bodies away for a proper burial.

He recognized the faces of his fallen comrades, but still didn't know their names. Now he never would. Orion's legs felt sore as he crouched down next to the closest man and started going through his backpack for food and water.

As he riffled through the pack, something else in the clearing caught his eye – the glint of shiny metal reflecting a stray ray of light that had managed to break through the canopy. Steel that was somewhere it shouldn't have been.

Orion stood up and made his way towards another body that was twisted in impossible ways. As he drew closer, he could make out the features of the same soldier who had questioned him when he had faltered in the field. The soldier lay on his stomach, head turned sideways, his features streaked with blood. He had fallen from a leg wound, but it was evident that he died from a head wound.

The back half of his skull was missing, bloody bits dangling from the opening. And in the mess of brains and bone, something foreign peeked out. Something metallic, bristling with circuits.

Orion bent down and grabbed the edge of it and found that it was loose. It was evident that it had been placed there before a bullet had exposed its hiding place. He gave it a sharp yank. There was a sickening sucking sound as brain tissue gripped the object before it broke free.

Orion held it out and grabbed his canteen, using water to wash away the gore. Gleaming silver housing encased a microchip that was black as night, riddled with tiny gold channels. As he looked at its dark surface, Orion wondered what secrets it held.

He rose and faced the savage garden before him. Blood seeped into the hungry soil, its odor a beacon to predators who had already begun to arrive on the scene. Huge ants formed lines, marching from unseen nests, likely to fight another war in the coming hours. And there were surely other things – larger things – waiting for Orion to leave.

Just as he looked over the backpacks, about to continue his own scavenging, a wave of dizziness hit him. He dropped to his knees, and the jungle spun all around him. As darkness began to cloud his vision, he could only think of one possibility – that there was some sort of biological agent in the air.

He felt himself falling to the ground among the dead, struggling to remain conscious. But it was futile. Some unseen battle raged in his own body, one that he couldn't possibly hope to win.

012

Orion opened his eyes to near darkness. Four familiar walls surrounded him, the room dimly lit by a single lamp. He jerked his head to the side and noticed the tall nurse at his left arm with a syringe. The drip at his right arm had stopped, the bright blue liquid no longer running down the transparent tube. Dr. Serapis stood in a shadowy corner of the room.

"What's going on?" Orion slurred, his words still thick with medicine induced sleep. He couldn't tell if was day or night in the windowless room, but he had the impression that it was still night. There was a steady beeping from the machine connected to the sensors on his head.

"The stronger dose isn't working," Dr. Serapis said, "so we woke you."

Orion watched as the nurse tucked the syringe into a disposal bin on the wall, the bio hazard symbol on it making the contents seem sinister. He couldn't help but dwell on the bizarre nature of what was happening. Why couldn't they just let him sleep for the night? Why were they still there? How many fucking hours did that nurse work?

"We're going to move you to another area," Dr. Serapis continued. "Then put you back down for brain scans."

"What's the fucking hurry?" Orion asked. He meant for it to be louder, more expressive, but the drugs in his system reduced the words to a whisper. "Just let me sleep."

"You'll be sleeping again soon enough," the doctor said. "But we need to fix you. We're on a time line."

Before Orion had a chance to ask the obvious question, Dr. Serapis turned and walked out of the door into the hallway which was awash in harsh florescent light. The nurse bent down to release the wheels on the bed, then there was a lurch, and Orion began to move forward. Old wheels squealed in the quiet of the night.

The hall was empty, except for another nurse making rounds. Orion didn't often see the other patients. It seemed as though he was either in the examination room or in his own room, only spotting others during the brief back and forth. Even his meals were delivered to his room.

The bed rolled through a set of double doors, into a room filled with medical equipment, including a massive transparent tube poised at the entrance to what looked like a giant oven. Dr. Serapis stood next to the tube, typing something into a keypad.

A strange feeling came over Orion just for a split second – a fleeting memory. He lifted his head from the bed, straining to look around with a furrowed brow.

"Is something wrong?" the doctor asked.

"No… just déjà vu," Orion said.

"I'm quite sure that I've never ordered these scans for you before."

Orion shook his head, letting it drop back down to his pillow. He felt the restraints on his arms loosening as the well manicured hands brushed against his skin. Then the belt across his waist was removed. He tried to sit up, but profound weakness held him down. He couldn't rebel, even if he wanted to.

"Take it easy," the nurse said. "I'll help you." She placed a hand behind his back, pushing upward. She guided him into a sitting position, helping him to swivel his legs off of the bed. She had to help support his weight as he took a shaky first step, his body dipping down towards the floor.

Dr. Serapis opened the top of the transparent tube, which was held in place by invisible hinges. It was at waist level, and the nurse helped ease Orion back into a prone position until his back was cradled inside of the cylindrical shape.

"There we are," she smiled down at him before crossing the room and returning with two syringes.

"What's that for?" Orion asked, craning his neck into an upright position again.

"One is a cocktail that will have the opposite effect of the REM inhibitor," the doctor said. "It will enhance the REM phase of your sleep, allowing the scanner to get stronger readings."

There was the sound of manicured nails clacking against steel. Clear liquid shot out into the air, then a soft hand gripped his arm. The bite of steel pierced his skin.

"The other should put you right out," Dr. Serapis gave him a half smile. "Nothing to be concerned about." The smile faded from his face as he turned back to the keypad.

For the second time in what seemed liked minutes, Orion felt darkness creeping into the edges of his vision. Whatever was in the syringe, it worked fast, probably piggy backing on the drugs already in his system.

Dr. Serapis' wrinkled face appeared at the end of what was quickly becoming a dark tunnel. "This might be last time you dream for a while," he said. "Make it worth it." The face disappeared, leaving only a bright light overhead at the end of Orion's tunnel vision. It was blinding, making Orion want to shut his eyes even more, adding to the steady tug of the medication on his eyelids. But he didn't want to give in.

"Sweet dreams," was the last thing he heard the doctor say before the darkness finally swallowed him whole.

013

There was another dark tunnel with blinding light at the end – but it was daylight. There was a familiar heat. Soon the canopy overhead filled Orion's vision.

He became aware of the sound of footsteps. Not distant ones, or even ones that were nearby. They were right next to him. Without moving his head, Orion closed his eyes quickly, only leaving a sliver of vision, and glanced to the side.

Boots. Legs draped in familiar camouflage. One of his own. He could hear others. The support squad had finally arrived to remove the bodies. They likely had not expected to find Orion there and had assumed he was just another corpse. Now he knew that a bio weapon hadn't caused him to black out; it was Dr. Serapis forcing him back into reality.

There was a slight grunt and the sound of leaves shifting as someone lifted a body off of the ground. Orion took a moment to listen, trying to ascertain how many there were, and what their positions were. He had surprise on his side. And fortunately, his fingers were still wrapped around the hot steel of his gun that refused to cool – even in the shade. He made one final assessment of the area before lashing out.

Orion swung his gun barrel right into the knee of the man standing next to him. There was a satisfying crack and a surprised yelp, then the man went crashing down. Without standing, Orion pointed his gun in the general direction of the others and opened fire. Chaos reigned as he jumped to his feet. The others had dropped to the ground, most of them confused, searching in all sorts of directions to find the threat that had suddenly descended upon them. But those who saw Orion yelled out and fumbled to get their guns into position.

Orion knew that he only had seconds before a spray of bullets erupted behind him. He pointed his gun backwards and opened fire as he took off running, hoping to sew more chaos and keep the others down on the ground. By the time the first bullet hit a tree next to him, Orion was already far enough away that he was pretty sure they wouldn't be able to hit him as long as he kept moving.

So he ran and ran, eventually diving into another hiding place as soon as he spotted one. It would be several hours before he would be able to emerge safely.

014

The sun was setting as Orion marched despondently through the jungle. He no longer knew where he was going or why. It would be night soon, and he knew that he was never going to make it home. Earlier, he had fished a picture of his wife out of his backpack, and he now held it in one hand, occasionally glancing down, wishing he could travel over continents and through time to be with her again.

There was a break in the trees, and he found himself standing before a gradual drop in the terrain that stretched for miles. From where he stood, he could see the jungle stretching out over mountainous terrain to infinity. He stared at the sea of green between him and home, and his shoulders sagged. He let his backpack slip off and clatter to the ground. Then he threw his gun down. Nothing mattered anymore.

He slumped to the ground with his back against a tree, then held up the picture of his wife against the sunset. She was out there somewhere, across the beautiful green expanse that was filled with countless horrors. He lowered his hand and watched the final rays of the sun.

Then he suddenly remembered another sunset, one that had marked the day he went home in real life.

After two tours out in the deep jungle, he had marched with two other men back to base camp, shadowed by a support squad the entire time. His group would be going home and three more men, newly arrived and finished with environmental training, were going to follow the squad back into the bush.

He then waited in base camp for two whole days, constantly on edge like someone was going to sneak up behind him and slit his throat. Even in the relative safety of the camp, well on their side of the disputed territory, it was hard to relax. He had no idea how he was going to sleep at night once he got home without knowing that a platoon mate was always watching over him.

At the end of the second day, he had stared into a matching sunset as the black forms of stealth helicopters appeared on the horizon. He could barely hear them, even as they touched down, kicking up billows of debris. He looked around one last time, then walked over to one of the helicopters, his discharge papers in hand.

And that was the last thing he remembered.

After that point in his memory, he was already home. There was no flight back, nor could he recall an exit interview. It was puzzling, but he had always brushed the huge gap in his memory aside. He had his wife and daughter, so it didn't really matter.

As the sun finally dipped below the horizon, Orion stood up to continue along a road to nowhere. For some reason, perhaps due to his training, he did pick his pack and gun back up. And for some reason he decided to find a safer place to sleep.

After about half a mile, when the light was almost faded, he spotted a dilapidated shanty. He determined that the structure was uninhabited with a quick sweep for signs of recent passage. As the rickety wooden door shut behind him, he wondered who had it built it and what purpose it had once served. Upon further examination, it seemed that the shack must have been some sort of outpost, but God only knew how long ago. Photo developing equipment that looked like it was decades old lay strewn out across a wooden counter.

He wedged his backpack against the door to hold it shut, then moved to a corner where he sat down on the floor. There was a familiar tug on his eyelids. Sleep was like clockwork when night descended in his dream world.

He had the sinking feeling that time was running out – but for good. Orion supposed that he shouldn't be sad; he wasn't actually leaving his wife. She was far away, inaccessible. He was only leaving the war behind. But there was a promise that he wasn't able to keep. A promise that he'd be back.

As soon as his eyelids closed, the picture of his wife fell from his hand, and his pupils began to move rapidly back and forth under his eyelids.

015

Orion opened his eyes in a different world – familiar, yet somehow distant. He was laying on his back in the transparent tube, the innards of the brain scanner closing in all around him. It was dark inside; the machine seemed to be turned off. Dim, ambient light leaked in from the surrounding room, but only enough for Orion to see the close quarters that he was in. Enough to make him feel claustrophobic.

There was no PICC line in his arm, and his mind was clear of any drug induced haze. He pushed up against the top of the tube, and suddenly the whole thing began to move, sliding out of the brain scanner like a snake was regurgitating troublesome prey that refused to stop moving inside of its belly.

Orion quickly saw that something wasn't right. He was alone in the room, the overhead lights turned off except for a single bulb that looked like it served as an emergency backup. He tensed as he sat up and stepped out of the tube onto the cold tile floor. It was like he was at war again, but a different war. He silently crossed the room to the double doors and slowly peeked out into the dark hallway where only every fourth florescent bank blazed like islands in a sea of darkness.

The civilian in him was tempted to call out and say hello to see if there would be a response. But the soldier in him knew that wasn't a good idea. He stepped out into the hallway, one foot after the other, just as he was trained.

Even though he wasn't intimately familiar with the facility, he had the impression that the hallway went on for longer than was possible. At one point he turned and looked back, but the double doors of the brain scanning room were nowhere in sight. He kept moving forward past one closed door after another, trying some of the handles, but they were all locked. He thought about trying to break them down, but didn't know which door would be worth the effort.

Eventually, in the distance, there was a lone door that was ajar. A dull, greenish light spilled out onto the white tiles of the hallway from inside. Orion tensed up even more, his hands balled into fists as he walked forward. There were clinks and clatters from inside of the room – the sound of metal hitting metal, then the brief whir of a saw.

He peered inside and saw Dr. Serapis perched over a man who lay on an operating table. The room was dark except for a single light on the end of an articulated arm that hung over the patient's face. Orion studied the man's features carefully. He had seen him somewhere before. But where?

Then it hit him. It was the nameless soldier who had confronted him in the field. The soldier's head was cut open, blood spilling out like it had in the jungle. Only this time, he wasn't dead. His chest rose and fell at the behest of a machine while Dr. Serapis dug around inside of his skull.

On a metal tray next to the table was the same gleaming silver casing that Orion knew to house a microchip that was a black as night.

He suddenly felt dizzy again, as he had in the jungle when the doctor had forced him to wake up. He just gave in this time. There was nothing there for him… except unanswered questions.

* * *

Orion's eyes fluttered open again. A blinding light hung inches from his face, and he knew that he was in a different place. But as he tried to sit up, he realized that he was actually still in the same room. Only he was the one on the operating table – the gleaming silver casing next to him.

Everything in the room appeared as a blur. Drugs impaired his ability to see or think. He lifted his hands weakly, noticing the tangle of wires and tubes coming from his body. An incessant beeping filled the air, and there were people talking in raised voices.

"…resistant to sedatives," he heard in one snippet. Dr. Serapis spun around and looked at him. Then he felt hands pulling him back down onto the table.

"Double the dose," Dr. Serapis said, "He's barely lucid."

There was the familiar pin prick of a needle going into his arm. Long black hair. A tall nurse. Soft manicured hands.

And then there was darkness.

016

When Orion woke for the third time, he found himself still inside of the brain scanner, but this time the machine was on, and he could hear others in the room. The memory of himself waking up on the operating table was still fresh in his mind, playing back over and over again. Somehow he knew that it wasn't a dream, but an actual memory. If it were true, it meant that Dr. Serapis wasn't actually a shrink at a nut house. Orion wasn't sure what was real anymore.

There was a mechanical click and then a whir as the transparent tube began to roll out of the scanner. Dr. Serapis and the tall nurse waited for Orion. A wave of panic hit him when he saw that she brandished yet another syringe.

Once the tube came to a stop, the doctor flipped it open and smiled down at Orion. "You woke up on your own this time, a resistance to the sedatives." The nurse took a step toward Orion, readying the syringe. "But not to worry, we'll have you back to sleep in no time."

"Where's my wife?" Orion asked. He had other questions, but felt that one was the most pressing.

The smile fell away from Dr. Serapis' face, and he looked genuinely concerned. "At home I would imagine. Are you okay?"

Orion never answered. Rather than get poked again, he jumped to his feet and pushed the nurse out of the way. A second later he was in the hallway.

The doors flying by in his peripheral vision could have just as easily been the foliage of the jungle whizzing by. Orion was running again, this time for real. There was nothing left for him in his dreams, nor at White Sands. The two had blended together into one hopeless reality. So he ran.

Soon a klaxon sounded throughout the building, and red lights started blinking along the walls. Dr. Serapis' voice came over the intercom. "Private, we have you surrounded." Orion turned a corner at full speed, running into a nurse who tended a couple of early risers. They barely slowed him.

"Surrender or we will be forced to shoot!" the doctor's voice blared over the intercom. Orion couldn't put his finger on it, but something wasn't quite right with the sound.

He turned another corner and skidded to a halt as he saw two orderlies at the end of the hallway. Blue arcs of electricity danced at the end of tasers. He thought about his training – how he should have been able to easily neutralize the threat. But his muscles were already giving out, a byproduct of being constantly drugged. And even if he could get past those two, there would be more.

There was a familiar sinking feeling in the pit of his stomach. He realized that no matter how far he went, he would still never get to where he was going. The two orderlies began to advance on his position.

He ducked into a bathroom and shut the door, locking it behind him. This was surely the end. Sooner or later they'd get through the door, then there would be no more dreams. No more war. No wife or daughter. Nothing.

There would also be no more memories of people he had never met, nor inklings of something being off, or the flashback of lying on the operating table under the knife. If they had made him forget once, they could, and would probably make him forget again. Or maybe he really was just crazy.

"This is your last chance," Dr. Serapis said over the intercom. "Surrender or we're moving in!"

The problem with the voice struck Orion in that instant: it didn't actually belong to Dr. Serapis. Yet he somehow thought that it should have. It was like he was in a dream.

He quickly moved to the mirror and brushed a hand through his short cropped hair. He could feel something under his fingertips. He leaned in closer for a better look.

Through parted hair, he could make out a scar on the right side of his head, right behind his ear. Right where he had found the silver casing and black microchip in the unnamed soldier's blown out skull. He felt the slightly raised ridge, saw the angry red line where something foreign had been placed where it shouldn't be.

Someone outside rammed the door, and Orion flinched in surprise. He wondered what he would do once they were inside. But he wasn't able to think for long before a blinding light shone into eyes.

Then he woke up.

017

Orion held his hand in front of his face, shielding his eyes. He was back in the shanty, the sounds of the jungle all around him.

"Don't move," a man said, moving the light out of Orion's face. Three black clad forms stood in the room with him, and red dots danced across his chest. He raised his hands in surrender.

"Get up," the same man said as he took a couple of steps back. Orion quickly weighed his options and decided that he had none. If he was right, the three men in black were Specters, elite soldiers who would hand his ass to him. Orion had heard rumors about them, talk that they weren't even completely human anymore – their bones laced with steel and their movements guided by wired reflexes. They belonged to a new branch, and if anyone was even more ghostly than the unit he belonged to, it was them.

Orion got up onto his feet, feeling for the first time that what he was seeing was all too real. He couldn't take his eyes off of the red dots, actually concerned that bullets might fly in what he had once thought was a dream.

One of the Specters stepped behind Orion and yanked his arms back, then zip tied them together. "Private, you are under military arrest," the man whispered into his ear.

"Is this real?" Orion asked. But there was no answer, only blank stares from two faceless black clad forms. And the red dots.

Orion felt cold steel against his neck. Another pin prick. More God-damned drugs. These were fast – injected right into his neck, rising to his brain almost instantly. The room began to spin and he felt incredibly sleepy, two strange sensations all at once. Suddenly there were four Specters instead of two in front of him, their expressionless visages mocking him.

His knees began to buckle, and he probably would have fallen if not for the man behind him holding him up with one hand in an iron grip.

As his body sagged downward, so too did his eyelids. Impossibly heavy. And once again he found himself asleep.

018

Orion woke up to the steady hum of an aircraft all around him. It was a gradual process as the drugs slowly metabolized in his system. He drifted in and out of sleep, discovering new details each time he popped back into consciousness.

There were restraints holding him down on a soft bed. A military doctor and nurse sat nearby, strapped into their seats. They all appeared to be in the wide open bay of a cargo plane or bomber. Once he was able to look around a little, Orion realized that he was the only payload on board.

He didn't bother to try speaking to the pair, and they were only slightly interested in him as he came to – certainly not enough to say anything to him. It was just as well. Orion figured that either his questions would be answered, or they wouldn't. He would be sane, or crazy.

As he had slept, there had been no dreams. Only blackness. He was slowly realizing what that meant. The war wasn't a dream – the nut house was.

And... he didn't dare to think. If the war wasn't the dream, then maybe, just maybe, his wife and daughter could be alive and well. A wave of excitement cut through the groggy haze, and Orion felt his heart rate increasing. It must have registered on some unseen instrument because it got the military doctor's attention right away. He unstrapped himself and walked over to Orion. Another pin prick. The darkness didn't overtake him quite as fast. Instead of tunnel vision, it was like a slow sunset. As his eyelids closed more and more, Orion could only think of one thing: his family.

This time, there was a dream. A memory of the past. Orion stood in the front yard of his suburban home in full uniform, a duffel bag slung over his shoulder. It wasn't his real uniform – that was top secret. It was the dressy one for show.

A taxi waited behind him at the curb as he faced his teary eyed wife and daughter. Orion reached out and caressed his wife's face, brushing away a tear with his thumb. "I'll be back," he spoke that same promise again, even though he had already said it countless times.

He leaned in and kissed her. There was something cold about it, a sadness. Then he looked down at his daughter.

"Say goodbye to daddy," his wife tried to sound cheerful.

Orion crouched down and looked his pouty daughter in the face. She wasn't old enough to fully realize what was happening, but still knew that something was wrong. She sucked her thumb as he pulled her close and gave her one final hug.

He stood up, fighting back his own tears. "See you soon," was all he could manage before he forced himself to turn around and walk towards the taxi. He had to be the strong one. His wife might question his promise if he cried.

Once inside of the taxi, he kept his head low, only glancing up once at the final sight he would ever have of his wife and daughter in person.

His dream continued as an extrapolation of that memory. He arrived back home in the same taxi. There were tears again, but not the same kind. His wife and daughter were out in the front yard, smiles on their faces. There was no more war.

Movement jolted Orion awake again. The plane was landing, its frame jerking and lurching as it slowed to a stop on a runway somewhere. The doctor and nurse stood up and removed the straps that had secured Orion's bed during the flight. Then they rolled him out of the plane.

It was a private airport with only two runways. Theirs was the only plane. A pair of MPs escorted them towards a large building that looked like a hospital. Orion strained his neck to look around.

His heart sank when he saw a sign on the building looming in the distance. It read: *White Sands Army Research Laboratory.*

019

One of the MPs stood over Orion as they entered the building and came to a stop. "Private, we'd like for you to walk the rest of the way. But no funny business. Think you can do that?"

Orion nodded. He was more curious than anything, and he knew that if he wanted answers, fighting wasn't the best course of action. He lifted his arms up and stretched as the tight restraints were lifted, then he stood up. He was no longer in uniform, his body covered by plain gray clothes.

It was surreal as he walked down the same hallways where he had been confined after killing his daughter. But ironically that was a dream, and that place had been a nut house, not a military installation.

A vision of the surgery flashed in Orion's mind again – and a different kind of training. The memories were fleeting, dancing in the back of his mind and refusing to come into the light. They walked right past the room where had met with Dr. Serapis and the tall nurse every morning in the dull gray light. Another doctor walked into that room to greet a different young man who was seated nervously on an examination bed.

Orion's heart froze as he was ushered into an office. Dr. Serapis, in the flesh, sat on the other side of a desk, motioning for him to sit down. He could feel the two MPs standing at his back, waiting for him to comply. His training was kicking in again, and in his mind he was already going through the motions of dropping both of them.

Instead, he sat down across from the doctor.

"It's been awhile Private," Dr. Serapis said.

"Who the fuck are you?" Orion blurted out. He felt the presence behind him draw closer to his back, then felt a hand on his shoulder.

The doctor gave a dismissive wave to the MPs. "It's fine, his reaction is understandable." Then he leveled his gaze at Orion again. "You shouldn't remember me, but I understand that your implant is malfunctioning."

Orion's hand subconsciously moved up to the scar at the back of his head, its raised ridge pressing against his fingertips. "This is real?"

Dr. Serapis slid a thick stack of papers across his desk. Orion looked down at the sheets, recognizing his own signature on a few. He finally looked back up at the doctor.

"This is your contract for voluntary entry into the sleeper cell program," Dr. Serapis said.

"The what?"

"The program relies on GUILD – Guided Unconscious Initiated Lucid Dreaming. It was designed for people like you."

"Like me?" Orion asked. "Why would I volunteer for this?"

Silence.

"You don't remember that part?" the doctor finally asked.

Orion just stared.

"Where do you think your family is?"

Orion shrugged. "I don't have any fucking clue, that's the problem."

Dr. Serapis sighed heavily. "Well, no need to sugarcoat I suppose." Nevertheless, he seemed to hesitate.

"They both died in a car accident two days before you were discharged from regular duty."

More silence. The tears didn't come right away, held back by disbelief.

As though the doctor had known what Orion's reaction would be, he grabbed a folder and tossed it at Orion. It contained copies of the obituaries and death certificates. There were also pictures from a car crash that resembled a war zone. Blood and brains were smeared on the windows and seats, the features of disfigured faces barely recognizable. But Orion had seen enough dead soldiers to be able to recognize his wife and daughter.

As he sat there holding the obituary, he remembered holding that same obituary on another day. Then it all started to come back to him.

He sat in his living room, which was no longer quaint. It was messy and unkempt, a reflection of his disheveled hair and stained clothes. Countless empty beer bottles punctuated his sad state. The obituary was in his hand as he looked up at Dr. Serapis and a neatly dressed military officer.

"Sorry for the mess," Orion offered.

"No, we're very sorry about what happened to your family," the officer began. "We always think that we'll be the ones to die first. But when something like this happens instead… it's the worst."

Orion nodded, a distant look on his face.

"What if I told you that it was possible for you to be with your family again?" the officer asked.

"What do you mean?"

Dr. Serapis stepped forward. "We're here to talk to you about a new program. Sleeper cells."

Yes, it was all coming back now. A flood of memories that had been locked in the recesses of his mind. At White Sands, Orion looked up from the obituary.

"As to why you would want to join, those in the program are at war by day," Dr. Serapis said, "but every night they dream that they are back at home with the loved ones that they lost. Only the process is designed for you to think that the war is a dream."

Dr. Serapis sat back in his chair, the wood creaking. "It's a win-win. The soldiers get something that they need, and the Army gets elite platoons that aren't afraid of anything because they think they're dreaming."

"I wasn't exactly living the dream," Orion said.

"We're still making modifications to the implant for variations in personality and the subconscious. The mind can be a moving target. It seems that yours was creating scenarios to trigger memories that should have been suppressed."

"Not erased?" Orion asked.

"It's impossible to erase, as you can tell." Dr. Serapis looked down at his hands as he fidgeted for a moment. "The real question is," he finally looked back up. "Do you want to see your wife again?"

Silence.

Orion sat up in his chair.

"You can reenter the program, and we'll give you a fresh start." Dr. Serapis reached into a desk drawer and pulled out a folder filled with papers in a neat stack.

"But that means I won't remember anything," Orion said.

"Exactly." The doctor slapped the folder down in front of him, opening the top flap.

Orion looked down into his lap and shut his eyes for a moment. He was in bed again, and his wife was next to him, propped up on an elbow, smiling down at him. He opened his eyes again to a colder reality. "What else do I have?"

Dr. Serapis handed him a pen. "Sign on the dotted line."

020

Orion opened his eyes to a grayish morning light that filtered through the drapes of his bedroom window. He was in his suburban home. Quaint. White picket fence. His wife smiled down at him.

"How did you sleep?" she asked.

Orion paused for a moment, trying to retain a dream that was fading away by the millisecond, erased by wakefulness. He looked up at his wife.

"I had the weirdest dream," he muttered.

BUTTERFLIES

021

1983.

Charlie's eyes were playing tricks on him. Small shapes seemed to flit around the edges of his vision – there, but not there. He shut his eyes for a moment, then opened them wide, trying to give his photoreceptors a fresh start. But he already knew that it wouldn't make any difference. He supposed that the seven watt light bulb dangling from the ceiling that they used for photo printing was better than sitting in utter darkness. That didn't change the fact that everything seemed different when awash in red. Eerie even.

Charlie heard the scrape of a boot against the old wooden floor as Tommy shifted his weight and fished something out of his pocket. A lighter. And a pack of cigarettes. A couple of flicks later and fresh smoke rose towards the red light, creating a haze in the rafters. Charlie glanced over at Tommy – he hated it when Tommy smoked.

They had sealed the exterior of the decrepit wooden shack to prevent light leaks, and that theoretically should have also prevented the smell of cigarette smoke from wafting out into the jungle. But Charlie felt like every time Tommy lit up, it was an irresponsible roll of the dice. There were already so many ways they could die without tempting fate. Nothing was supposed to escape the confines of their tenuous sanctum and give them away.

Not only was radio silence strict, but the two men barely talked. When they did, it was in hushed whispers. Charlie and Tommy were just like the small shapes that persisted on the fringes of Charlie's vision. They were there, but not there. Two lone operatives, deep in enemy territory, who would slink out of their hiding place in the dead of night to reconnoiter forbidden things and record them on film. Once a week, a runner would pick up their developed prints and drop off fresh film rolls and rations.

They weren't alone out there, but mostly so – far away from the fighting that didn't exist on official records. The "war" had been over for years, but people were still fighting. People were still dying. Communism was just the cover story.

Charlie lifted a camera from his lap and looked through the viewfinder. Suddenly everything was better. It was as though he were no longer sitting atop his sleeping bag on the floor of a hell hole. For an instant, however slight, it was like he was looking in from the outside. Tommy stared angrily into the lens.

The other man was younger than Charlie. Blond patches of hair dotted his face in lieu of a full beard. Charlie often felt that Tommy was more boy than man, rushed to the front because he enjoyed killing things in video games. Or perhaps it was the blond hair and blue eyes. He was a poster boy for what *Us* was supposed to look like. Corn-fed Midwesterners. Wholesome family men. Except that Tommy wasn't wholesome. His cold blue eyes were for killing.

Charlie had almost forgotten what his own face looked like. He avoided mirrors, not wanting to remember. The last time he saw himself was an accident – a glance as he passed a shard of mirror that Tommy had left propped up behind the developing trays. For a split second, he had panicked, thinking that a stranger – one of *Them* – had somehow gotten inside of their refuge. But the sunken black eyes and corpse-like hollow cheeks had been his own.

The ambient red glow seemed harsher as Charlie lowered the camera and was forced to stare at his companion through his own eyes. He looked away, placing the camera into a small case right next to its night vision attachment. Acrid smoke burned Charlie's nostrils, and he silently cursed Tommy again, wondering again how the younger man had ended up there in the first place. They were supposed to be an elite unit, and he wouldn't have expected such amateur mistakes.

Charlie was supposed to be the commanding officer, but with it being only the two of them, so far away from the front, his grasp of the situation had slipped. He feared that his grasp on reality was also slipping. The constant silence didn't help. Of course the 'silence' actually consisted of the incessant sound of insects. It pressed in all around them, almost deafening, yet forming an inane cloud of white noise that added to the constant disquietude. Sleeping by day had an even more adverse effect. An exclusively nocturnal existence warped reality – not that the jungle needed much help. It was a place so filled with predators that even they were prey.

Charlie leaned forward and turned a dial on their field radio. There was a click, and a soft static broke the silence. He was careful to keep the volume low, almost imperceptible to his own ears. It was inconceivable that an enemy soldier lurking outside in the darkness, surrounded by the cacophony of insectoid noise, could possibly hear it.

"You're not going to get anything out here," Tommy's voice sliced through the tension. "Unless you're trying to call someone."

Charlie just stared at Tommy.

"But you know better than that," Tommy added.

"I'm fucking bored," Charlie said, ignoring the snub to his seniority.

"I'd turn it off."

Charlie didn't feel like pulling rank, so he turned until the dial clicked off – a submission to Tommy's control. He instantly regretted it. In fact, he knew that he had to stop or their roles would end up completely reversed. "I wouldn't smoke if I were you," Charlie finally said.

Tommy shrugged and ground his cigarette against the floor. "Time to go anyway."

Charlie glanced down at his watch. Indeed it was finally dark out – time to become a predator amongst a sea of predators. This brought a sense of both relief and dread. Every time they slipped out, there was the risk of never coming back. Yet the jungle, the war, was their only escape from the confines of the shack.

022

Charlie traded the dull red of the shack for the eerie green glow of night vision. The jungle came to life. Analogue noise danced against the backdrop of night, filling his vision with yet more flitting shapes. As the weight of the clunky night vision rig pulled against his neck muscles and a rubber seal tugged at the skin around his eyes, Charlie cursed Tommy for the twentieth time that day.

The younger man had been outfitted with experimental ocular implants that allowed him to see in almost total darkness without additional aid. Charlie had been told that due to the experimental nature of the implants, it was best to try them out on a younger recruit – one who was more expendable. There had also been secret orders to terminate Tommy and destroy his eyes, should something "strange" happen out in the field. Charlie had already been tempted several times to just pull the trigger and write it off to something strange, but instead he continued to endure their strained partnership.

He couldn't hear Tommy's silent footfalls as the other man crept into the jungle, more predator than prey. Sometimes Charlie wondered if Tommy was sporting more than just ocular implants. The young man was downright scary in the field, stalking the dense landscape like a jungle cat. Despite his amateur mistakes, it was clear that if there was one thing he was good at, it was killing.

When the two men were out in the jungle, Tommy's very presence sent chills down Charlie's spine, which is why the more seasoned veteran was happy to get away from him as early as possible on their nightly trek. The routine was always the same: they went the first half mile together before splitting up, then separately approached the enemy installation which was a few miles away in a massive ravine.

Their success on any given night depended heavily on two factors. The first was the density of outer perimeter guards, and the second was their ability to slip past those guards undetected. Fighting wasn't an option. Security would instantly be doubled or tripled, and kill teams would be sent out to hunt them down.

Most nights, they managed to slip past – especially Tommy. Then they would hide next to the ravine, each man at a very different vantage point, telephoto lenses at the ready. They hoped for some kind of outdoor activity at the facility. Anything. Faces that could be tied back to scientists, or pieces of equipment entering or exiting the place. Some nights were deathly quiet. Others were filled with activity.

One thing was clear to Charlie. The installation, which was mostly underground, wasn't just a hidey-hole, or even a headquarters. Something big was going on there, although he wasn't sure what. The perimeter guards were most definitely special ops of some kind – at least as sophisticated as the enemy was capable of. Charlie reminded himself not to underestimate them. Despite their relatively primitive technology, they had somehow managed to drag the war out for over three decades.

There were whispers from some soldiers, especially the old timers, that the enemy was in tune with some kind of primal magic. Charlie knew that was nonsense of course – jibber-jabber reserved for scaring greenies at camp. But the stories had taken on a life of their own, passed from soldier to soldier, creating a web of legend. In many of the tales, soldiers saw things in the jungle that shouldn't have been there, especially at night. Or they stumbled across places where something was living – or had been – and it wasn't the enemy.

One story that Charlie found particularly creepy was a tale of two men out at a listening post on strict radio silence. As the days went on and they waited for some sign of enemy approach, they began to hear bizarre things in the jungle – like dinner parties and social gatherings so loud that the two soldiers could have been guests. Except that nothing was there. Eventually they cracked and called in an air strike, lying about hearing enemy troops marching towards their position. That story always hit a little too close to home for Charlie, except that he and Tommy didn't have the option to call in an air strike.

Charlie sometimes thought he heard things out in the bush, but he chose to ignore them. He would tell himself that he was imagining things, or that it was just a small animal making a racket. But he knew full and well that his trained ears weren't lying, and that the only things that dared to make a sound were at the top of the food chain. Or part of a horde, like the insects. Even if some became prey, the great masses would live on. Sometimes he even told himself that it was just Tommy lurking out in the darkness, which was both reassuring and frightening at the same time.

The truth was that Charlie had no idea what sometimes made strange sounds in the night. All he could do was clutch his gun more tightly and try to reassure himself that he would have a fighting chance. There was also a slight consolation in the fact that Charlie wasn't out there alone. There were far more perimeter guards, and he hoped that statistical probability favored him in the event that there really was something out there preying on soldiers.

He shook his head, letting the steel of his gun bite into his gloved hand to snap him back into reality. Such thoughts were foolish; he wasn't a child hiding under the blankets. There was nothing out there more dangerous than those who fought the war. Yet a sigh of relief came when he spotted an enemy guard and suddenly felt a strange camaraderie, happy to no longer be alone.

The figure was still three hundred yards away. The enemy's use of first generation night vision made them burn like beacons in the night – at least from Charlie's point of view. An infrared light was mounted on each enemy soldier's helmet like a spotlight. They had to produce their own whereas Charlie's more advanced model picked up natural infrared light. He was hidden and they were not – as long as he didn't step into their beam of invisible light.

Charlie circled, leaving a wide berth between him and the enemy, careful not to crunch or break things underfoot. It was an exercise in slow, deliberate movement – painfully slow. It felt more like crawling or treading water than it did walking. The trick wasn't necessarily to be silent so much as it was to blend into all the noises of the jungle. It was a maddening routine that made Charlie feel like something other than himself. Unnatural movements redefined his gait, and every single thought had to be dedicated to not accidentally slipping back into a natural rhythm. The whole pattern was an echo of the war. Normal lives disrupted by the disharmonious frequencies of constant conflict.

He finally found himself at the far side of the sentry and picked up speed again, on the lookout for the next. On a bad night, it could take hours to reach the ravine. Charlie always had to be careful to leave himself enough time at the end of the night to return. If he was still outside when the sun rose, the slough back to his hiding place would be glacial – if he made it back at all.

A part of him wanted him to purposely mess up and let the sun sneak up on him. It would theoretically be good for the mission to be able to snap photos of the facility during the day when it was presumably more active. But more importantly, Charlie would be able to break free from an existence under the cover of persistent darkness. The last several weeks had transformed him into a creature of the night, and he hated it.

His limbs slowed again as he spotted another perimeter guard and stepped into a different existence. Another abysmal progression. To pass the time, he tried to imagine what kind of animal he was most likely mimicking. But he came up short. His movements were an aberration of nature, something only cold calculating thoughts were capable of creating.

He was the product of a darkness that was beyond the simplicity of lower mammals which were only tuned into survival.

Charlie could have been a crab, or a spider, or a great cat. But the jerks and contortions of his appendages didn't belong to any of them. His mind reeled with the idea that war was uniquely human, yet the most dehumanizing thing one could do. He somehow added speed to his movements, wanting to rush through the required motions and get to the ravine.

Only then could he lift the camera to his eyes again and pretend like he wasn't there.

023

Even in broad daylight, it would have been entirely possible to walk through the ravine and not even realize there was a base hidden there. That is if one were allowed to pass through without being gunned down. Charlie carefully eyed the six hidden pillboxes that lined the high ground on each side of the ravine. Each contained gunners pointing heavy artillery to both the interior and exterior of the deep gash in the earth. He generally assumed that the guns pointing down below were there in case an invading force managed to descend into the ravine. But sometimes Charlie wondered if they weren't also meant to keep something inside from escaping.

Some nights, he thought he heard twisted squeals or growls coming from below. He tried his best to ignore the sounds, but the tale of the two soldiers at the listening post kept creeping back into his thoughts. After so many nights of thinking that he was hearing things, he knew that he had to discount it or risk going crazy. His mind was surely playing tricks on him, the strange noises conjured up by his fears. At least that's what he kept telling himself.

Charlie tried to focus on the job at hand, affixing the night vision attachment to his camera with a firm click. Then he lifted it to his eyes and began to scan the area. Since the canopy thinned out over the ravine, great precautions had been taken to conceal the base from aircraft flying overhead. That notwithstanding, his government obviously knew the location of it.

He placed his back against a rocky outcrop and slowly lowered himself into a sitting position. While he went through the familiar motions of searching for any signs of movement, he pondered the mystery of the enemy base for what seemed like the millionth time.

There was something thoroughly baffling about the operation that he and Tommy were a part of. If the Army knew the location of the base, but the enemy didn't realize it, why not just paratroop in and take over the facility? There were no anti-air guns, presumably because that would have given the location away, and the base was remote enough that any response would have taken a long time – days even.

It was as though Charlie's government were waiting for something to happen. Something he and Tommy were supposed to photograph. But why wait? Why leave the enemy to their own devices? Couldn't their scientists simply be captured and forced to continue working? What if Charlie and Tommy missed whatever it was they were supposed to immortalize in film?

Charlie guessed that whatever the enemy did there, it must be somehow rooted to the location itself. If that were the case, the scientists couldn't simply be relocated, and the base itself would be too difficult to hold onto that deep in enemy territory. Charlie wondered what could possibly be there under the thickly carpeted jungle floor.

It seemed to Charlie as though none of his photographs had captured anything of significance, but perhaps Intel was able to extrapolate information that he couldn't discern due to his limited perspective. As he continued to scan the ravine, it was quickly becoming apparent that any photographs from that very evening promised to be lackluster. Nothing stirred at the bottom except for the occasional sentry shifting weight between legs, waiting out the night. No one stood near the main entrance, which was shut and mostly concealed by vegetation.

After he completed an initial sweep, Charlie turned his attention to the opposite side, wondering where Tommy was hiding. He had never managed to spot his partner before, nor should he have, but he still found himself searching out of boredom. At that point, he felt as though he had some idea of the happenings of the facility, and there were usually telltale signs that movement of some sort was about to occur. He knew that he probably shouldn't let his attention slip, but his mind was veiled in solitude and wanted an escape.

There was too much inaction in his daily life. Nothing to do but sit under a dim red light and wait for nightfall, then arrive at the ravine only to sit and wait some more. Even his nightly trek back and forth was repetitive. One foot after the other – motions he had long memorized. His mind screamed to be free.

But he was trapped out there, in the war. He tried to imagine what it might be like to be sitting in a hypothetical backyard somewhere in the suburbs, watching hypothetical kids playing. For a moment, he could almost feel the sun beaming down on his pale white skin. But there were no kids back at home to greet him. Or a wife. Even if he went back there, wherever that was, he didn't know what his life would look like. He'd been in the Army for too long. So long that he didn't perceive an existence that predated his service.

The night around him suddenly felt empty, and a lump rose in his throat. He wanted to jump up and run around, screaming at the top of his lungs. He was tired of the pervasive lethargy that had overtaken him and was now working on his mental faculties. He was tired of not doing. He was tired of not living.

Charlie wondered why he couldn't be like other soldiers who had pictures of their family tucked away in pockets for just such an occasion. He couldn't even conjure up an image of his long deceased parents. Much of his childhood had been spent going from foster home to foster home. The thought had crossed his mind that perhaps the reason why he entered the service as soon as possible was because all he had ever known was how to surrender control of his life to another. And when there were no more foster homes, he needed someone else to take charge.

Things weren't that bad, he supposed. Tommy didn't have a family either, at least not that he mentioned. The younger man had been recruited while still in high school. But there was one blaring difference between them: Tommy loved being in the Army. To him, every night of their mission was a game to be won. Charlie just wanted to go home. Except that there was no home to go to.

The unsettling glow of night vision shone through the camera's view-finder as Charlie lifted it back up to his eyes for another pass. He tried again to focus on the task at hand, knowing that he couldn't let his mind linger in such dark places or it might never get out. The ravine was still quiet, the main entrance still shut tight.

Usually nothing of note happened unless it opened. Sometimes people left, and other times things were brought in. The whole facility was sort of ridiculous, out there in the middle of the jungle with no roads in or out. There wasn't even a helipad. Charlie wondered how they had even managed to build the damn thing.

Perhaps he was overestimating the quality or nature of the construction. He had been in one of the enemy's underground cities before, albeit aban-doned, and it was nothing more than connected rooms dug out the earth and held up by wooden support beams – hardly a marvel of modern engineering. However, the entrance to the base below was bordered by old stones that had been set in place long ago and were even decorative in nature, each featuring elaborate carvings. Charlie imagined that the site had once been something else, maybe even a temple of sorts abandoned by ancestors. The enemy could have piggybacked on the existing infra-structure to dig out more tunnels and chambers like an army of lethal ants.

There was no telling how many of them were down there, but it was certainly enough to require a regular supply line. Any time enemy porters brought things to the base, they wound down the side of the ravine in a long dark line, carrying various objects wrapped up against prying eyes. Charlie couldn't be sure how lively the base was by day, but he imagined that most activity actually happened at night, lest a spy plane spot something.

But nothing was happening that night. Charlie had not snapped a single photograph, yet the character of the night was already changing. The insects sounded different, and the air was cooling, carrying with it a scent that bordered on refreshing. The dead of night waned as morning approached.

After packing his camera up and refitting his night vision rig to his face, Charlie rose and headed back.

024

One foot after the other. Familiar repetition was becoming more of a liability than an advantage. Charlie had already moved past what he believed to be the last perimeter guard and was quickly approaching the last half mile that led back to the shack. His mind wandered again, so much so that he didn't notice the corpse until he was about to step on it.

He froze in his tracks, and a chill ran down his spine into his core. This was no place for the dead, even if it was a war. The corpse wasn't part of the mind numbing sameness that Charlie had become accustomed to. An enemy uniform hung loosely on the damp flesh of the cadaver.

Sweat. This one was fresh.

Charlie raised his gun and whipped it around, searching the jungle for a killer. But there was none. He was only greeted by emptiness filled with flitting shapes.

Charlie finally directed his gaze back down to the dead man whose eyes were shut as though he were sleeping, mouth slightly agape. There was no blood. No gunshot wounds. No signs of struggle.

A horrifying thought slammed into Charlie. He pointed the barrel of his gun squarely at the man's chest and bent down, finger poised over the trigger. The man's chest didn't seem to rise and fall, but Charlie had to be sure. Controlled, shallow breathing would have eluded the casual observer, especially if that observer had just assumed that the man were dead.

All of the noises of the jungle were eclipsed by the pounding in Charlie's ears. He wholly expected the man to spring up at him at any moment, so he was afraid to even blink. He was far too close and should have kept his distance. But the body had been underfoot so quickly. The product of a mind elsewhere. An amateur mistake.

Charlie tried to maintain a cat-like stare, fearing that he might miss a subtle movement of the man's chest if he blinked. Still, the body didn't seem to budge. Or did it? Even with the night vision, the darkness was playing tricks on Charlie's eyes. Small flutters, almost imperceptible. The green glow that filled Charlie's vision writhed with noise.

He finally poked the man's chest with cold steel. No reaction. Not even a flinch. Charlie ventured another thrust, pushing the barrel against the man's sternum – hard enough that there was eventually a sickening crack. Still no reaction.

Charlie straightened out, breathing a silent sigh. The immediate threat was over, but it left a thousand questions in its wake. Soldiers didn't just drop dead in the jungle, and predators usually left marks. Regardless of how the man died, Charlie was sure that it wouldn't be long before the sentry was missed.

After another quick survey of the surrounding area, Charlie found himself staring at the corpse's face. His attention was increasingly focused on the man's lips, parted in a final gasp. He had seen dead men before, even killed them himself, but had never really taken a good look. There had never been the time or the need. It had always been more important to keep moving.

Charlie suddenly had a strange impulse. The strap of his camera bag slithered over the material of his black uniform as he unslung it. He knew the equipment by feel and was able to affix a fifty millimeter lens and its night vision attachment to the camera, all without taking his eyes off of his newfound companion.

It only took a moment to remove the night vision rig from his head, temporarily drowning his sight in utter darkness. Charlie wondered if that's what it was like to die – everything suddenly going black. But his camera promised a rebirth for him, quickly bringing the night back to life as soon he looked through the viewfinder.

He bent down again, filling the frame with a view of what used to be a man's face. With a click of the shutter, the deceased was immortalized. As Charlie rose, he tried to wrap his mind around why he felt compelled to take such a picture.

Just then, the hairs on the back of his neck stood on end – something was wrong. His body reacted before his mind could, trying to lift his gun from his side and spin towards an unseen threat that lurked in the inky blackness. Once the camera's viewfinder fell from his eyes, he was blind, but he could feel someone standing right next to him.

An arm shot out and grabbed his, a knee blocking the pivot of his body as he tried to raise his gun. There was no conscious thought on Charlie's part, only a visceral reaction that tapped into his primal instinct to survive. He was about to grab the assailant's arm and attempt to reverse their roles when a familiar voice whispered from the emptiness.

"It's me," Tommy said. "What the hell are you doing?"

Charlie fumbled to get his night vision rig back into place, suddenly feeling silly. And stupid. "Just headed back." Once Charlie got his visor back into position, he could see that Tommy stared at him coldly – ice blue eyes appearing freakishly white in night vision.

"You walking home blind?" Tommy asked, keeping his voice so low that it was almost lost in the white noise of the insects all around them.

"I just took it off for a second." Charlie felt the edge of his boot against the corpse's leg as he shuffled his stance. "I thought Intel might recognize the face." Charlie shrugged, absentmindedly fingering the camera which still dangled from his neck.

"I don't care about the fucking picture. Why did you kill him?"

"I didn't," Charlie spat out before he could think, his face elongating into a mask of surprise.

Tommy squatted down and examined the corpse, lifting its head and moving it side to side, then rolling the body over slightly to check under its back. Apparently satisfied with his inspection, Tommy stood back up and managed to look Charlie right in the eye, despite the visor that separated them.

Charlie shivered in the jungle heat. He hated when Tommy looked at him that way. It was like the younger man could somehow see right into his soul.

"Then what the fuck killed him?" Tommy asked.

"I don't know," Charlie turned his head to search the surrounding area once again. "I didn't see or hear anything. You?"

Tommy shrugged, raising his hand to his mouth as if to take a drag, then letting the empty gesture transition into rubbing his chin for a second. "No," he shook his head.

A moment of silence passed between them. Charlie kept glancing away, but every time his gaze returned to Tommy, it was met with that same intense stare that bored into him.

"We have two problems then," Charlie started as he looked around for the tenth time. "There's a mystery killer out here, even though it's just supposed to be us and them." He reluctantly looked back at Tommy. "And a not so mysterious killer is going to come looking for us as soon as they find him." Charlie shook his head. "It's over." He didn't quite know what that meant. They weren't allowed to abandon the mission, nor could they call in support. They couldn't even radio HQ to get new orders. The only way to communicate was through the weekly runner, if they survived that long.

"I guess we just go back and wait," Charlie said as he started to take a step in the general direction of their hideout.

"Wait." Tommy reached out and grabbed Charlie's arm again. "We need to hide the body," he said, the hint of a smirk dancing around the corners of his mouth. Charlie just stared at him.

"It's one thing if they find the body. It's another if the guy just disappears. Leaves more to the imagination. They're on radio silence too."

Tommy stared off, playing out some scenario in his mind. "It'll be spooky as hell." He smiled.

"That still leaves the first problem," Charlie said flatly, wondering if they really were alone.

Tommy leaned closer to him as though he were about to whisper some profound truth. "Whoever killed him is after them, not us." Tommy backed away again. "And whoever killed him doesn't even know we're out here – because we're not." He squatted down and grabbed the man's shoulders, glancing up at Charlie. "Let's do this. I know a good spot."

Overhead, the night continued its relentless crawl towards morning, and Charlie knew they didn't have much time before they were sitting ducks. He reached down and grabbed the corpse's feet, keeping his other questions to himself.

Tommy led them through the jungle, each step overburdened by the dead weight of the body. Charlie regretted every crunch and snap, imagining the entire enemy army could hear them clear as day. But it was less risky than just leaving the body out in the open. He wondered how far they were going just as beads of sweat began to roll across his skin and fatigue sapped his arm muscles. The underbrush had become incredibly thick, slowing their progress even more.

"Almost there," Tommy whispered.

"This is right by our camp," Charlie objected. "If they find the body, we'll be at the center of their search."

Tommy came to a stop and glanced up at the steadily brightening canopy overhead. "You have a better idea?"

Charlie wished that he did. He shook his head angrily.

"Don't worry, this is a good spot."

As they continued deeper into the underbrush, Charlie wondered just how Tommy had discovered this "spot." Progress had become painfully slow, the way forward barred by thick vegetation and thorny vines that had hardened like tree branches. The greenery had become so dense that Charlie couldn't see Tommy or the front of the body anymore.

All of sudden, they were standing in a small clearing at the base of a gargantuan tree. Charlie hadn't quite seen anything else like it in the jungle. Its imposing stature and gnarled bark suggested that it was a child of antiquity, which was odd in a place that constantly teemed with new growth.

Tommy tilted his head to indicate a large hollow at the base of the tree. They stuffed the body inside, shoving it out of sight. Then they began to grab desiccated leaves and bits of dead branches to further conceal the fallen soldier. Not only would one have to practically crawl inside the hollow to see the body, but that someone would also have to remove the natural debris covering it.

Tommy emerged from the hollow and nodded at Charlie. It was finally time to return to a familiar, dull existence.

025

The world was red again. But before stepping back into the four suffocating walls of the shack, Charlie had seen a rare thing. The inky blackness of night had begun to brighten into the hazy blue of morning – something he hadn't seen in weeks. Or had it been months already?

The sight of a different light, a different world, almost caused something to break inside Charlie. Familiar green and red worked to keep him bound to duty, but deviations threatened to destroy the forced rhythm.

As Charlie had stood at the base of the five steps leading up into the shack, waiting as Tommy entered ahead of him, he wanted to break into a run and leave everything behind. War was a simple equation. Us and Them. There and somewhere else. Even though he had nowhere to go, he knew that didn't want to be there. But in the end, he had slowly marched up the steps and closed out the blooming dawn.

Now Charlie and Tommy sat across from each other as they always did, Tommy smoking, Charlie trying to avoid the other's gaze. A dull ache had welled up inside of Charlie's chest and refused to leave. Some part of him wanted to cry, but tears were something from a distant past that no longer existed in his world. Without any release, the ache persisted. Charlie eyed the entirety of the shack which had become the entirety of his world. If he had nowhere else to go, had this become home?

"You gonna develop that picture?" Tommy asked.

Charlie shook his head slowly. "It's the first one on the roll."

Tommy gave a single nod in recognition, then silence descended upon them once again. The truth was that Charlie wanted to develop the photo, but he had no intention of doing it while Tommy watched him. The impulse to snap the photograph had been strange to begin with, and now his desire to develop it felt like a guilty pleasure. It was something that he shouldn't have been curious about.

Charlie sat up and started to unlace his boots. He hadn't yet decided if he was going to wait until Tommy fell asleep, or if he'd return early the next night. But if he did decide that he couldn't wait, the sound of removing his boots later would likely wake Tommy. His heart started to beat faster as he placed the first boot in the corner with a thud. It was like he was back out in the bush, up to dark deeds.

He dared a glance over at Tommy as he started to remove his second boot. The other man was already sitting there in his underwear, hopefully oblivious to Charlie's intentions. But even in the split second that they made eye contact, Charlie felt like Tommy could see right through him.

Next he removed his t-shirt, then laid on top of his sleeping bag and stared up at the ceiling like he was disinterested, even though adrenaline pumped through his veins. The sensible part of his brain warned him that he should concerned about his morbid fascination with the photo, maybe even worried about finally going off the deep end. Yet a cold, calculating part of him was already planning how he would develop it secretly. There was a tug of war, and he feared that some inner demon was taking control. Why did he feel like he had to do it without Tommy knowing, and what did the desire even mean?

The rafters overhead were dark, left in shadow by the positioning of the dangling red light bulb. Amorphous forms coalesced there, an optical illusion beyond the reach of Charlie's human vision. The more he stared, the more it seemed like something might actually be moving up there in the shadows – maybe an insect that had flown in when they had opened the door.

Charlie frowned. That couldn't possibly be true. If it were an insect, it would be bumping up against the light bulb constantly. As it was, a cloud of smaller bugs swarmed around it. Technically, they should have already turned off the light to conserve battery power, but there was an unspoken preference to sleep with the light on. Fortunately, they had found a good perch for their solar panel that caught sunlight most of the day.

Charlie heard the soft scraping sound of Tommy putting out a cigarette, then finally laying down. It was too hot for either of them to climb inside of their sleeping bags, which was just as well. The rustling from getting out of it would have likely waked Tommy as well.

Bedtime was usually Charlie's favorite part of his meager existence. Unlike many soldiers he had known, he never seemed to have nightmares. There were only vague dreams of a home he couldn't consciously recall. Of a bed he couldn't remember sleeping in. And a wife he never had. But in that moment, he decided not to indulge the fantasy that his subconscious had conjured up in favor of the waking task that had arrested his interest.

More and more justifications kept popping into his head, making the task seem less bizarre. He was just bored, he kept telling himself, and the excitement of a series of unlikely events had roused his numbed senses. Developing the picture was merely something to do.

After several minutes, Charlie rolled onto his side to face Tommy and feigned droopy eyelids. Tommy didn't seem to care, or notice. The other man already had his eyes shut, but Charlie knew that it would be better if he waited for a while so Tommy could enter a deeper phase of sleep.

As the minutes rolled by, Charlie found himself wondering what the other man dreamed about. Tommy had never bolted upright in the middle of the night screaming as other soldiers occasionally did. He sometimes even had a vague smile, which made Charlie wonder about the perversity of his dreams. Was it possible that one man's nightmares were another's pleasure?

Finally there came a noticeable change in Tommy's breathing. It had become deeper, more time elapsing between breaths. But it was a change that had to be visually measured. The man was just as quiet in his sleep as when he was stalking through the jungle. Never a raspy breath, never a snore.

Charlie waited another half hour before he finally sprang into action. He had purposely left his camera bag unzipped earlier, and after sitting up, he deftly removed the roll of film without making a sound. Then he stood up.

His progression was slow. Painfully slow. A long rehearsed symphony of sluggish movements designed to evade detection. Tommy had suddenly become one of Them, and the shack was no different than the bush. Tommy's rifle was mere inches away from his hand, and it was for this reason that Charlie usually avoided getting up during the day. A soldier with cat-like reflexes might shoot first and ask questions later if he woke and mistook an ally for an intruder. Charlie purposely avoided looking at Tommy, fearing that he might invoke a feeling of being watched – a sixth sense that he knew to be real.

Soft footfalls glided across the old wooden floor, somehow evading spots that would have let out plaintiff creaks in alarm. Over half of the shack was devoted to development and print making. The original plan had been to exclude this from the mission, stripping it down to only snapping photos, then having the runner take the undeveloped rolls back to HQ. But someone had been concerned that if the recon photographers were unable to review their work, they might fail to notice finer details and later miss a photo op because they had dismissed something as insignificant. While orders could have been sent from HQ about things to watch for, there would have been a two week delay with the runners' schedule.

Of course developing photos in the field made the whole mission more complicated – and treacherous. An abandoned structure had to be located, and power supplied. Runners had to carry chemicals in addition to other supplies. Charlie was glad that such a decision had been made. Developing gave him something to do.

He partially unwound the roll of film, snipping off the only exposed image from the head before slipping the rest of the roll into a pocket.

Developing the entire unused roll would have meant evidence to dispose of and more explaining to do. The single print sank into the chemical bath where a couple of gnats had landed and drowned at some point. Charlie made a point of listening carefully while he waited, still not wanting to look over at Tommy. Nothing seemed to stir.

The waiting was the worst part, but Charlie used the time to walk through the rest of his plan again. As soon as the print was made, he would grab it and the negative, then retreat back to his sleeping bag where he would hide them. If Tommy later asked about the photo of the dead soldier, Charlie would shrug and blame it on a camera malfunction. Even though he had already rehearsed these things while he still lay on the ground, he couldn't stop them from replaying over and over again in his head. Sometimes the excuse he gave to Tommy was slightly different, finessed a little more to hide his lie.

As soon as the negative was developed, he carefully removed a blank print from a sealed package. He had performed the task of printmaking so much that it was now something he could do mindlessly while his thoughts raced in other directions. He slipped the negative into the enlarger, then flipped it on. He made a point to only look at the fringes of the ghostly image for sizing and focus – he didn't want to spoil anything until he could see the actual image in print.

After exposing the blank paper, he moved over to a row of trays. Fortunately, they hadn't thrown the fluid out yet. That would have complicated matters, necessitating an outdoor disposal once he was done so Tommy didn't wake up to full trays that had been empty. Not to mention the fluid that would have been missing from their scant supplies.

Charlie placed the exposed print into the first tray, then began rocking it gently to agitate the developing fluid inside. Although there was a timer on the work bench behind the trays, Charlie had luckily acquired the ability to time things perfectly without it. The incessant tick-tock would have had Tommy awake instantly.

He anxiously leaned over to watch as a faint image began to appear on the paper – the immortal remains of a man who had already begun to waste away. For an instant, he imagined what the face would look like on the cover of *Time* Magazine. Then he remembered that he was fighting in a war that didn't officially exist. There would be no accolades or recognition. If he died, there would be no return home. It dawned on him, just then, that perhaps it wasn't a coincidence that he nor Tommy had families.

But before his mind could drag him too far down that line of thought, something caught his attention in the photograph. Just as the black and white image was fully coming into being, there was a striking feature that stood out like a sore thumb. Above the man's slightly parted lips was perched a butterfly.

Charlie stared into the developing tray, probably leaving the print in for too long. It seemed that his eyes were playing tricks on him again. There hadn't been a butterfly there when he had taken the photo… or was there? It should have been plain as day through the green glow of the viewfinder. How had he missed it?

As he moved the photo into the stop process tray, a distant part of his mind screamed out silently that he was indeed going crazy. The fact that he had been obsessed with developing the morbid photograph was disturbing enough without factoring in what he was – or wasn't – seeing. Charlie's stomach fluttered at the possible implications. Weren't serial killers the only people obsessed with such things?

The fixer and rinsing stages flew by, and Charlie was all too happy to creep back over to his sleeping bag and shove the picture out of sight.

026

Charlie tossed and turned all day between fitful bouts of sleep. His imaginary home in the suburbs refused to welcome him. Instead, he kept trying to picture the corpse's face, hoping to remember a butterfly being there. But it just hadn't been.

He ran through ludicrous scenarios – like his lens being dirty and somehow creating a pattern that looked sort of like a butterfly. But no – the image was crystal clear, the pattern on the wings elaborate and possessing a ghostly beauty in black and white. It was a butterfly, not a Rorschachian impression conjured up by a greasy smudge.

It took extreme willpower, but he resisted the urge to fish the photo out of his pack. If he were slipping into a depraved mental state, finally cracking under the pressure of war, it was going to be his secret. As far as he was concerned, the photo didn't exist. It would not be given to the runner when he arrived in two days, and Tommy sure as hell wasn't going to see it.

Charlie felt sick to his stomach, like someone who was committing a perverse crime and knew it – but still kept doing it anyway. He lost track of time, his thoughts splintered, and his one sleepless day seemed longer than the entire war. Each second was excruciating, separating him from the moment when he could examine the picture again.

Tommy finally stirred, rising to urinate in the container that they used in the corner. Charlie shut his eyelids, deliberately waiting a few minutes before pretending to wake up. It had to appear as if nothing was amiss.

Tommy lit up and glanced over at Charlie. "What's the plan?"

A pause. "What do you mean?"

"We going out?" Tommy asked. "Or laying low?"

Charlie sat up on an elbow. He had been so concerned with the photo that he hadn't considered the enemy response to a missing soldier.

But he had to find a way to be alone.

"They must know he's gone by now," Tommy said as he flicked ash against the wall.

Charlie nodded. "We shouldn't just sit here though," he eyed Tommy. "I'd at least like to know if they're coming. Have a fighting chance."

"Back to the bush then," Tommy shrugged, unable to hide a sparkle in his eye. "You gonna develop that picture first?"

Charlie shook his head slowly. "I'll wait until the roll is full."

Tommy put out his cigarette and stood up, grabbing his pants.

"It's still light out," Charlie said.

"I know," Tommy said. "Just getting ready. Nothing better to do."

Charlie let himself fall back onto his sleeping bag. More waiting.

027

When they finally emerged from the shack under cover of darkness, there were no pleasantries or hand signals. They just split up, and Tommy was swallowed whole by the jungle moments later.

After their brief exchange when they woke up, no more words had cut through the silence, no plan developed. Charlie just wanted to be alone, and it seemed as though Tommy was just as anxious to escape into the open night. It was foolish that they didn't have a plan. But what could they do? If kill teams had been mobilized, they would just have to dodge them and stay invisible as they had been for weeks.

Charlie still felt like he was falling off of a cliff, ignoring protocol and common sense. Something was slowly snapping inside of him, and he felt a strange sense of finality creeping into his being. He feared that one way or another, the war might be over for him soon.

He had transferred the print from his pack to his camera bag when Tommy's back had been turned, but he hadn't managed to sneak a glance. Now he trudged through the jungle, seeking absolute privacy before finally satiating his curiosity.

Once he was deep in the bush, he crouched down to set his camera bag in front of him. A moment later, he had the photograph out, comparing it to the image burned in his mind. Seemingly, his memory of it had become more fantastic. He remembered the pattern on the wings being more elaborate and thought he had seen hints of other vague, fluttering shapes in the darkness.

Charlie tried to picture the man's face again – the way it had looked to his eyes before the click of the shutter. It seemed that his memory had failed him completely, because he didn't remember seeing a butterfly there.

He shook his head as he stuffed the photo back into his camera bag, thinking about the fact that butterflies aren't even supposed to be out at night.

It probably didn't matter anyway. The man was dead. Who gave a fuck if there was a butterfly there? And so what if he had somehow failed to see it. What mattered was survival. Charlie resolved to refocus his efforts as he continued on his nightly trek, one foot after the other.

028

It had been a normal night, like so many other nights, spent sidestepping perimeter guards, then waiting next to the ravine for nothing to happen. Charlie was bored.

Either the facility had not missed the dead soldier, or they didn't care. Charlie supposed it was possible that they had chalked it up to natural predators. It wasn't uncommon to cross paths with great jungle cats or crocodiles as long as three men. He could see how one disappearance could be written off, especially since the body was missing.

Charlie couldn't dismiss it as easily. Natural predators killed for food, their claws and teeth shredding flesh to a bloody pulp. The only reasonable explanation was that the man had dropped dead from a heart attack or a deadly snake bite. But there was nothing reasonable in war. Charlie knew better.

He shifted his attention away from the ravine and to the surrounding area, trying to discern what might be lying in wait beyond the dancing noise in his visor. An icy feeling of vulnerability ran through his veins, a chill that electrified the hairs on the back of his neck. He debated whether he should trust the feeling, not knowing if it was the same intuition that had kept him alive all over the years or just paranoia.

He put his camera away and slipped the night vision rig back onto his head. The unbending steel of his gun felt good in his hands, a reassurance that he was making the right decision as he stood up. There was a killer out there, and the roles needed to be reversed before he wound up dead.

Breaking the nightly routine wasn't part of his orders and would certainly be frowned upon if ever a disciplinary review came of it. But survival was more important than his orders, even if HQ would disagree with that sentiment. Besides, it was something different to do.

Charlie decided to start by circling to the other side of the ravine. His footsteps were no longer well-rehearsed as he strayed from his familiar path. He felt alive again, shaken from a dull banality that had settled like a layer of dust over his sharpened senses. Walking along the edge of the ravine required extra care. Each pillbox had an array of infrared lights that shone like the sun, at least in night vision. If he were spotted, he'd be ripped in half within seconds by the heavy gunners.

As he reached the head of the ravine where it seemed to start, he wondered if he'd spot Tommy as he walked along the other side. He wanted to spot Tommy, to keep tabs on everyone and everything around him, but he knew that if the other man was well hidden, he might just walk right past and never know it.

And indeed, as he wound his way along the opposite, unfamiliar side, he was only greeted by the bright lights of the pillboxes. It was a quiet night where nothing seemed to stir, like there was a dread hanging in the air that signaled horrible things to come.

When he finally arrived at the foot of the ravine, he spotted a deep gash carved into a tree trunk which he knew to be the enemy sign for an invisible roadway through the jungle. He spotted signs of passage and realized that he was following the path used by supply runners coming to and from the secret facility. He and Tommy had found it their first week there, but avoided it to minimize the chances of contact.

Suddenly the path was more alluring to Charlie. The basic runners were unguarded villagers, probably laden with simple cargoes of food or gasoline. They would be the lowest hanging fruit and the least likely to be missed. Of all the places he could randomly search in the jungle, it seemed slightly more probable that he might find the killer there.

Charlie was careful to moderate his movements, even though a natural chemical high rushed to his head. He felt like he was on to something, his sixth sense responding to some unseen threat again. He stopped, listening carefully for something that didn't belong – some telltale sign of an apex predator lying in wait.

His vigilance was rewarded by a distant, almost imperceptible sound. It sounded like a twig breaking underfoot, but it was so faint that it was difficult to tell.

Charlie stayed perfectly still for several minutes, waiting for some other sign. But there was none. It had been fortuitous that he had even heard what he heard. He finally decided to approach the general vicinity from which the noise had come.

The normal ambiance of teeming life seemed to diminish as he drew closer, as though repulsed by some unnatural force – something that didn't belong. The vegetation thinned out along the path where countless runners had crushed new growth underfoot, and there was another deep gash through the bark of a tree where yellowish ichor had spilled out like tears and hardened.

It didn't take Charlie long to spot a crumpled form that used to be a man on the ground. Before paying any attention to his find, Charlie took several minutes to ensure that he wasn't about to become the next victim. But there were only signs of careless footsteps and scrapes. The stealthy killer had blended evidence of its own passage into the well-worn path.

The corpse that lay on the ground was just a villager who never had a chance. A spilled cargo of foodstuffs lay on the ground next to him. Charlie searched for an obvious cause of death, but there weren't any marks or puncture wounds of any kind. Not even a drop of blood had been spilled. This time, he took the opportunity for a more thorough examination, looking for snake bites on the legs. Nothing was there.

The body was still warm, its appendages still limber. Another fresh kill. Charlie stared out into the night, wondering what secrets it held.

Then his gaze settled back on the gaunt features of the deceased. Like the first body, its lips were agape, as if to try to inhale one final breath. Charlie waved his hand back and forth over the mouth.

"No Goddamn butterfly," he muttered to himself. This time he was going to make sure that he took note of exactly what he was seeing. He had his camera prepped moments later and examined the same face through the viewfinder of his camera.

No butterfly. He chopped the air over the corpse's mouth again for good measure. After one click of the shutter, he decided to take a second photo, then a third from a totally different angle. And after the last one, he visually inspected the area over the mouth one last time.

He finally stood up, debating whether or not he should try to hide the body. All alone, there was only so much he could do. He would have made an awful lot of noise dragging one side of the body through the underbrush. He supposed that he could carry the body over his shoulder, but the extra weight would strip him of any hope at stealth – which would in turn make him an easy target.

As he slipped his headpiece back on, he decided that he would at least remove it from the main trail. The regularity of the runners' schedule was uncertain, and Charlie had no idea where they came from, but assumed that a missing food delivery would raise less red flags than a dead soldier. But not if the body was right in the path of the next runner.

He slung his gun and camera bag over a shoulder, then squatted down and pulled the limp body up into a hug as he hoisted it over his shoulder. Dry wood cracked underfoot, his step less certain. The thinned out foliage of the trail quickly gave way to waist high growth. Charlie tried his best to not crush any of the tall stalks underfoot, counting each step to gauge how far he had traveled.

Charlie spotted a depression half covered by a fallen tree and dropped the body inside. Then he started gathering dead leaves and covered the slivers of flesh and clothing that were still visible.

A check of the time revealed that the night was only halfway over. If Charlie had still been at his position on the edge of the ravine, it would have been another two hours before he needed to start heading back.

But now there were more pictures to be developed, and he didn't relish the idea of another sleepless day as he slinked around while Tommy slept. He checked his compass and decided set off in the direction of the shack for an early return.

029

The return journey had taken longer than Charlie had wanted. He wasn't familiar with the part of the jungle that he had wandered into, and he ran afoul of several guard posts unexpectedly. In spite of that, he was still early. By his estimations, Tommy should have just then been leaving the ravine and should have been at least an hour away.

But as soon as Charlie approached the perimeter of the shack, a familiar odor hung in the air – fresh cigarette smoke. He paused, taken aback by the apparent presence of the other man. And he now knew without a doubt that those damn cigarettes would eventually give them away.

Charlie trudged up the front steps and slowly opened the door, not wanting to spook Tommy. Notwithstanding, as soon as he slipped through the open doorway, he was greeted by the sight of a gun barrel leveled right at him. He stopped until Tommy lowered the gun.

"What are you doing back so early?" Charlie asked.

Tommy sat there shirtless, a half smoked cigarette dangling from his lips. "Tried to make it to the ravine, but there were too many guards. I'm surprised you didn't come back sooner."

Charlie weighed his words, thinking that perhaps Tommy was referring to the guard posts that he himself had encountered. But he had no way of knowing what the normal amount of activity was leading up to the other side of the ravine. Instead of responding, Charlie just set his gun and camera down.

He sat across from Tommy, glaring at him. "You know, I could smell that fucking cigarette a hundred yards away."

Tommy just shrugged, taking another drag.

"Where do you get them from anyway? You should be out by now."

"Made a deal with the runner," Tommy said.

"You need to stop. It's a dead giveaway."

Tommy pushed what was left of the cigarette up against the floor then tossed it in the corner. "I'll cut back."

"If you want to risk your life, go do that shit outside – somewhere faraway from here," Charlie said. "I don't want my brains blown out because you can't kick a habit."

Tommy just nodded, then removed a straight razor and a can of shaving cream from his pack. "I already got us fresh water." He stood up and walked over to the far end of the workbench where he had propped up the shard of mirror on top of a wooden beam. He flipped the blade out, then dipped it in a basin of water. Shaving cream escaped the can with a hiss.

"I didn't get very far either," Charlie finally said.

Tommy glanced over as he lathered the cream over his face. "Oh?"

"Yeah, found another body. Had to hide it."

The straight edge of the razor slid down the side of Tommy's face, making a loud scraping sound. Charlie watched him, noticing how the other man didn't even wince, even though shaving without hot water was always painful. But Tommy just kept swiping the straight razor across his skin, stripping away evidence of manhood and leaving behind the face of a twelve year old.

"You see anything while you were out?" Charlie asked.

"Nope," Tommy answered, "just guards." He splashed some water on one half of his face, washing away the remains of the lather before moving the razor to the other side. "You sure like to talk all of a sudden."

"Since you already gave us away with the damn cigarette smoke, I figure it doesn't hurt to talk. At least until the smell clears out."

Tommy looked at him via the reflection in the mirror. "You get any pictures tonight?"

Charlie suppressed a wave of panic. He shook his head slowly. "Nothing worth seeing."

A silence settled over the room, only broken by the scraping of the razor against dead cells. Charlie was annoyed that Tommy was there. He had an urgent desire to verify that he wasn't crazy and that the first photo had simply been a lapse in observation. Then he could return to the business of dealing with whatever was stalking men in the night.

Tommy swished the razor around in the water, then gave his face a final rinse. Drops made red by the overhead light rolled down the sides of his clean shaven face, dripping back into the pan. He crossed the room and put his things away, then grabbed his pack of foreign cigarettes, a satchel and his gun.

"Still got a bit before first light. I'm going to take your advice." Tommy motioned towards Charlie with the pack of cigarettes, then moved to the door. "Don't worry, I'll be plenty far away."

And with that he was gone.

030

Charlie sat in shock for a minute, wondering just how much time he had alone. Everything in him wanted to grab the camera bag and run over to the workbench. He forced himself to wait five minutes, lest Tommy return after having forgotten something. It took a great deal of self-control, like he was a child on Christmas morning waiting for his parents to wake up.

Once he was fairly certain that Tommy wasn't returning anytime soon, he sprung up and placed his camera on the workbench. Just as he had done before, he used scissors to remove only the exposed frames, spooling the rest up for the next shot. The negatives sunk down into the development bath as Charlie shifted his weight from one foot to the other impatiently.

As he waited, he checked the print trays, then prepped the enlarger. A giddy excitement fluttered through his stomach. He had thought he'd have to wait hours for Tommy to go to sleep, but instead he was able to indulge this guilty curiosity immediately.

As soon as he removed the negatives from the bath, he held them up to his eyes, trying to discern the tiny images. But the dimness of the red light overhead didn't favor small details. He contemplated grabbing a flashlight and taking a look, but decided he was just wasting time.

He moved the first blank print into position under the enlarger, then slotted the developed negative into place. He avoided looking at the projection of the negative image, once again just glancing at the corner of the frame for sizing and focus. He replayed the scene in his mind, recalling just how purposeful he had been to remember exactly what was and wasn't there. If anything had been over the corpse's mouth, he would have swatted it away with his hand.

He carefully placed the print inside of the developing tray like a holy man placing a relic upon an altar. Then he began to rock the tray, disturbing the placid surface above the blank white paper. His heart pounded in his ears as he watched a faint outline appear from nothingness. Every second was agonizing, but as each passed, the image became clearer.

And so did a small winged form perched above the dead villager's mouth. Charlie stopped rocking the tray, his own mouth agape. It should have been impossible, yet there it was. The pattern on its wings was completely different from the one in the first photograph. Charlie staggered back, light headed, as he stared at the reality shattering image that sat at the bottom of the tray under swirling fluids.

As seconds turned into minutes, the image turned black, ruined by the same chemicals that had given it life. Charlie rushed back over to the work bench and grabbed the other two negatives, anxious to prove to himself that he wasn't crazy. Surely the butterfly wasn't in all the pictures. Or maybe the alternate angle would reveal some trick of the light.

Yet as the second print developed, the butterfly was still poised over parted lips, mocking him. This time, he didn't even let the print finish developing before he slipped the next into the tray. In the scant seconds before the image started to materialize, Charlie felt a mix of resignation and desperation. The final print had to prove something, but he already knew that it wasn't going to be what he wanted to see. From his alternate angle above the villager's face, the butterfly was just as clear, spreading its wings as though for the camera.

Charlie ripped the print out of the tray and set to cleaning up the workbench. He stuffed the ruined negatives and prints into his camera bag and ran back over to his sleeping bag to grab his gun and night vision rig. A crazy idea was forming – one that he knew he shouldn't pursue. But he had to know. Once his headpiece was secured, he exited the red pallor of the shack and entered the waning darkness of night.

031

Charlie had no idea where Tommy had gone off to, but he wasn't so much concerned about the other man anymore. He retraced the steps of the morning before when he and Tommy had shouldered the burden of the dead in an attempt to stay alive. The underbrush had already recoiled from their steps, springing back up to conceal the path they had taken. But he thought that he still knew the way.

As he recklessly crashed through the tall vegetation, he imagined that he might have been a young boy running through a backyard or a young lover dashing through the trees to find his sweetheart – anything but what he actually was. His existence had become a verisimilitude of a nightmare; instead of laughter or gentle kisses, horror lurked in the darkness beyond.

The thing that scared Charlie the most wasn't the silent killer, but the invisible shapes that he thought he saw in his peripheral vision. The killer was at least something real, something expected. The strange shapes shouldn't have been there, and at that point, Charlie could no longer tell if they really were or not.

He suddenly emerged from the bush and found himself standing before the strange tree where they had hid the first body. An eerie silence hung over the place, and Charlie noticed for the first time that nothing seemed to be growing around the tree. It was like a ring of death had spread from its trunk long ago, leaving behind dry husks and fallen leaves. As Charlie eyed the hollow at its base, the green glow of night vision took on a sepulchral air, and a chill ran down his spine.

It was one thing to kill a man, but another to handle a day old corpse. Charlie stooped down and crawled into the hollow, leaving his backside exposed as he reached out to grab the fallen soldier. The body was stiff, and Charlie could feel small things angrily crawling onto his hands, their meal disrupted.

He pulled the body far enough out so that he could clearly see its face, but not an inch farther. The clammy dead flesh writhed under his fingertips. Even though the body had been hidden from the eyes of men, scavengers had begun to feast upon it, taking with them small bits of skin and flesh. The heat and dampness of the jungle had also given rise to microscopic predators, and the smell of rotting meat filled the air.

Charlie didn't want to breathe, nor did he appreciate his tactile senses at that moment. Every fiber in his being rebelled against his proximity to the thing that he feared he might become. Everything seemed wrong. Charlie could have been a grandson paying respects at the casket of a grandfather. But instead he was there on his knees desecrating the remains of a man he didn't know, yet had so much in common with.

No butterfly, Charlie reassured himself as he swiped the air above the lips of the deceased. But there were ants, flies, and other writhing forms that he didn't recognize. He tried not to gag as he readied his camera, but it didn't work. Normally, looking through the viewfinder was a welcome reprieve, a false separation from reality that Charlie enjoyed and even relied on at times to keep his sanity. But as he framed up the lifeless face, there were too many reminders of where he really was for him to suspend reality. The smell of rot. The buzzing of flies. And a sense of dread.

The click of the shutter brought a sense of finality to the investigation. Whatever had been captured on the negative was now there, trapped forever. All Charlie could do now was develop the truth. He rose to his feet and kicked debris from the jungle floor over the corpse's face, not wanting to lay hands on it again. He fought an overpowering urge to run. Not only was he possessed of a powerful sense of revulsion, but the clearing around the tree felt alien. It was not a place for life – not to mention the fact that he could feel someone or something watching him.

As soon as the body was sufficiently concealed, Charlie turned to leave, searching the surrounding underbrush for some sign of his invisible stalker. He was so concerned with what was hiding beyond his vision that he failed to watch his own feet. The steel plate on the inside of his boot ran right into a stone with a dull thud.

Charlie glanced down and realized that it wasn't just an amorphous stone shaped by nature. It was actually a waist high pillar, shaped by men. A heavy growth of vines obscured it, explaining why he hadn't noticed it before. Despite wanting to run, Charlie felt compelled to take a closer look. He ripped away clinging vines, exposing the worn face of the stone.

His blood ran cold as he recognized the carvings there. They were the same sort of ancient sigils that adorned the stone structures down in the ravine. In that instant, he recalled all of the strange noises he often heard from down below while watching the facility, and he wondered what the connection was to the clearing and the gnarled tree.

But it wasn't something that he pondered for long. He finally let his primal instincts take over and dashed into the underbrush, not bothering to look back.

032

Charlie gingerly navigated the series of tripwires set up around the perimeter of the shack. Being more elaborate than a normal setup, it always slowed his progress but insured that it was highly unlikely anyone would be able to get close to the hideout without them knowing about it. If one didn't know the location of each and every wire, it was damn near impossible to not hit one. Charlie had to twist his feet sideways in some places and tiptoe in others, an unnatural sequence that he had memorized.

When he arrived at the doorway, he could sense that someone was inside, which meant that Tommy had returned before him. Charlie cursed silently. There was a new photo that needed developing, but now it would have to wait.

Charlie opened the door cautiously, expecting to come face to face with the waiting barrel of a gun again. Instead, Tommy glanced over at him from the back corner. The other man stood across from the workbench, handling something that sat on a small shelf.

"You needed a smoke too?" Tommy smiled.

"No," Charlie said as he the shut the door. "I was scouting our perimeter." As he drew closer, he eyed the object on the shelf that Tommy still had his hands around. It was a ragged square of cardboard bristling with a few sewing needles that had been pushed into it. "What's that?"

Tommy glanced down at the piece of cardboard. "Nothing." He left it on the shelf and stepped away, heading for his sleeping bag. "Just bored."

"Yeah," Charlie said, resigning himself to the agonizing passage of time to come. But there was nothing to do but wait.

033

Charlie watched the rise and fall of Tommy's chest, trying to catch any irregularity that might betray a feigned sleep. He still wondered how it was possible that he had been able to develop the first photo the previous night without getting caught. Even though Charlie doubted Tommy because of his youth, watching him move through the jungle told a different tale. Tommy was dangerous, and he should have woken up the previous night. Charlie was starting to think that everything was not as it seemed.

Yet there Tommy was, his breathing regular, perfectly modulated by the sleep cycle. Charlie knew that he wouldn't be able to sleep unless he developed the photo, but knew that doing so probably wasn't prudent. He weighed the options. If Tommy was faking it, then he probably already knew that Charlie had been developing prints. The main question that weighed on Charlie's mind was why Tommy would pretend to be asleep in the first place. Why not just confront him?

Some other part of Charlie wondered why he cared. So what if Tommy woke up? So what if Charlie had been snapping photos of dead men? The war would go on. Their mission would continue as it always had.

With that, Charlie decided to rise. He still did so ever so slowly, playing along with the ruse if there were one. And if not, he didn't want to wake Tommy. He grabbed his camera on the way up, then moved silently over to the work bench.

Unloading the roll, snipping the negative, watching it slowly descend into a chemical bath – another process that had become a mindless activity of the war. But unlike the others, this task was twisting Charlie's stomach into knots. He was aware of an increased heart rate, shallow breathing. Paranoia.

He wanted to look over at Tommy as he moved the developed negative to the enlarger, but still didn't dare. Tommy was either asleep or he wasn't. Charlie pressed on, his hand trembling as he flipped on the enlarger, casting faint beams down onto a blank print.

He took great care to not under or overexpose, still grasping for some technical glitch that might explain the anomalies in the other photographs. He turned off the exposure lamp and grabbed the print reverently. He held it above the tray, examining the blank canvas which harbored something invisible beneath the surface – something he couldn't see with his bare eyes. Chemicals were required to tease the image out.

As he finally placed the print into the developing tray, he didn't know what to expect. His eyes had lied to him thus far. Why wouldn't that trend continue?

Fluid waves rolled back and forth in the tray as Charlie rocked it, right over the faint traces of an image that had begun to form. He was just as taken aback as he had been with all of the other photos, but this time the surprise was different. The dead soldier's face was clear in the image – albeit ravaged by insects. What was left of the lips were still parted in a final gasp. But there was no butterfly.

Charlie held the print up to his eyes before placing it into the fixer. Just as with the previous photos, he doubted what he was seeing. He had come to expect the flitting forms that seemed to play in the fringes of his vision and dance among the video noise of a green night. But now suddenly there were none.

He took his hand off of the fixer tray.

He didn't care anymore.

The fluid in the tray settled over the print. Charlie was inclined to simply leave it there in its watery grave. Knotting his fists into balls of frustration, Charlie rocked on his feet instead of pacing. He wasn't sure what to do next.

In a fleeting moment, his vision grazed the mirror that Tommy had set up for shaving. Panic jolted him before he even realized what he had seen. Or what he thought he had seen.

In the reflection sat the piece of cardboard that Tommy had set upon the opposite shelf. Speared under each bristling pin was a butterfly – three of them.

When Charlie looked back at the mirror, they were gone. It was only a normal piece of cardboard again with pins pushed into it. He spun around to examine it with his bare eyes, but still there was nothing. He even picked it up, feeling around each pin, but his prying fingers were only met with empty air.

Then it hit him. He reached over and grabbed his camera, fumbling to get the film loaded again. After a couple of mechanical winds, the loose film was pulled tight again. He snapped the back of the camera shut and turned back to the shelf. But there was a problem. He realized that the ambient red light wouldn't expose the film, and there was no natural infrared light in the room. He'd have to take it outside if he wanted a photo. He snatched the cardboard square from the shelf and turned.

Tommy stood there, at end of the workbench, staring at him. Charlie almost fell backwards in shock.

"What the hell are you doing?" Tommy asked coldly.

Charlie looked down at the piece of cardboard in his hands, trying to find words that wouldn't come. It was the stark reality of truths coming to light – a husband caught cheating on his wife, or an elected official finally caught stealing public funds. Only Charlie's predicament wasn't so mundane.

"Put it down," Tommy said, subtle menace lacing his words as he eyed the piece of cardboard.

Without taking his eyes off of Tommy, Charlie placed it on the work bench. He followed Tommy's gaze as the other man looked over at the photo still in the fixing tray.

"Sick fuck." Tommy took a half step towards Charlie, a smile on his face.

"You're the one who's killing them out in the jungle," Charlie accused.

Tommy glanced back over at the photo. "It doesn't look that way. That's some serial killer shit – taking pictures." He took another step forward.

For a split second, Charlie considered if such a thing were even possible. Had he gone so utterly crazy that he could possibly be responsible for everything? He shook his head in silent answer.

"Don't try to pin this on me." Charlie motioned to the cardboard square. "Who was the third?"

"HQ warned me something like this might happen."

"What the fuck are you talking about?" Charlie raised his voice, not caring if the outside world heard.

"I'm afraid I'm going to have to relieve you of your command," Tommy said. A dark blade appeared at his side, produced from some hiding place. He lunged at Charlie.

Pure reflex kicked in, and Charlie threw himself backwards against the wall, avoiding the blow. His actions were no longer conscious, and he was only able to reflect upon them as he watched his movements play out. In the scant moment it took Tommy to recover from the lunge and position his body for another, Charlie swiped the shard of mirror from the wall and in one fluid motion ran it across Tommy's exposed neck.

For a split second, time seemed to stop. Tommy just looked at Charlie. And then there was blood.

Tommy clutched at his throat, trying to stem to flow of his own life running out. He was incredibly well composed, not staggering backwards in the least. There was no surprise or regret in his eyes. Only a cold resignation as he stared unblinking at Charlie.

"You win," was all he managed before his words were replaced with a sick gurgle. He removed his hand from his neck and slowly got down on his knees, never once taking his eyes off of Charlie.

It was disturbing how inhuman Tommy's movements were, and Charlie subconsciously backed away until he felt the wall behind him. In that moment, Charlie somehow knew that he was still human, despite the war It was Tommy who was beyond hope. To the cold blooded killer, there was no need for theatrics or panic. Death was no stranger.

Tommy's eyes began to drift, his mind finally in a different place, then he fell backwards. Charlie just stared for a long time at the other man's face. Another face of death, mouth slightly agape.

034

Charlie cradled Tommy's lifeless form in his arms as he used his boot to push the door to the shack open. The sun was blinding, and he quickly shut his eyes against lances of pain. He knew that he had become a creature of the night, and as he tried to walk down the steps with his eyes closed, he wondered if he would ever dwell in daylight again. His vision slowly adjusted, and he could finally see if he squinted.

A tear fell, coming unbidden, and Charlie soon found himself sobbing uncontrollably. He should have been a father watching his son's softball game on a summer day. Or a husband porting a picnic basket through a park. But he wasn't those things.

In spite of that the day was welcoming, bringing him closer to that imagined life. He walked out into a different world, even if he was carrying dead weight. After a difficult trek through the tripwires, Charlie found the perfect spot to bury his lost companion.

As he set the body down on a small patch of earth clear of underbrush, he couldn't help but think that death had made Tommy human again. Charlie didn't blame him for going crazy. The war was responsible, or perhaps the training that had forced a child to grow up too quickly. Tommy's final words still resounded in Charlie's mind. To the other man it had all simply been a game. But as far as Charlie was concerned, they had all lost. *Us. Them.* Everyone.

Remembering his orders, Charlie grabbed a knife and cut out Tommy's eyes, placing them into a small plastic bag that he could send back with the runner. After he was done with the grisly task, he couldn't bear to look at Tommy's face any longer. The eyes were the windows to the soul. But instead of seeing one there, Charlie could only see pitch black orbits that were devoid of humanity.

He grabbed a field shovel from his side and unfolded it, deciding that he didn't care about protocol and that a shallow grave would do. He made quick work of the digging, then rolled the body into the hole. He made sure it was face down so that he didn't have to see the horror that Tommy's face had become as he threw dirt over the body.

A profound sadness settled into his being. Even though he had hated Tommy, their tenuous connection was better than being alone. It made it easier to dream of a family that Charlie didn't have.

035

The door to the shack swung shut, closing out the daylight. The dim red light made it easier to look at the bloodstain that covered half of the floor. As Charlie surveyed the overturned trays and developing equipment, it occurred to him that he hadn't bothered to take a picture of Tommy. It was just as well, he decided. It was time to put what had happened behind him.

He slumped down into a sitting position and fished something out his pocket. Besides the eyes, Charlie had only taken one other thing from Tommy – the cigarettes. He examined the foreign writing on the pack and wondered what city they might have come from before being smuggled out to the bush. Despite the humidity, the cigarette lit up just fine.

An overwhelming sense of solitude enclosed Charlie as he looked around the shack. He had known a brief freedom outside in the daylight, but now he had returned to the world of red and green. He looked at the empty sleeping bag across from him and imagined Tommy sitting there, watching him. And he felt a little less alone.

Even though the shack was tightly sealed, something had found its way inside. Charlie looked up and saw a butterfly repeatedly bumping into the red light bulb overhead.

DEAD PIXELS

SCORE 000230

036
1962.

The Jungle was a shade of dark gray, as always. A monochromatic wash over 8-bit trees.

Anders could see the barrel of his gun floating in front of him as he turned back and forth, searching for the next enemy. He had only managed to shoot a few Trogs, but he knew there were Morlocks underfoot waiting to reach up and grab at his legs. If only he could spot the subtle shift of pixels that gave away their underground movements, he might have a fighting chance.

He had only made it to the Jungle two other times before, and both times the Morlocks had been the death of him – literally. It was always disappointing when he died that far into the Game. Since they only had one life, it always meant starting over.

He was finally getting really good at beating the Forest, its dull greens almost comforting in comparison to the digital night of the Jungle. The River was still tough. He was usually overrun by Lizard Men or surprised by a Croc. But occasionally, he could beat the River too.

Anders desperately needed more practice killing Morlocks, but he was just going to have to get faster at beating the first two levels. He found himself spinning in circles, terrified to move forward in any one direction. If only the enemies would just come to him as they were apt to do in the Forest. All Anders had to do on that level was stand there, only advancing between waves of Trogs. But Trogs were stupid compared to the other enemies, or so his classmates had told him.

His score loomed in the bottom right of his view, unchanging. It was quickly becoming clear that his inability to move forward wasn't luring any enemies to him. They were all out in the Jungle, waiting patiently for him to make one misstep. Even though he knew the Game wasn't real, chills electrified every hair follicle, and a lump formed in his stomach at the mere thought of creeping through the underbrush.

His palm felt clammy against the moist plastic joystick. The edge of the trigger scraped against his index finger as he nervously moved his digit back and forth. It had taken him some time to develop this particular tick without actually wasting bullets. Anders found himself doing it anytime there was idle moment of indecision.

Finally he pushed the joystick forward, and his view advanced through the digital landscape. Pixels warped at the edges of his peripheral vision, and all too often he mistook it as sign of a Morlock trying to sneak up on him. He kept stopping and spinning around to face the perceived threat. But the Jungle was strangely quiet. It was like the Game was able adapt to his fears, creating the most unsettling scenario possible.

He had heard rumors from some of the older kids that when all the other enemies stopped showing up, it was likely that Dead Eye was about to arrive. But Anders didn't really believe in Dead Eye, so he moved forward again after a mental shrug.

That's when a clawed hand finally burst through the ground in front of him. If his reflexes hadn't improved since his last foray into the Jungle, it would have been Game Over. He jerked the joystick back and hit the trigger. The arms were easy to miss, so he fired off more shots than he cared to, even after he had already hit it.

His heart pounded in his ears as he watched the rest of body erupt from the ground. The Morlocks were squat and hairy, their features out of a warped fairy tale. This one was pissed – its blown off arm lying on the ground behind it. It charged at Anders.

One invisible bullet after another hit it square in the chest, causing it to stagger back slightly with each impact. But it never stopped. Its good arm took a swipe at Anders' face, but once again he managed to pull back on the joystick just in time. The digital gun barrel recoiled multiple times in rapid succession as he backed up blindly. He knew that the tactic was folly; he could run into something else lurking right behind him – but it was hard to think about that when certain death was right in front of him. In the Game, one hit and you were out.

Finally the Morlock stopped and melted into a crumpled pile of gray pixels on the ground, barely recognizable if one hadn't seen a dead Morlock before. The score in the corner of the screen jumped up ten points, and Anders felt a familiar elation – a comfort he felt anytime his score went up.

Suddenly the Jungle was quiet again, and as an afterthought Anders swung around to check behind himself. He made a mental note that it shouldn't have been an afterthought. He should have done it the moment he saw the Morlock start to go down. But before he had even completed the spin, he knew that nothing was behind him. If there had been, he'd already be dead.

Dark gray pixels lurched into motion as Anders continued forward again. Soon there was a clearing in the canopy, and he could see The End in the distance. It was the same lonely tower that he had seen from the Forest and the River, mysteriously looming from some faraway place. Perhaps it was just his imagination, but it seemed like the tower was infinitesimally closer than it had been the last time he saw it at the River.

Among all the cadets, no one had ever made it to The End, or so Anders had heard from his peers. Although it seemed like an unattainable goal, they collectively postulated that it must be possible to get there. Otherwise, what was the point of the Game?

The tower itself was the subject of much speculation. They all desperately wanted to know what was inside and what would happen if they finally managed to reach it. The most popular theory was that the player would feel a hundred times better than he felt when he killed a regular enemy. At least that's what they hoped would happen.

A Trog made the mistake of rearing its ugly head. Without thinking, Anders had already taken aim and fired. One bullet to the head, and it went down. Another jolt of elation hit him as he took note of his bullet count.

The problem with all the levels was that everything looked the same. There was no path to memorize or landmarks to remember. Anders would wander aimlessly until he finally caught a glimpse of the tower, then head in that direction. When he first began playing the Game, he had a tendency to be trigger happy, but then would frequently find himself out of ammo and still meandering. It was a balancing act to score as high as possible yet finish the level before running out of bullets.

Even though his real body was sitting in one place, he was running in his own mind, his breathing noticeably heavier than it should have been. It didn't help that the Game seemed to be toying with him again.

Another clawed hand ripped through the pixelated ground, and Anders almost ran into it. He heard himself gasp as he pulled back, the joystick slick against his palm. This time he didn't shoot at the hand, even though it meant that the Morlock would continue to follow him from underground. Something just felt different; there was a slight tingle at the back of his neck. He spun around just in time to see another hand grasping at the air right behind him. Even though his stomach jumped into his throat, he still breathed an audible sigh of relief. If he had allowed the first Morlock to surface and charge him, the situation would have been unmanageable.

As it was, he didn't really know what he was going to do. He made a half turn and ran away from both enemies. Even though he had narrowly avoided a Game Over, he now had to deal with two Morlocks chasing him. While he could evade them easily enough, he was no longer moving forward cautiously and knew it was mistake.

He swung back around just in time to catch the second Morlock before it pulled its hand back underground. There was a slight vibration in the joystick as he took a shot. And missed.

Fuck. He bit his upper lip which had a faint taste of salt on it. He scraped his finger repeatedly across the trigger as he slowly backed up, looking from left to right for any sign of his pursuers. He noticed a faint disruption of pixels along the ground in a line and took a shot. The pixels stopped shifting, and his score jumped up dramatically. He knew that he had been awarded a one shot kill for managing to hit it while it was still underground.

The resulting elation was just enough of a distraction that he missed a new line of shifting pixels moving towards him. On the edge of his vision another a hand reached up out of the ground, close enough that he knew he couldn't simply back away. In the half second before the hand took a swipe at him, he tried to turn and take aim, but it was too late.

Gray pixels flashed to red, and the words "Game Over" appeared on screen. Anders instantly felt deflated, all of his energy drained, and a foul mood crept over him. He slowly took his hand off of the joystick and pulled the semi-circular visor from his face.

Austere white walls closed in around him, and he suddenly felt suffocated. The air conditioning was cold against his damp skin, and he could feel an icy ring of sweat all along his collar. He eyed the IV tube hanging from the ceiling that was connected to the PICC line in his arm that got changed out once a week. They had been told that the IV was to keep them hydrated during the long hours they played the Game every day. It was hard to tell if there was even anything inside of the tube, but Anders reasoned that water would be impossible to see anyway.

There were no clocks inside the small room where he sat, and he wondered if there would be enough time left for another game. All he could do was sit and wait during the mandatory stand down, bored, tired and cold.

Finally the intercom in the room crackled to life.

"Re-enter the Game," a disembodied voice said.

Anders excitedly grabbed his visor. Within moments, a monochromatic green landscape filled his vision, and he was back in the Forest.

037

An instructor droned on somewhere in the back of Anders' consciousness. "Troglodytes represent the lowest common denominator in the field. The easy kills."

Even though he was sitting in a classroom, Anders couldn't focus on real life. The white cinder block walls of the windowless room somehow seemed less genuine than the vectorized landscape of the Game.

"You shouldn't be killed by the lowest common denominator," the instructor went on. "Eventually, you should be able to evade all enemies in the Game."

A couple of cadets in the back muttered quietly.

The instructor stopped pacing and turned in their direction. "Is there something you'd like to say?"

The two cadets stopped, their heads snapping to the front of the room. "No sir," one of them, a boy named Gentry, meekly volunteered. Of course the boy's real name wasn't Gentry, just as Anders' name wasn't his own either.

"Questions perhaps?" The instructor pressed, making the two cadets squirm in their seats.

Gentry just shook his head and gulped loudly.

Anders suppressed a sigh and wondered when they were going to get back to the Game. The lack of clocks in the classroom made the wait interminable. After ten weeks at the Academy, Anders could barely remember what his real name had been. His former life seemed inconsequential. Parents. A house in the suburbs with a white picket fence. The Game was so much more fun.

Their days were divided into one of three activities: physical training that usually took place in the morning, classroom instruction, and the Game. Always the Game. Classroom time reminded Anders of the school that he went to before the Academy, only now the subject matter was darker. They still studied things like math and science, but only as they related to war.

Biology had been reduced to the location of major arteries and vital organs. Math was used to calculate the trajectory of mortar shells. Chemistry was a mix of fatal agents. Every subject was shrouded in death. But only occasionally did they openly talk about the Game.

"There will come a time when a culling will be necessary," the instructor continued. "Not all of you will make it." Anxious feet shuffled against the floor as the instructor seemed to pause for effect. "Not all of you will be good enough to make it to The End."

Gentry raised his hand in the back of the room, cautious to not begin speaking until the instructor called on him. "Is it even possible to make it to The End?"

A wry smile crossed the instructor's face. "Of course it is, in time. What you all need to focus on in the next couple of weeks is getting as far as you possibly can. Those who have not made it beyond a certain point will be..." There was a slight hesitation as the instructor seemed to be searching for the right words. "Relegated to alternative service."

More shuffling of feet. Another cadet named Sims raised his hand. "What's the cutoff point?"

"If you have to ask, you probably haven't passed it," the instructor responded. His cryptic answer resonated in the room, and Anders could sense the weight of every cadet trying to decipher what that meant. He didn't even bother – he knew that he needed to try harder. He was so close to getting through the Jungle.

"But I will say that if you are still getting killed by Troglodytes, you had better shape up," the instructor said.

Even though everyone else's attention was fixed on the front of room, a sixth sense tugged at Anders and drew his gaze to the floor. There he spotted a small insect – a baby roach, antennae swaying in a wide arch. Without making a production of it, he silently lifted a boot. Then it came down with a satisfying crunch, and he felt an ever so slight jolt of happiness.

038

When Anders finally beat the Jungle, excitement coursed through his veins. The dull gray pixels in his field of vision were replaced by the purple landscape of the Temple. Ancient crumbling structures were draped by hanging vines, and the ground was choked with familiar underbrush.

Up to that point, he had only heard about the Temple from some of the other boys. It was the home of the Faceless – strange humanoid figures with indiscernible facial features. Except for being exceptionally creepy, they didn't seem to have any special abilities.

Anders spotted one approaching from the background and took a shot. He smiled when his score rose. There were more lurking ahead, and he was tempted to rush forward for a series of quick kills, but he remembered the other enemy the boys had warned him about.

Specters weren't terribly common until later levels, but he had heard that it was possible to encounter them in the Temple. The only telltale sign of their approach was a faint shadow on the ground, the pixels only a shade off from the surrounding ones. They wouldn't appear until they were right in front of the player, and by then it was usually impossible to dodge their shot.

Anders scanned the ground ahead for any signs of subtle movement. Despite his excitement, he knew that he needed to take the Temple slowly until he got used to it. More Faceless approached, and he quickly dispatched them, careful to never take his attention fully away from the ground. With the immediate vicinity clear, he took a moment to spin around and make sure he wasn't being followed.

Specters supposedly only moved when they weren't being watched. It was possible to catch one if the player quickly spun around, but it was best to learn how to recognize its stationary shadow. Anders strained his eyes shifting his gaze from pixel to pixel. After a while, they all seemed to dance in his vision, every little bit of movement a harbinger of doom.

He turned back around and moved forward again. More Faceless were on the horizon. He wondered about the point of them in the grand scheme of the Game. The enemies had gotten more difficult on each successive level, but the Faceless were pretty easy to kill. Almost as easy as a Trog, except that they moved a lot faster.

As he passed a massive stone column in the ruined temple, he noticed a strange symbol on its surface. Something else to wonder about. Anders found himself pondering the creators of the Game and all the subtle nuances they had woven into the programming. It was clear that the cadets were being trained for something, but that something wasn't entirely clear.

Anders still remembered the first time the men in suits came to his old school. He was sitting in a ninth grade math class when they showed up with the principal, and he was called out of the room. Apparently he had done exceptionally well on a special test that he hadn't even realized was special.

They took him to a classroom where ten other boys already sat, then one of the strange men shut the door in the principal's face. All of the boys were given another, longer test.

The questions had been bizarre, asking what they would do in certain situations or what they had done in the past. It was all fill in the blanks or short essay. The boys were told that their parents and teachers would never see the tests; they were to answer as honestly as possible. Anders had paused at each question, wondering what it was really asking.

Have you ever sneaked out of your room at night?
Why?
Were you ever caught?
Have you ever intentionally hurt a pet?
In what way?

Why?

Have you ever killed a living creature?

What kind?

Then there had been another test that seemed more general in nature. Math, English, Science. Still no multiple choice.

The next day, there were only five of them seated in a waiting area outside of an office. A man in a black suit stood watch over them – they had explicit instructions not to speak.

When it was Anders' turn, he went into the office where he took a seat across from another man in a suit who mercilessly questioned the answers to his first test.

"You indicated on your assessment that you like to kill insects?" the man asked him.

Anders just nodded.

"You don't see anything wrong with that?"

Anders hesitated, the words stuck in his throat.

"It's okay, you can tell me the truth." The man's lips rose into a twisted smile. "I used to pull the legs off of grasshoppers and leave them next to the bird feeder."

Anders laughed, then stopped himself.

"You like that idea?" the man asked. "What kinds of things have you done?"

"Sometimes... I use firecrackers to blow up ant piles," Anders said as he stared down at the floor. "When there's too many of them swarming, I use smoke bombs to make them dizzy." He finally looked back up at the man.

The man in the suit must have liked what he was hearing, because he jotted down several notes. "What about people? You ever hurt someone?"

Anders shook his head. "That would be wrong... wouldn't it?"

The man shrugged. "You tell me."

Anders thought about it for a long time. "It depends," he had finally said.

By the third day of testing, there were only two boys left, and Anders had been the only one invited to the Academy in the end. He wasn't sure why, but his parents had been crying when they told him goodbye.

He suddenly remembered that he wasn't doing a very good job of keeping an eye out for Specters. There would be time to dwell on such mysteries later when he wasn't trying to survive in the Game. Two more shots, two more Faceless dead.

As a matter of course, he spun around to check behind himself. It was hard to tell since all the pixels were spinning around him, but it seemed like something had been moving right as he turned. Panic washed over him. He wanted to turn and run, but then he noticed The End above the tree line. It seemed closer than it ever had been before.

He cursed to himself and spun back around, took a few steps forward then turned again. Something had definitely been moving. He spent longer than he should have scanning the ground, trying to differentiate what he imagined would be slight variation in pixel shading. He thought about taking shots in the general direction of what he thought he had seen, but decided against it. Even if that tactic worked once, it might not the next time. He had to be smarter than that.

A half turn and a pause, then he swung back towards the direction of The End. This time the movement continued for a split second longer, and Anders took the shot. The Specter became visible for a split second before tumbling to the ground. It was the most human thing Anders had seen in the entire Game. A sinister mask covered its face, but it otherwise looked like a man in a suit of sleek body armor.

Anders gasped as his score jumped up a hundred points all at once, and a sudden jolt of excitement rocked his body. After the rush, a general feeling of calm and well-being washed over him. He just wanted to sit there forever, basking in sensations he had never felt before. But even more so, he wanted to kill another one.

A few more steps closer to The End. Another strange symbol like the one on the stone column. More circular sweeps – searching for shifting pixels. The feeling in his veins was fading, and he wanted more. Oddly, there were no Faceless around either. Nothing to kill. Nothing to make the score go up. Slow and cautious gave way to abandon as Anders ran towards The End – until a Specter materialized right in front of him and took a shot. Game Over.

Any sense of well-being that still lingered was quickly replaced by fatigue and a general feeling of illness. He slipped his visor off and entered the mandatory stand down, waiting to return to the Game.

039

"I swear I saw him," Gentry said to a group of boys huddled around his lower bunk. It was past lights out, and the pale moonlight coming through the window was barely enough to see by. Anders rolled onto his side and looked down at the group from the adjacent top bunk. Gentry was ashen white.

"No way," another boy said. "What did he look like?"

"Just like a person," Gentry choked, "but instead of eyes he just had black holes."

"Dead Eye's not real," Anders said dismissively from above, drawing looks from the boys below. "Nobody's ever died for real in the Game."

"How would you know?" Gentry asked defensively. "You haven't been here that long either."

"The older cadets just want to scare us," Anders said. "You ever heard an instructor say anything about Dead Eye?"

Gentry pointed to himself, stabbing himself in the chest repeatedly. "I. SAW. HIM." The other boys muttered.

"Then why are you still here?" Anders asked. "Everyone says he's the one enemy you can't beat."

Gentry shook his head, tears forming in his eyes. "I don't know."

"But if Dead Eye didn't let anyone get away, then nobody would know about him," another boy spoke up.

Anders laughed, but the truth was that ever since he had heard the story of Dead Eye, he had been terrified. If anything, he was harassing Gentry to reassure himself about the whole thing.

As the boys whispered down below, Anders recalled the first time he had heard the story. They weren't the first batch of players in the Game;

there were older kids who had already been at the Academy for a lot longer. The different age groups didn't mix very often, but when they did, the younger boys always asked the older ones what they knew about The End or other enemies in the Game.

Dead Eye was the first rumor that Anders had heard shortly after arriving at the Academy. He still remembered the older kid who had told him the story in the exercise yard as the sun was setting one day. Deep shadows had played under the boy's eyes, setting a ghastly tone to their exchange. According to the tale, the Game once caused a player to go into seizures, and he died with his visor still on.

"I don't know how it happened," the older cadet had explained, "but the dead guy got stuck inside the Game."

"W-what do you mean?" Anders had asked as a chill autumn wind blew across his skin.

"Like he's stuck in the Game! He shows up sometimes as an enemy."

"Has anyone ever killed him?"

The older boy had shaken his head. "You can't. All you can do is try to run to the end of the level before he catches you. If he kills you in the Game, you die in real life."

Anders pulled his bed sheet more tightly around himself as he remembered those words. He was starting to think that maybe he shouldn't be making fun of Gentry. He rolled back onto his side. "What level were you on?"

Gentry looked up. "The Ravine."

Anders felt a little relief at that, but also a tinge of jealousy since he hadn't made it past the Temple yet. He didn't want to end up among the culled.

"How did you manage to get away from him?" someone asked.

Anders' ears perked up as Gentry explained.

"Once Dead Eye showed up, there weren't any other enemies, not even Specters. I just ran and got lucky. Once I spotted The End, I didn't even turn around."

At that moment, a bunk monitor flung the door open, and the boys scampered back to their beds. "What's going on in here?" he swung a flashlight beam around the room. No one dared to speak, but not everyone made it back to bed in time.

The monitor sneered. "That's going to cost you a half hour of sleep and a two mile run in the morning. I don't want to hear another peep out of you tonight." The door slammed shut, leaving them in an eerie silence.

040

Anders dreamed of the Game that night. He was trapped in the mono-chrome blues of the River, unable to make his way towards The End. He killed one enemy after another, but his score never changed, and there wasn't the familiar feeling of accomplishment.

It was tedious, and he felt a desperate need to advance to the Ravine to avoid the culling. Try as he might, he couldn't seem to get anywhere no matter how many Lizard Men he killed. But he kept killing them anyway.

Until there were no enemies and he was alone.

Only he could sense that he wasn't. Someone or something was watching him. But his silent observer didn't seem to be in the immediate vicinity. It was a gaze that pervaded the entire Game. He suddenly felt like if he didn't get out, he never would.

He searched for enemies so he could commit suicide, but there were still none in sight. No easy way to provoke a Game Over. No way to get out other than to find The End.

Anders could feel himself starting to panic, the oppressive stare beating down on his back from both everywhere and nowhere all at once. There was an endless digital landscape before him, constantly renewing itself and expanding, algorithms creating slight variations in the terrain. Yet there was nowhere to run. Whatever watched him was right on his heels. He normally would have spun around, finger carefully poised over the trigger mechanism of the joystick – but at that moment, he didn't dare. It was too close.

Then he realized it was himself.

He awoke, gasping for air, almost hitting the ceiling above his top bunk. At first, all he could see were white spots dancing in the darkness

– his eyes playing tricks on him. Gradually he was able to make out the faint outlines of the other bunks and sleeping cadets. Wind whistled outside, slamming against the sole window in the room and rattling its panes. Anders felt like he couldn't breathe. Like he needed to get out of his bunk. Out of that room. So he did.

As he flung his foot over the edge of the bed onto the top rung of the ladder, he imagined a room full of Specters lying in wait below. If he wasn't absolutely quiet in his movements, they would detect him, and it would be Game Over. He managed to silently descend the bunk ladder and then tiptoed across the room towards the door.

He already had a plan – a simple trip to the bathroom. If the monitor caught him, it wouldn't be good, but perhaps excusable. Once he reached the door he stopped a mere inch from it, straining to hear any signs of movement out in the hallway. It was quiet. Deathly quiet. Just like the Game.

He turned the knob ever so slowly, willing his hand to move at an unnaturally glacial pace. There was no sound as he allowed the mechanism to finally fall into place, and the metal door slowly swung open.

The hallway was incredibly antiseptic, like they could have all been in a hospital instead of the Academy. It was also devoid of any signs of life. Anders became aware of his own heart pounding in his chest, fueled by a rush of adrenaline. He wasn't quite sure why he felt the way he did; it was just a trip to the bathroom. Yet he found himself scanning the hallway for signs of subtle movement – like a shadow, or a displacement of the floor tiles.

Anders smiled at his own foolishness – surveying his surroundings for uncommon enemies. He found that it kept him hyper alert. If he was concerned about Specters and Morlocks, the stupid monitor would be akin to a Trog and easily dodged.

One foot in front of the other, a series of silent footfalls across the short distance to the communal bathroom. He pushed his way inside and shivered. The temperature seemed to have dropped dramatically from when they were out the previous morning. It didn't help that someone had left a window propped open in the bathroom.

Even though he didn't really have to go, Anders decided to go through the motions to make his story more plausible. As he stepped up to the trough style urinal with his penis in his hand, he pondered his next move. He didn't really have a plan, but he didn't want to return to his bunk either. Just as a few drops of urine spattered in the old metal trough, Anders noticed that he wasn't alone in the room.

A large male mosquito fluttered near the open window, too stupid to escape. Anders wondered what it was doing out so late in the year. Once he was done peeing, he crept over to the insect. He spent a long time watching it, aware that it was unaware that it was being watched. He wondered if that's what it was like to be a Specter. Or a Morlock. Or Dead Eye.

In a silent flash of movement, Anders reached out and plucked off one of the mosquito's wings in mid-air, then watched it drop to the floor and flutter around in circles. Then he crushed it with his toe, attentive to its final shudder.

He felt a sudden rush, as sure as if he had just killed an enemy in the Game. So easy to separate life from a corporeal form. He yearned for the feeling of killing a Specter again. And with that thought, he resolved to stay up a little longer, searching for something else to kill.

041

The next day all Anders could think about was the Game. As he and the other boys went on their punitive two mile run, he imagined himself running through the Forest, headed to the River. And then to the Jungle. It made everything easier if he pictured himself somewhere else.

In class, he imagined himself inside some sort of prison camp, just going through the motions that were expected of him while he plotted his escape later that afternoon. Suddenly class became easy. He got all the math problems right when he ceased to think about them.

As an instructor went on endlessly about subtropical plants, Anders wondered why they couldn't just live in the Game. They were already set up with an IV. Why not rig up a way to go to the bathroom too? It was clear that the Game was the most important part of their day, why not treat it that way?

When the bell finally rang in the early afternoon to signal Game time, it took everything Anders had to not run to his assigned chamber. Instead, he calmly fell into line as the boys walked single file down the hall. There was quiet excitement in the air as each boy stopped in front of a sealed steel door and waited. Loud clicks resonated all along the hall, then the boys entered.

Anders sat in a large console chair and waited for a nurse to stop by to connect his IV before he finally slipped his visor on. His muscles were tense as the dormant pixels inside the visor screen flared to life.

Something was markedly different on that particular run of the Game. The enemies seemed easier to kill and less able to sneak up on him. He breezed through the Forest, more concerned about advancing than he was about upping his score from killing Trogs. Now that he knew how many points Specters were worth, many of the earlier levels weren't even worth his time.

The River took a little longer than he wanted because Lizard Men had a tendency to rush en masse. But even killing them in rapid succession didn't award the same high that killing a Specter had. Crocs tended to be single kill enemies when they decided to show up, so Anders felt like they were an even bigger waste of time. The Jungle couldn't come fast enough.

Whereas he used to take pleasure in wandering and killing in the early levels, and was terrified of the later ones, now everything was simply an obstacle between him and hunting Specters. The Morlocks had become trite – easy enough to spot and even easier to kill. They were more nuisance than anything, forcing him off track every time he had to run backwards from a charging Morlock.

When he finally did arrive at the Temple, he was surprised by how predominantly populated it was by the Faceless. He searched and searched, but couldn't find a Specter. He cursed his luck on the previous day to have stumbled across not one but two almost right into the level – not to say that he wasn't thankful. The Game seemed different now, like it wouldn't even get started until the Ravine.

Anders decided to change his objective. Instead of looking for Specters, he decided to speed to the end of the level as fast as he could. In one dead run, between waves of Faceless, he felt the hairs on the back of his neck stand on end as a familiar chill crept into his being. He spun around and instantly recognized a shadow moving along the ground for a split second before it stopped. He didn't even think. He just fired. And hit.

A wave of pure euphoria washed over him as the Specter materialized and died. His entire body tensed up, then relaxed profoundly. He almost forgot to keep moving, but eventually turned back around to face a distant view of The End through the trees. The tower was mysterious as ever, and although he couldn't be sure, he thought he saw a flash of movement in one of the windows. He ran forward again, taking shots at Faceless without even slowing. Soon the purple field of pixels faded to black.

Anders ran his finger nervously over the trigger attached to the joystick, applying more pressure than usual since he was between levels. Soon another view flared to life. "The Ravine" appeared over a backdrop of pixels so dark that Anders could barely see the outlines of trees.

Even though he was anxious to begin, he paused and surveyed the dark landscape before him. Whereas the Jungle was shades of dark gray, the Ravine seemed to be shades of black, if that was even possible. Anders wondered how he was supposed to spot shadows moving along the ground if there was barely any light. Fear gripped him – not fear of failure, but a fear of not being rewarded for killing things that he couldn't see.

He took one tentative step forward, and the screen suddenly lit up. For a split second, Anders could see all the details of the Ravine – the trees, the roots along the ground and the same strange symbols that had appeared in the Temple. It took him a moment to realize that the source of light had been a bolt of lightning that had appeared in the top right corner of the screen.

Another flashed, barely visible through the thick canopy. This time he spotted a hint of movement along the ground and fired, but missed. He couldn't help but marvel at the genius of the Game's creators – to hide shadows within shadows. Then he had the sneaking suspicion that the Specter could still be advancing since technically he couldn't see it.

He expected panic to cloud his thoughts, but instead he remained calm. It was just a game, and he was no longer the prey. They should be frightened of him. What pixels he could see, he kept a close watch on. He was rewarded when he noticed one in particular change to slightly different shade of dark gray. He fired and almost leapt out of his seat in excitement as he saw his score jump up. He wanted to bask in the chemical reaction that was taking place in his brain, but knew that he couldn't leave himself vulnerable.

Another flash of lightning and he was on the move again. One step after another, gun barrel floating in midair. Hunting. He spotted another Specter, and then another. Three kills in a row and he felt as though he were hovering like his disembodied gun barrel.

He squeezed his legs together in response to an unexpected stirring between his legs. The three rapid kills had somehow given him an erection. He squirmed in his seat, but there were other, more important things to worry about. He needed another kill.

As the seconds ticked by, turning into minutes, there was no sign of another Specter, and his excitement slowly drained away, and he could sense the beginnings of a slight headache.

"Damn it," he muttered to himself, wondering where all the enemies were hiding. Was it possible they were afraid of him? He reminded himself that there had been other times when the Game uncannily seemed to sense how he was feeling or what he was thinking and adapted, throwing the worst possible curve ball it could muster at just the right time to get him killed.

Lightning flashed again, and he saw something in the distance. Something he didn't recognize. His heart skipped a beat as he tried to make sense of the cluster of pixels he had just seen. *It couldn't be.*

Another flash, as if on cue, and now the something was closer – close enough to see a light gray face and two black pits where its eyes should have been. As the screen went dark again, Anders' instinct was to turn and run. But a single thought kept nagging him. If killing a Specter was the best thing he had ever physically experienced, what would it feel like to kill Dead Eye?

He braced himself, eyes raking the expanse of the screen several times per second. When the screen lit up again, Dead Eye was closer. Anders fired repeatedly, quite sure that he was hitting the mark based on how good he had gotten at hitting Specters blindly. But there was no reward.

Within three seconds of the previous flash in the pixelated sky, there was another. Dead Eye appeared right in front of Anders' face, having moved an impossible distance in that span of time.

Anders screamed, and his entire body slammed into the back of the console chair. The face was clear now. It was a human boy, not much older than Anders, with two empty sockets above his slender nose.

Even though Anders was in a state of utter panic, his hand had a mind of its own, and cold instinct kicked in like muscle memory. He had the joystick pulled back as far as it would go, the trigger fully depressed. In the half second that he could clearly see Dead Eye, it was obvious that bullets didn't seem to affect him in the least.

He expected the screen to flash to dull red and see the words "Game Over" any second. Or worse, he expected his consciousness to fade into the darkness of true death. But neither came.

Presuming that the only imminent danger was Dead Eye, Anders backed up as fast as he could with reckless abandon. Normally such a move was suicide, and he surely would have run afoul of another enemy, but the stakes had suddenly risen.

As he continued to run backwards in the eerie silence of the Game, heart pounding in his ears, he began to wonder why he was still alive. Dead Eye clearly was capable of catching him. Yet there he was, still running away. A bolt of lightning finally lit up the screen after what seemed like forever, and Dead Eye was nowhere in sight.

Instinctively, Anders swung around to check behind himself, but when the screen lit up again the only thing he noticed was The End. The tower was closer than ever, but still in the distance. Anders made a mad dash for it, and soon he arrived at what looked like a massive entryway. He paused for a second, surveying the shadows to make sure nothing was lurking on the other side, then he crossed the threshold. The screen changed, indicating the end of the level.

He didn't realize how tense he was until his muscles finally unclenched. He could feel sweat pooling against the edges of the visor. A million questions filled the scant seconds between levels. He recalled that Gentry had also seen Dead Eye in the Ravine, and he began to wonder. But lots of other boys had made it to that level before and never seen him. Surely the level couldn't be that short. It must have been dumb luck that he found the doorway. His thoughts were cut short as the screen changed again.

The next level was a blood red that reminded Anders of the Game Over screen. "The Base" flashed briefly before blinking out. For the first time in the Game, Anders found himself inside of a structure. He wondered how he would be able to spot The End with a roof over his head. Rumor had it that the facility, unlike the other levels, was a randomly generated maze that changed each time a player entered it.

Before he had any more time to think, an enemy appeared from around a corner. It was a naked woman, her nipples single pixels in the center of her breasts. Despite his befuddlement at what he was seeing, he still took a shot. Her demeanor instantly changed as soon as the bullet made contact, her face warping into a mask of evil. Then she charged Anders with incredible speed. As he struggled to line his gun barrel up with her form, he noticed two long fangs protruding from her mouth. He tried to dodge her advance, but he hadn't quite figured out her movement patterns. She lunged at him, and the screen became an even deeper shade of red as "Game Over" appeared.

When Anders took off his visor, he realized what a horrible state his body was in. He was drenched in sweat, shivering, and his head was pounding. For the first time, he wasn't anxious to get back to the Game.

042

As the boys shuffled single file away from the gaming chambers and towards the cafeteria, Anders eyed the other boys, searching for any sign of distress in their faces. All of the others seemed to be perfectly at ease, if not somewhat depressed to have to walk away from the Game. Business as usual.

Anders looked at his own face as he walked past a closed door with a glass panel. He couldn't be sure if the reflection was making things appear worse than they were, but he seemed especially pale and gaunt.

Up to that point, he, like the other boys, had treated the Academy like a vacation from real life. It was more fun than school, and it was easier to respect instructors and officers than it was one's own parents. And where else could one play a game for four to six hours a day?

For the first time since his arrival, Anders began to wonder what was really going on. Clearly there was more to the Game than any of them thought. If it wasn't important, they wouldn't be allowed – no forced – to play it so much. There wasn't even a reprieve on the weekends, which most everyone was thankful for. They had never been told what exactly they were being trained to do at the Academy, but it was becoming increasingly obvious that they were been taught how to kill on a level far above that of the common murderer.

Anders originally thought that his parents had been crying when he left as the result of saying a temporary goodbye. But now he was beginning to wonder if there wasn't more to that as well. After all, he had never been told when he might be returning home.

He waited patiently in the cafeteria for his food. As he moved down the line, workers placed various meats and vegetables on his plate. They weren't allowed to pick their food, and being on a strict dietary regimen meant they were also required to eat everything on their tray – even the sickly sweet gruel that was served three times a day at the end of the line.

Anders watched as a worker scooped some up and dumped it into a small bowl on his tray with a plop. He glanced along the line one last time before turning away. It always struck him as odd that everyone at the facility was male. At his high school most of the cafeteria workers were women. Everything seemed so different at the Academy, although he couldn't quite put his finger on what exactly it was. He scanned the cafeteria and noticed a group of boys gathering around Gentry. He headed that way and placed his tray on their table.

"I saw him too," Anders said, ignoring all the other boys and looking right at Gentry.

"What?" Gentry replied, distaste lining his voice.

"Dead Eye."

Gentry crossed his arms and leaned back in his chair. The other boys were silent.

"I saw him in the Ravine," Anders insisted.

"Fuck you," Gentry said.

Anders was a little surprised by the response. He had expected more camaraderie, perhaps a willingness to talk about their shared experience. Instead Gentry just glared at him.

"What?" Gentry shrugged.

Anders took a step closer. "No, I really did see him." His voice went up an octave.

Gentry reached out and planted his hand firmly on Anders' chest, pushing him away. Anders, still in shock over Gentry's animosity, stumbled back and almost fell.

"Go find your own table," Gentry said. He glanced down at Anders' tray like he was considering the possibility of flinging it from the table, but he just sat back down instead.

Anders took a tentative step forward to test the waters, then moved back to the table to retrieve his tray, never taking his eyes off of Gentry. Then he finally turned and walked over to another table where no one was sitting.

For the first time in ten weeks, he sat alone.

043

Once they returned to the bunks, Gentry continued to ignore Anders. Not wanting any problems with the monitors, Anders decided it was best to just leave the other boy alone for the time being. While the others huddled into small whispering groups before lights out, Anders ascended the ladder next to his bunk, laid down on top of his perfectly made bed, and stared at the ceiling.

He was starting to feel a dull ache in his body that was slowly growing. Everything around him was inconsequential; his mind kept drifting back to the Game. He shut his eyes, and the encounter with Dead Eye played over and over again. Dozens of alternate courses of action ran through his mind, and he played through each, imagining different outcomes. Even though rumor had it that Dead Eye could not be killed, Anders was clinging to the idea that he could. The lore also claimed that one couldn't survive an encounter with Dead Eye, but clearly that wasn't true either.

Anders was starting to think of Dead Eye less as a myth and more as just another part of the Game. As he ran though scenario after scenario of how he could have done things differently, he started to yearn for the Game even more. He desperately wanted to play again, speeding through the early levels as quickly as possible so he could search for Dead Eye again. But then he realized that Dead Eye was simply the lure of the unknown – whereas killing multiple Specters in a row was a repeatable phenomenon. Anders needed that rush again.

With his eyes shut tightly against the overhead fluorescents, he pictured his gun barrel floating through the Ravine. He concocted new strategies for spotting their movement and imagined a series of successful kills. Even though he desperately clung to the memory of the subsequent high, the only thing coursing through his veins was the dull ache that continued to amplify itself.

He was so engrossed in his fantasy that he didn't hear the monitor enter the room, or the boys rushing to their beds. But he did notice when the overhead lights finally went out. His eyes fluttered open, and he stared at spots dancing in the darkness. A hush had settled over the room.

A terrible boredom afflicted him despite the fact that his heart was racing and his mouth was dry. He thought about the odd side effect he had experienced earlier in the gaming chamber, and in an attempt to recreate some semblance of what he had felt, he reached down and grabbed his penis through his trousers. It was something that all the boys did after lights out. Even at that moment, Anders thought he heard a stifled grunt from a nearby bunk. His penis stiffened a little, but he quickly realized that masturbating wasn't going to take his mind off of the Game.

Then he remembered killing the mosquito the night before. And the adrenaline rush from stalking down the empty hallway until he became too frightened to continue any further. While it was nothing like what he had experienced after his triple kill, it was the closest he could get to those feelings without playing the actual Game.

But he knew that he would have wait awhile longer for all the others to fall asleep. His chest felt like it would explode from the anticipation. He resolved to go farther this time.

He had to find something else to kill. Something bigger.

044

As he finally crept down the ladder from his bed, not daring to breathe, Anders pictured a score in the lower right corner of his vision that was set to all zeroes. He figured that he would spend some time exploring parts of the Academy that he had never seen, like levels he had yet to attain. But he also remembered seeing a stray cat in the exercise yard.

He had a cat back home in another life, a life he suspected he wasn't allowed to return to. In the back of his mind, he knew that he should probably be repulsed by the murderous thoughts running through his head. He also knew that he was no longer the same little boy who enjoyed the kitty curled up into a soft ball of fur next to him.

An image of the naked woman from the Base flashed in his mind, and he considered her duality – beautiful and calm at first glance, but a blood sucking killer none the less. He had never paid much attention to the killing rampages of his cat growing up, but once he thought about it, he recalled so many dead things: insects, mice, even a bird once. If felines were capable of doling out so much death, then perhaps they deserved to die themselves.

Anders scanned the outlines of beds and sleeping forms in the near darkness. It was like he was back in the Ravine, only able see some of the pixels. For all he knew, there could be an invisible killer in the room – and it could have been any of the other boys.

He spun around to examine his sleeping bunk mate. The boy's pale flesh glowed in the darkness, the features of his face easily distinguishable. His mouth was slack, hanging open, and there was a faint chortle every time he breathed in and out.

Satisfied, Anders swung back around and slowly picked his way through the room towards the closed door. Expertly placed footfalls on the cold tile only whispered of his passing. The cold steel of the door knob finally met his palm, a sobering reminder of what he was about he do. He spent a long time turning the handle until he felt the door release. Just as he began to open it and a sliver of light cut through the darkness, he heard a noise behind him in the room.

There was the unmistakable feeling of being watched. He turned and looked into the dark room, but nothing stirred. Everything was as he remembered it, each luminous face appearing to be asleep. Except for... one boy had rolled over in bed. Gentry. Right across from Anders' own bunk. But nothing seemed amiss.

After watching the room for five full minutes, waiting for any would be observers to slip up and open their eyes, Anders finally opened the door silently and stepped out into the hall. Even though it was empty, and there were no signs of approach, Anders decided to start with the bathroom so he had an easy alibi if a monitor was near. As he walked into the room tiled in sickly greens, the temperature seemed to drop twenty degrees and he could feel his balls shrivel up.

The bathroom had been cleaned since the previous night, but there was still a stray mosquito wing sticking out of a crack in the tile. He searched the area around the propped open window, but there were no signs of life. Nothing for him to kill.

Even though it wasn't a pressing need, he urinated. Anders had no idea how long he would be and didn't want the physical distraction of a stretched bladder to dull his other senses. It reminded him of how the bathroom was always full before the boys left for the gaming chambers, even if some of them could only eke out a squirt or two. The four to six hours that they were allotted to play each day were precious, and they didn't want to have to stop once they started.

Once he was done, he fastened his pants and moved to the doorway where he paused to listen. There were no sounds of movement, only a steady buzzing coming from the overhead lights. Anders exited the bathroom and decided to head in the general direction of the gaming chambers.

He moved just as he did in the Game – a few steps forward at a time before turning to assess his surroundings. He also stopped frequently to listen for auditory cues that didn't exist in the Game. He was cold and methodical, just as much as he was in the Jungle or the Ravine.

As he approached an intersection of two halls, distant sounds broke the silence. He froze in his tracks. It wasn't a lone stalker trying to hide its approach, nor was it a monitor. Instead, it was a large group noisily making its way towards the intersection. He quickly wedged his slender body into an alcove containing two water fountains and placed his back against the wall closest to the intersection.

He recognized the rhythm of people walking in a single file line, but their steps were more disorganized than he would have expected. They were mostly orderly, like people trained to march in time with each other, but periodically a misstep or two would stick out like sore thumb. Anders dared to peek around the corner of the alcove.

A line of disheveled older boys came down one hallway and turned towards the gaming chambers, heading away from Anders' position. They looked like they had been rushed out of bed, hair uncombed and shirts half untucked. A monitor came into view, walking alongside the main line as they always did, escorting the group through the facility. Anders ducked back behind the concealment of the wall.

He wondered why they were being taken to play so late. A clock on the wall indicated that it was after midnight. He listened until the end of the line had filed past and the footsteps receded into the distance. After another moment, he heard a succession of distant doors shutting.

After checking the hall for monitors, he slipped out of his hiding place and faced the intersection, pulse racing. When he and the younger boys had been down that same hallway before, they had always gone straight. But he decided it was best to steer clear of the actual gaming chambers since they were occupied, and there would be monitors milling around the hallway.

So he turned at the intersection and went in a new direction.

045

Most of the doors that lined the endless hallways were shut and locked. Those with glass panels revealed nothing more than the fact that the lights inside were off. Occasionally Anders would spot strange pinpricks of blinking light and would press his face to the glass, trying to discern what was inside. But the details were beyond his reach. Even if he could see into the rooms, he wasn't sure he'd know what he was looking at anyway.

He kept careful track of where he was going through the labyrinth of unfamiliar halls. Fortunately there were landmarks and room numbers that he could commit to memory, unlike in the Game. He had gone in a giant square, looping back around to where he imagined the game rooms would be. At one point, as he tried one doorknob after another, he had stumbled into a room of sleeping boys who appeared to be slightly older than his group. The setup was the same, and there was a familiar bathroom just across the hall.

He turned another corner and found himself in a hallway that was far nicer than all the others. The standard lackluster tile ended and gave way to lush carpet. There were plants and sitting areas outside of what appeared to be offices. The walls were adorned with large framed photographs of uniformed men in various settings – some even in front of the White House. But Anders didn't recognize anyone. He started reading the golden plaques affixed to the bottom of each picture, and some of the names seemed familiar. Anders racked his brain, thinking to back to history class, but he kept drawing a blank.

His curiosity waned, the same dull ache from earlier settling back into his core as he moved past a succession of closed office doors. He pictured his imaginary score again, painfully aware that all the numbers were still zero. While he had wanted to explore, he was hoping that he might stumble across another insect, or even a rat as he slinked through the hallways. It was a strange itch that he just had to scratch.

He was about to turn around when he heard voices. In an instant, he ducked behind the side of a couch. By his estimations, he was approaching the general vicinity of the gaming chambers, and for a second he wondered if two monitors were loitering while they waited for the boys to be released.

He peeked over the arm of the couch and was able to localize the source of the sound. A heavy door was ajar down the hall. Anders could see multiple forms shifting in place through the crack – instructors and officers from the looks of it. The overhead lighting in the room seemed to be dim, but lots of light was coming from what appeared to be the walls.

After watching the door for a few minutes, Anders gathered that the men inside were working, their attention diverted. Right next to the room was a darkened sitting area with plenty of furniture to hide behind. Anders slowly rose, and in a series of cat-like steps he approached the room. As he placed his eye up to the cracked doorway, he could see that the entire back wall of the room, from floor to ceiling, was made of screens that looked like television sets. On each was a view of the Game as a player would see it, except that the screens lacked peripheral vision. Anders watched jealously as thirty different views displayed a myriad of levels and enemies, and most importantly, constant killing.

Ten men or so were seated at a long console that ran the length of the room, a mess of cables behind it running into the floor. The entire surface of the console was covered with buttons, knobs, and smaller screens full of words and charts. The ten men watched the wall of monitors intently, occasionally making adjustments to the controls. Two officers in uniform stood behind them chatting softly.

Anders was frozen at the doorway, taking in the impossibility of what he was seeing. As one of the officers idly started to pivot towards the doorway, it was like it was happening in slow motion. Anders perceived the beginnings of the turn and was already moving to his predesignated hiding spot before the man could spot him.

The smooth wall of the sitting area pressed against his back as he sunk into the shadows. He purposely slowed his breathing despite his pounding heart so no one would hear him. There was slight rush to his head when he did it, but he managed to keep things under control.

He kept waiting for someone to step out into the hallway, but it never happened. Then there was a burst of laughter in the room. He envisioned the officer again, pivoting in place towards the door – just a turn and glance perhaps. Maybe the officer had a sense that he was being watched.

Anders decided that it was time to head back the way he had come. There were far too many people nearby who could disperse at any instant. He might be able to evade the glances of one or two, but not everyone.

He stepped back out into the hallway, then ran silently along the carpeted floor back to the beginning of the executive hallway. After stopping and listening at the place where tile met carpet, Anders whipped around the corner into a less threatening hall.

In order to get to the exercise yard, he was going to have to pass back by his bunk room – which meant a somewhat long journey. It wasn't because it was a long distance, but because he had to move forward at a cautious pace, constantly picking out potential hiding places in the event that someone suddenly appeared.

He kept thinking about the wall of screens in the mysterious room. All the cadets assumed that the Game was something that just happened, the players being the only ones who had a controlling stake in its outcome. But now it was obvious that the Game was controlled in a God-like way.

That line of thinking only led to more questions, like how phenomena like Dead Eye were even possible if the controllers could see everything. Then it dawned on Anders that they had created Dead Eye – and the rumors of his existence. There was a sinking feeling in the pit of his stomach as he realized that he was just a puppet in a bigger game.

Or a player. He smiled.

He relaxed as the bathroom and his adjacent bunk finally came into view. Nothing seemed amiss as he floated past, his feet barely touching the floor. There was only the sound of a steady drip coming from a pipe in the bathroom.

046

A disquieting calm made the familiar seem unfamiliar. Even though Anders was in a part of the facility that he knew well, it had taken on a completely different air in the dead of night. The infirmary where they went for weekly checkups was full of instruments of torture and death. The instructors' offices were places where unspeakable things were planned. And the classrooms were where they were being taught to kill. He quickened his step, wanting to arrive at the exercise yard as quickly as possible.

Anders wondered what other secrets the facility was hiding. The maze of hallways seemed endless, and he had only explored a small section. He had already decided that he was going to sneak out of bed every night, getting a little farther each time – exploring new levels. The only thing that would make it better is if there were enemies.

As he approached a long line of classrooms, he suddenly got goose bumps – it seemed that his wish had been granted. The untrained boy in him wanted to stop and look around fearfully, but the person he had become continued moving forward as though he had no idea that he was being watched. It was like playing cat and mouse with a Specter. Anders couldn't look back until he knew that his stalker was fully committed.

He waited until what he thought was the right moment, then abruptly turned around. But the white hallway was empty.

After a quick assessment of the number of open doorways behind him he realized that there were plenty of places to hide. Anders was baffled by the possible identity of his stalker. A monitor would have been less stealthy since he would have nothing to hide. There would be nothing to lose by screaming across the distance for Anders to stop and succumb to questioning. But there was none of that. Only the empty hallway and the steady buzz of ballasts overhead. Anders' mouth was dry, but his emotions soared at the prospect of an enemy. A real enemy. The stray cat in the exercise yard would still be there another night.

Anders' pulse quickened as he turned back around to move forward, excitement in his veins and a twisted smile on his face. He pictured the hallway ahead as a field of pixels. Any fear that he had melted away. It was all just a Game.

But there was one very real problem. No matter how hard he imagined himself a soldier, he didn't have a weapon.

The goose bumps returned. He didn't quicken his pace in the least. It was unlikely that his stalker had a gun, otherwise Anders would already be dead. The lack of a projectile weapon meant that there was no reason to rush. Nor reason to show any sign of weakness.

He turned into one of the dark classrooms as nonchalantly as if he were simply going through his daily routine and filing in with all the other boys. The door was propped open, allowing some light to spill in from the hall. Anders almost didn't need it, his eyes adjusting immediately to the darker space. He searched for a weapon, but the room was bare except for desks, chairs, chalk, an eraser... and an American flag at the front of the room.

He considered searching the instructor's desk, but time was short. There was only one option.

The flag pole felt thick as he hoisted it out of the brass holder on the floor. It was merely an unwieldy blunt object in its present form. Anders wanted something more deadly – something sharper. He pictured himself trying to break it in half and failing. If he were back in his former life, a freshman in high school, his classmates would have laughed at him. A weakling. Pimply faced. No training.

Surprisingly there was a loud crack as solid oak gave way in Anders' grasp like a thin piece of rotten wood. For a split second it was as if some kind of spell was broken. Anders suddenly felt very sober, aware that as much as he was living within a fantasy, something impossible had just happened. He looked down at his own hands – at every vein raised slightly from the surface of his skin.

What's happening to me?

The moment of sobriety passed as he remembered that he wasn't alone. There was a reason why he had just snapped a flag pole in two. He examined each end quickly to determine which side was sharper.

Without a sound, he placed the blunter of the two on the chalk holder beneath the board, then grasped the other half in both hands and moved deftly to the doorway.

He thought carefully about how someone would enter the room from the same direction he had, and once that image played repeatedly in his mind, he hid in the shadows, poised to strike. Even though Anders couldn't see anything, he could feel something approaching the open doorway slowly. Unnaturally slow. The same way he would have moved.

It couldn't possibly be a monitor.

But then who was it?

A part of the Game, of course.

The polished wood felt slick in his sweaty palms. He ran his index finger back and forth across its surface. Along the floor outside of the door, a faint shadow rippled across the flawless shine of the tile floor – a shadow so faint that an untrained eye would have surely missed it. By the time the figure stepped into the doorway, Anders was beyond the point of no return. Before he could assess the situation his body was in motion, the new found strength in his muscles propelling the makeshift weapon forward.

It met with resistance. Hardness. Followed by a sickening crack. Then softness. Wet, sticky warmth began to cover Anders hands as he still clung to the flag pole. There was also a gasp. Sheer surprise that trumped pain.

Anders looked up into Gentry's face. The other boy's mouth was agape as he stared down at the pole protruding from his chest. Blood flowed from around the edges of the wound like rapids. Gentry started to speak, but had to stop when blood welled up in his throat and dribbled down one side of his mouth. He seemed to take a moment to compose himself, then spoke.

"I..." he began, having to stop again. A slight shudder wracked his small frame from deep within, then his gaze fell to the ground before he looked up again at Anders. "I just wanted to talk to you."

The two boys, not more than a foot away from each other, stared into each other's eyes. Anders could see intelligence, thought, and a trace of fear. A soul. But after the space of a dozen heart beats, those things began to fade from Gentry's eyes. What had been the windows to an inner self were reduced to sclera, irises, and faltering pupils that seemed to flicker like dying lights. When Gentry fell forward, he was no longer a cadet. No longer a boy who used to live in the suburbs. No longer a son. It was just skin filled with flesh and bone.

Anders stepped to the side and let the corpse fall to the ground. He suddenly felt dizzy and tried to place a hand on the wall to steady himself, but only succeeded in staggering back a few steps and falling into a sitting position. The room spun as pure euphoria overtook him, ten times greater than anything he had experienced in the Game. It was so intoxicating that almost a minute passed before he even realized that he had an erection and that an orgasm was approaching. He realized there was nothing he could do to stop it, and he shuddered as he ejaculated in his pants. After that, the feelings started to fade.

It took a while for the stark reality around him to sink in. He felt cold and wet, but his mind was clearer than it had been all night. His arm quivered as he pressed against the ground to push himself into a standing position. Except for a slight nausea, Anders felt much better than he had while he was still lying in bed staring at the ceiling. The dull ache had gone away.

There was blood everywhere, including on Anders, his once white socks a horrible shade of red. A tackiness pulled at the skin of this index finger and thumb as he pressed them together and pulled them apart. The mass that used to be Gentry lay face down on the floor.

Anders couldn't stop staring at it. He took a step forward and reached out with his foot, prodding the shoulder with his big toe. The body moved slightly when Anders pushed on it, but always fell back into the same position as soon as he moved his foot away. He took another step closer and crouched down next to the body. He grabbed the shoulders and twisted it around until the blood streaked face was exposed. Gentry's eyes were still open, his mouth frozen in one final gasp of surprise.

Tears welled up in Anders' eyes, and he soon found himself sobbing uncontrollably. Without thinking, he brushed a blood-soaked hand across his face to wipe the tears away, then pulled his hand away in revulsion. A former life flashed in his mind. A home. Parents. Friends. A not so distant past when he used to play with toys. When he used to just be a boy. And now everything had changed.

At first he assumed that he was crying because he had violated one of the greatest taboos of humanity. But the more he cried, the more he realized that wasn't actually the problem. He was disturbed not because he had killed another human being, but because he had liked it.

He stared at his hands. The hands of a killer.

As the minutes went by, his sobs started to subside as he became more comfortable with the realization. He knew that he wouldn't be able to change who he had become. The choice was to either spend time fighting himself, or he could indulge his desires. He pondered how something that felt so good could be wrong.

A final tear rolled down his face, then he knew that it was time to clean up the mess.

047

Anders finally stood up and began to think of his next move. If he didn't want a Game Over, there was work to be done. He ran through several possible scenarios, hitting dead end after dead end. His resources were limited, the possibilities slim.

That's when he decided to leave the body where it was. There simply wasn't any good way to dispose of it. No matter where he left it in the facility, it was still going to be discovered in the morning. There also wasn't a way to clean up the mess since the janitorial closet was probably locked. The most important thing, he decided, was that he didn't get caught.

A clock on the wall in the classroom ticked away, the hands creeping towards two AM. He wasn't familiar with the monitors' schedule, but he doubted that any would be around at that hour. It seemed like the time of night when they would shirk their responsibilities and doze off in an office somewhere until five or six in the morning.

Anders stripped off his clothes, the cool air on his naked skin further awakening his senses. He saved his blood-soaked socks for last, thankful that he hadn't been wearing shoes. As he peeled each away, he was careful to place the mostly clean soles of his feet on a patch of floor devoid of blood. The last thing he needed to do was leave footprints behind.

With clothes draped over his arm, he took one last look at his first real kill. The body would surely be whisked away and the mess erased. He carefully tiptoed towards the door, wiping his toes on the back of Gentry's pants before stepping back out into the hall.

Cold air whipped around his thin frame as he ran to the laundry room. A uniform left behind at the scene would have given him away instantly, but he also knew that keeping a bloody one in the bunk was just as dangerous.

He started by rinsing the clothes out in a basin while the gore was still fresh. Fortunately, their uniforms were dark in color, and Anders had to strain to see any traces of blood. Next he placed them in the washer and began the cycle, cringing at the sounds that echoed in the room and surely out into the hallway. He was betting on everyone being asleep.

Before he turned the corner back to the hallway where his bunk was, he paused and listened for anyone making a late night trip to the bathroom. But the only thing he could hear was the faint drip. It occurred to him that he shouldn't be able to hear such a thing through a closed door from a hundred feet away. Yet he somehow could.

He ran as fast as he could to the bathroom door; if he were spotted by a fellow cadet, blood all over his naked body, it was Game Over. Fortunately, no one emerged from the bunk door.

There was an even bigger sigh of relief when he found the bathroom empty. The hot water against his cold skin was exquisite. The steady stream of water whisked red ribbons down the drain and restored him to a presentable state. Despite how good it felt, the shower was noisy and would be heard from across the hall if anyone was awake. He made sure not to linger.

By the time he returned to the laundry room, it was time to move his clothes to the dryer. The forty-five minutes or so that he had to wait were the worst. The metal button on his pants clanged loudly against the dryer drum, resonating in the room and in his mind. He felt like a sitting duck staying in one place, inviting discovery. But no one ever came.

He slipped the warm clothes back on, heart pounding because he was so close to safety. It would be a shame if he was finally caught at that stage of the Game.

At three-thirty in the morning, the halls were still empty. Eerie. Quiet.

Even though he practically ran back to the bunk, once he opened the door to the room he slowed to a preternatural speed. He wanted to get the door shut as quickly as possible to stem the influx of light into the room, but resisted. He knew that the way he was moving looked like a foreign organism, and even if a boy saw him in a half state of sleep, he was no longer recognizable as himself. Or anything human for that matter.

When the door was finally shut, he slinked through pools of darkness towards his bed. As he passed the sleeping cadets, he took a long look at each face, searching for any signs of consciousness. He was amazed at just how easy it was to perpetrate nocturnal sins – and how oblivious everyone was to his presence.

As he crept past the bunks of the some of the top players in the Game, a sick smile crossed his face. They might gloat by day about just how much better they were, but at that moment they were helpless. Anders imagined the warmth of their throats against his icy palms and their inability to fight him since he had ascended to an entirely different level. As much as he wanted to do something to them right then and there, he knew that there would be other chances. Other nights.

At the base of his bunk, he quickly stripped down to his underwear and t-shirt, carefully putting his uniform away. Before he climbed the aluminum ladder up to his roost, he turned and surveyed the room one last time. If someone was going to be a problem, he wanted to know it at a time when he could still fix it. But nothing seemed out of place, except for Gentry's empty bed and Anders himself. He felt like he could finally breathe as soon as he climbed into bed and slipped under the covers. It was done, and he hadn't been caught.

But there was the chance that he been seen by another cadet entering or leaving the room. Or perhaps he forgot a shred of evidence at the scene. Fear slowly spread through him as he considered the terrible possibilities. As he had moved through the room towards his own bed, he had assumed that he was anomalous among his peers. But he had failed to consider the fact that Gentry had followed him in the first place. What if some of the other boys were just as good and he was the late comer to this new game?

If that were the case, then someone surely must have feigned sleep and cracked an eyelid while Anders thought that he was unobserved.

He suddenly felt nauseated as his mind raced. Then it dawned on him that in all his time at the Academy, no one had ever disappeared or been sent away. Even if other boys were experiencing the same changes that he was, he had been the first to kill. And that thought made him smile.

He took a deep breath, assured that no one in the room had an advantage over him. Sleep fell over him like a heavy weight. On the edge of consciousness, he remembered something. He couldn't tell if it was the beginning of a dream or not, but he saw his score go up.

048

The morning was surprisingly banal. Anders didn't know what he was expecting to happen, but it certainly wasn't their regular morning routine. Around six AM, the other boys had already started to wake from habit and were in various states of dress when the monitor burst through the door and turned the lights on.

"Lights! In the yard in five!" he screamed.

Anders sat up on his elbows looking around the room. There was nothing out of the ordinary. No one even seemed to notice that one of their bunkmates was missing in the flurry of morning activity. As Anders descended from his bed, he eyed Gentry's which was seemingly conspicuously empty only to him.

Soon he found himself shuffling into the back of a single file line as the boys exited the room into the hallway. It was surreal walking the same path that he taken only hours before. He found himself searching the floor for traces of blood, but there were none.

As the line approached the last turn before the row of classrooms, Anders held his breath. The boys in the lead turned the corner, but instead of stopping, the line just continued forward with its normal precision. Anders wanted to break file and rush ahead. It took incredible discipline to just appear normal.

Finally he turned the corner and was able to see for himself instead of trying to gauge the reactions of others. The doors to all of the classrooms were still propped open as they had been the night before, and the hall was empty except for the boys and a nearby monitor. There were no officers, no doctors, and no military police. As he neared the doorway where he had killed Gentry, he dared to glance inside ever so quickly.

The floor was a pristine white, and a new flag sat in the brass holder at the front of the room. The faint smell of disinfectant made Anders' nostrils twitch. He wondered who had discovered the body and why no one seemed to be concerned.

The line turned down another hall that dead-ended in double doors leading out to the exercise yard. The boys silently filed past two monitors who stood just inside of the door. Still nothing out of the ordinary.

Just as Anders brought up the end of the line and began to walk past them, he felt a hand on his shoulder. He turned, and his gaze made its way along an arm and up into one of the monitor's faces.

"We need you to come with us," the man said, sending anxiety like a knife into Anders' stomach. The man guided Anders to turn around as the other monitor shut the doors to the exercise yard.

Anders thought about trying to fight, but then he spotted two other monitors watching them from down the hallway. Even if he somehow managed to get the upper hand, it wasn't the right time. He relaxed and let the man guide him forward. Perhaps there would be a better opportunity to escape.

The third and fourth monitors fell into formation with the first two, boxing Anders in as they continued forward. He felt so small next to the four soldiers, suddenly aware of how thin his arms were and how flat his chest was. At the same time, he couldn't help but wonder why they felt the need to have four guards escort him to wherever it was they were going.

Anders soon found himself walking over the plush carpet again, only now the hall was alive with activity. Most of the offices were now lit up, and uniformed men moved all about. He wouldn't have thought that the brass would be in so early, unless...

Before they could arrive at the room with the wall of screens, the four men stopped and turned to face a sealed steel double door. One of them swiped a card through a narrow slot, and a red light switched to green, followed by the release of a locking mechanism.

The corridor beyond was filled with doctors in white coats. As soon as Anders walked through the door, they all seemed to stop and watch him. It felt more like a parade than him being led to a punishment.

Anders looked around in wonder at the mysterious wing of the Academy, stealing glances through glass door panels when he could. Some rooms had operating tables. Others were filled with animals in cages. First there were rats, then dogs, and even a room full of monkeys. Anders flinched at the sight a massive gorilla behind bars, all alone.

Next they passed a large room that instantly caught Anders' eye. The walls were lined with screens, just like the hub where men controlled the Game – only the screens in this room showed live video feeds from around the facility. Anders' jaw dropped as he noticed his peers out in the exercise yard. He could see the hallways, the bunks, and even the bathrooms. Four men sat in chairs, watching the feeds.

He was finally ushered into an examination room where his escorts left him and shut the door. He searched the ceiling for any signs of a camera. It occurred to him that there would be no questioning or investigation. Only punishment. But there was something that didn't make sense. If they could see everything, why wasn't he apprehended before he returned to the bunk? He had sat and done laundry for over an hour for God's sake. Why was the whole incident even allowed to happen? Surely they had observed him and Gentry heading for their inevitable collision.

His thoughts were interrupted by a soldier with a gun entering the room. Then a doctor walked in and removed a syringe and a vial of clear fluid from a locked cabinet. After drawing the fluid up the thin needle, he took a step towards Anders.

For the second time, he pondered resisting. But the outcome of that potential scenario was obvious. Anders noticed that the soldier's gun already had the safety disengaged.

More than anything, Anders was curious. Why had there been no lecture from the head of the Academy? No one telling him that the act he committed was wrong?

Instead of fighting, Anders just watched as the doctor injected the fluid directly into his PICC line. It was like liquid ice ran up the length of his arm.

"You may want to lie down," the doctor said.

Anders was already feeling sleepy, so he obliged. Soon the world went dark.

049

Anders woke up to a series of beeps. His head felt heavy, but he slowly gathered that he was lying on a hospital bed and that there was an IV line hooked up to him. A myriad of other cables ran to and from his body, most of which seemed to be noninvasive.

The door to his room was ajar, and he could hear voices from beyond the threshold. Bits and pieces of conversation reached his ears.

"Serotonin levels are normal," one man said.

"His vitals are increasing," someone else said. "He's awake now. You ready for the test?"

This time, Anders spotted the surveillance camera looking down on him and imagined the men in the next room watching him. They were now silent as another sound reached his ears – a mechanical whine. He localized the source of the noise and noticed a small platform rising at the foot of his bed. On top of it was a crystal clear box with a snake inside, the only opening pointed right at Anders.

A rattling echoed from inside the box as a forked tongue tested the air. Anders jerked his feet away and sat up. He thought about leaping over the rails, but there were too many instruments crowded around the sides of the bed.

The snake slithered out the box towards him, the periodic rattle warning of danger. Anders realized that he could probably just stand up and jump over the snake, landing on the floor at the foot of the bed.

But it was clear that there was something they wanted to know. The rattlesnake wasn't the much awaited punishment, it was part of an experiment.

Why disappoint?

He imagined that it was just another enemy from the River. He didn't have a gun, but he knew that he wouldn't need one. He got on his knees and watched the snake as it warily inched forward.

Then Anders sprung. His hand shot out, and the snake tried to react, but it was too slow. He caught its head in mid-strike and snapped its neck. After a popping sound, the snake's body was no longer under its own volition. It twisted and writhed, but Anders knew that it was dead. As he tossed it onto the floor on the side of the bed, he experienced a slight spike of happiness.

A moment later, applause erupted in the next room. Anders just stared at the doorway.

"He's ready," one voice said before it was lost in time.

LIVING DEAD

050

1984.

It had been dark for almost an hour, and their commander was late.

Even though he had been informed of it during training, Gabriel had never quite believed that the jungle could get cold. Yet there he was shivering around a fire with the rest of his platoon. He knew that the tardy arrival was only putting off the inevitable, but he was glad for the fleeting pocket of warmth that was keeping the forty degree weather at bay. They were at the final outpost on the edge of the northern front; there would be no fires after that night.

Only nine months before they had been fresh out of the states, an elite platoon that had trained since they were all high school age. Gabriel felt that they were more ready for war than most – in fact they needed it. Yet on the eve of their first mission, there wasn't the usual jokes and small talk. But it wasn't because they were nervous.

Three locals sat around a smaller fire right next to them conversing in Vietnamese. Gabriel felt an innate aversion to the presence of the foreigners that they had all been trained to hate. When the platoon had first arrived at the outpost, they received strict instructions not to harass the trio because the other men would be joining the ranks. Gabriel watched his peers sneaking distrustful glances over their shoulders at the other fire.

"Hey," the platoon's Lieutenant finally called out to the three strangers. He was an imposing man named Riker who towered above everyone, especially the short foreigners. The trio abruptly stopped talking and eyed their counterparts. "You speak English?" Riker continued.

All three of the men nodded. "Yes," one of them said with a heavy accent. "My name is Vinh."

"You from the north or south?" Riker asked. The entire outpost suddenly seemed quiet.

"The north," Vinh said matter-of-factly. The Americans recoiled. Even the sounds of the surrounding jungle didn't seem to penetrate the silence.

Vinh smiled. "I said I was from the North. We're on your side now." In spite of the comment, the platoon was still visibly ill at ease.

"Are we missing something here?" Gabriel interjected. "You don't look like soldiers." Indeed, the three men were rail thin, their forms draped in plain clothes.

Vinh placed a thin pipe up to his lips and inhaled. "We're spies," he said as wisps of smoke erupted from his nostrils. "You'll need us to go into the villages for you."

"You know what the mission is?" Riker asked.

"You'll find out soon enough," a voice boomed from the darkness behind them.

They all turned to face an elderly man in night camo who was flanked by two imposing figures in black body armor wielding unusually long rifles. The two bodyguards wore full helmets with built in air filtration and solid black visors where their eyes should have been.

"You're my platoon," the man said, his voice confident and powerful despite his frail frame.

Riker saluted, followed by the others. "Second Lieutenant Riker sir. May I ask whom we have the pleasure of serving under?"

"The name's Kurtz. General Kurtz."

The silence was now something palpable. Gabriel dared to quickly glance at the faces of his fellows, wondering if he was the only one completely dumbfounded. But their stone faced glares revealed nothing.

"We move out tonight," Kurtz said, his voice both smooth and threatening. "Start breaking camp."

Gabriel had become so distracted by his curiosity that he had almost forgotten about the cold. Almost.

051

In a long series of night marches, they slowly made their way deep into the north. Walking wasn't the most efficient way to travel, but it was the most secretive. They could have hidden in the bottom of a barge and went up the river, but there would have been other boats, some of them military. A helicopter could have possibly gotten them close to their destination without getting shot down, but then their arrival would have been loud and clear.

Instead, it was easier to be swallowed whole by the jungle. They walked where men seldom went, and other than the occasional backwater village, they were utterly alone. But just in case, they only dared to move under the cover of darkness.

Temperatures continued to drop, and Gabriel had a chill in his bones that wouldn't go away. He desperately hoped that there would be some excuse for a fire, but purification tablets eliminated the need to boil drinking water. And even though they were supplementing their rations by foraging, there was no meat that had to be cooked.

Cold water. Cold food. No baths. It was life in the bush. No one else complained, so Gabriel didn't either. The long march was painfully methodical, and he found himself inventing ways that they could have arrived at their destination undetected. He knew that it was a silly thing to think about, but after a couple of dead end scenarios, it became a problem that he needed to solve.

His favorite idea was that they could have somehow hijacked a small cargo plane at one of the larger villages – the kind that peddled agricultural goods and livestock. The platoon would have had to pile into the back when no one was looking while one of their local spies climbed into the cockpit for takeoff – making the whole thing appear like a simple theft. Then they would have had to find a way to crash land the plane somewhere close to their destination. The plan wasn't perfect, but Gabriel was still working to iron the kinks out. There was nothing better to do, even if his crazy idea would never be heard.

Gabriel was just a Private, and there were bigger men among them. He frequently watched as the aged General picked his way through the jungle. By Gabriel's estimation, Kurtz had to be in his seventies or late sixties – at best. In spite of that, the older man kept pace with the twenty somethings like he was one of them.

The two bodyguards were even more enigmatic. Their uniforms bore no insignia indicating branch or rank – or even their country of origin. They never removed their helmets, and the duo always went off alone with the General to eat and drink. Or at least Gabriel assumed that was what they were doing. The pair never talked, and except for the general shape of their bodies, Gabriel had no evidence that they were even human.

When the members of the platoon found themselves alone, they only dared to talk about the General and his escorts in hushed whispers. It quickly spread around the very first night that none of them had ever seen or heard of such strange soldiers. Apparently they, like the war itself, weren't supposed to exist.

Gabriel constantly wondered about the nature of their mission. Even though Kurtz had said they would all find out soon enough, the venerable man hadn't said a word since they moved out. The only thing that he had given Riker was the coordinates of their destination. According to the map, they were headed to the dark heart of the jungle, far from any vestige of civilization.

As they traveled over a hundred miles on foot, the endless nights started to blend into one another. Gabriel barely felt alive – and barely in control of his own actions. He started to notice that he and other men were becoming terribly pale from a total lack of sunlight. It was like they had become creatures of the night.

The entire platoon was so out of touch with reality that it was a surprise when they finally did arrive at their 'destination.' It was unremarkable – just another swath of the endless jungle and the endless night. Dawn was still a couple of hours away when Riker suddenly called for a stop.

The General strode to the front of the group. "We'll make camp here," Kurtz said. "There aren't enough hours left in the night to do the work we came to do. But tomorrow, we begin." He gave a slight nod at the men, then started to walk away.

Every man in the platoon looked to Riker. The Lieutenant just shrugged. They still had absolutely no idea what it was they were going to do.

052

The following night was the coldest yet. Gabriel didn't want to get out of his sleeping bag, but he was tugged by an intense curiosity. Even though no one was saying anything, there was a buzz in the camp. The moon was full, and bright blue light filtered down through the canopy, catching their breath in white wisps.

Finally Kurtz emerged from a patch of darkness, still flanked by his two shadows. He moved to the center of the waiting men, all eyes on him. "Not far from here lies an enemy position of critical importance," he began. "They are far too entrenched to be overrun by force, and there are... peculiarities of the position that make it such that a bombing would not be appropriate. We are here to take control of that position using a different method."

Kurtz paused, looking from face to face. "You might be wondering why a General is out in the bush. It's because I'm the one who created this method and perfected it in the Philippines in the fifties. This position is so important to the war that I was summoned out of retirement to oversee this mission personally."

Gabriel didn't know why, but for some reason that statement gave him chills. He tried to imagine what such a man would have been doing in his retirement after what appeared to be a lifetime at war, but he came up short.

"The enemy position is supplied by a network of villages in the surrounding area. The only weakness that Command has identified is that the enemy is superstitious. Very superstitious. They believe that there are horrible monstrosities living in the jungle that only come out at night. We are going to capitalize on that belief. The objective is to scare them into abandoning the position through psychological warfare."

Kurtz paused again, searching the reactions of his captive audience. "It might sound ridiculous to you because you've only been trained to kill. But I know for a fact that this type of warfare is effective. Timing is everything, and it just so happens that people have recently been disappearing at night – both soldiers and villagers alike."

Gabriel shivered. He imagined that the others were equally terrified since no one dared to move an inch. He couldn't help but remember ghost stories told around the campfire at base camp. But this time there wasn't a fire – only the pale, ghastly face of the General under the full moon. The blackness beneath his eyes made him look corpse-like.

"About eight months ago, we even lost two of our own to unexplainable circumstances. They disappeared while on a recon mission of this very same position." The General paused again, seeming to relish the utter silence. "The enemy is already spooked. It's our job to now escalate it to an entirely different level. Either we scare the villagers off and starve the base, or we scare everyone off." He leveled his gaze right on Riker's ashen face. "Any questions?"

At first there was silence, only broken by a loud gulp. "Uh, how exactly are we going to scare everyone?" Riker asked timidly.

"There are going to be more disappearances of course," the General smiled. "But I'll save all the gory details for later. Anything else?"

"Any Intel on what's... actually making people disappear?" Riker asked, choking on the last part.

"I wouldn't worry too much about it. It's probably nothing," Kurtz said. There was another awkward pause as the entire platoon just stared in the wake of his response. "Like I said, they are very superstitious."

That follow-up didn't make Gabriel feel any less like a twelve-year-old in a dark forest. He turned his head and surveyed the jungle around them, which seemed darker and more ominous than it had before. It was really starting to set in that they were utterly isolated. Even though that was what they had trained for, now that they really were there facing the unknown, things had suddenly become very creepy.

"I need your best stealth runners," Kurtz addressed Riker.

Gabriel perked up.

With dread.

They all knew survival and fighting skills, but within the platoon there were various groups of specialists: snipers, medics, trackers, and heavy artillery, among other things. Gabriel was a stealth runner, which meant that he was good at moving around undetected. Very good. He was the ideal candidate for stealing things, or planting explosives behind enemy lines.

But now he was wondering just what Kurtz had in store for him.

053

Flames sputtered in the darkness below – beacons to the sleeping village. Gabriel crouched on a rise next to three other men. One was recon, eying the village through night vision binoculars, and the other two were stealth runners. Riker was behind them, somewhere in the jungle with Kurtz and his bodyguards.

The recon specialist squinted into his binoculars. "All of the lights are flame based, mostly oil lamps. It looks like there is one central lodge with a generator, but it's obviously not on right now."

"Any guards?" Gabriel asked.

The other man shook his head. "Why would they have any?"

Gabriel nodded at the logic. Then he spotted a black form on the edge of his vision and almost jumped at the sight of one of the General's body-guards. Gabriel stifled a scream. One of the tricks of the trade to being a stealth runner was that one generally was aware when he was being watched or followed. But it was like the other soldier hadn't even been there – until he was. Kurtz emerged from the shadows with Riker, neither man as sneaky as the bodyguard had been.

"You ready?" Riker addressed the stealth runners. Each man nodded.

"I need a child, roughly seven to ten years of age," Kurtz said. "The sex is irrelevant." He seemed even more ghastly than before. Branches danced in the wind, casting shadows across his face that made him seem even older than he really was.

"In what condition, sir?" Gabriel asked, horrified by his own question.

"I need the child alive, uninjured. Not even a scratch," Kurtz said. "No one is to know. I want the parents to wake up in the morning to an empty bed with no clue as to what happened. No sign of struggle whatsoever. Got it?"

The three men nodded again. Gabriel wanted to ask why they weren't sending one of the bodyguards instead, but he knew that would be out of bounds.

"Rendezvous here ASAP with the quarry," Riker said just as Kurtz and his men retreated back into the jungle. Gabriel knew that there were six other men stationed nearby, including heavy artillery, should things get hairy. But it was just a village, he reassured himself.

Gabriel was the lead man, and he was anxious to get moving in hopes of warming up. The other two runners followed him over the edge of the drop, and in moments they were at the outer perimeter of the village. Gabriel was thankful for the firelight. If they moved quickly, an onlooker might mistake them for optical illusions or shadows cast by the flickering flames.

They were clad in pure black from head to toe. Each man only carried a dagger and a small pistol, both of which were tucked into their clothing so as to not reflect light. Gabriel had always been annoyed at the way the pistol bit into his waist. Unlike the flat dagger, there was just no good place for it. It didn't help that the barrel was elongated to accommodate a silencer. The slight pinch was manageable, but a distraction that inhibited certain types of movement. He considered the weapon more of a liability than an insurance policy. But it was standard procedure for runners – should things get hairy.

All the members of the platoon knew basic sign language; it was essential to moving through the jungle without speaking. But the runners had a bigger vocabulary than the rest. The other two men watched as Gabriel held two fingers up to his eyes, then pointed those two fingers at various shanties. He then held his two hands back to back before parting them like a swimmer. Lastly, he held up ten fingers and pointed the ground. *Split up. Search the designated areas. Reconvene in ten minutes.*

As the other two men went in opposite directions, Gabriel moved towards a cluster of buildings that seemed to be nestled in a pool of blackest night. He was consciously aware of every step that he took, careful to never put too much weight on any given one. As a matter of course, he scanned the ground for trip wires or traps as he went, although he wouldn't have expected that there.

Soon he was standing outside one of the houses, if one could call it that. It was little more than an old wooden shack that was raised slightly off the ground. He approached one of the windows and peered inside. Everything seemed to be arranged in one central space, and it didn't look like there were any other rooms. A man and woman slept on floor mats with two children, perhaps ages three and five. The dim light from a dying fire undulated over their faces.

Gabriel shook his head to himself. Even if the kids had been old enough, the layout of the building wasn't conducive to stealth. He was hoping that not all of the shanties were the same.

He checked a few more and encountered similar results. There was no way to get to the children without entering a communal space. He stopped looking in windows along that particular row and decided to look for a different type of house altogether.

As he neared the center pavilion, a bit of movement in the darkness caught his attention, and he froze. Within a few seconds he figured out what it was – a pen full of pigs behind one of the shanties. That particular one seemed larger than the rest, so he headed in that direction.

He was hoping that sleeping in a communal space had more to do with socioeconomic status than it did with the culture of the village. Even though they had been taught about Vietnamese households and their practices, the villages were much different, like relics frozen in time.

One peek through a front window revealed that there was a main room that appeared to function as a living area, dining room, and kitchen. No one slept there. In fact, he spotted the entrance to a hallway in the back of the room. Now he only had to hope that whoever lived there had children in the designated age range.

As he walked to the back of the house, the pigs shuffled around nervously, and a few low snorts and squeals erupted from the pen. A dog emerged from a hutch, a low growl coming from its throat as it searched the darkness. Gabriel froze, cursing his luck. Animals were one of the difficult x-factors to mitigate – especially dogs. But it was not impossible.

He slowed his pace to an almost imperceptible crawl, becoming part of the scenery – black against the night sky. It was excruciating to move that way, but it fooled the dog until Gabriel finally arrived at one of the other windows. An elderly man slept next to a similarly aged woman. It was what he was expecting – that some of the wealthier individuals would be older. He then resumed his ridiculously slow crawl to the next window. Inside a younger couple slept with a baby.

Gabriel needed to check the two bedrooms on the other side of the house, but he didn't want to risk walking around the back right next to the animal pen. The dog was still eying him, trying to figure out what exactly it was looking at.

Gabriel looked ahead anxiously as the other two windows finally came into view after he took the long way around the front of the house. In the first bedroom slept two girls, probably aged about four and five. Not quite old enough, but they might have to do. The only problem would be kidnapping one without waking the other. But even as Gabriel tried to work out the logistics in his head, he spotted something more promising in the final bedroom – a boy sleeping alone who appeared to be about ten years old.

Because of the damn dog, Gabriel was a few minutes late back to the rendezvous point where the other two runners were already waiting. He made a sign at them to report. One just shook his head, and Gabriel imagined that he must have encountered nothing but single room homes. The other man held his hand out, palm towards the ground and rotated his hand side to side — *so so*. Gabriel gave them both a thumbs up and indicated that they should follow him.

Soon they were at the front door to the larger residence. Going through that particular entrance meant they would have to travel farther once inside, but Gabriel just didn't think it was possible to exit the back carrying a child and not have the dog go berserk. He stood silently as one of his partners in crime crouched in front of the door knob, lock pick in hand. The third kept watch nearby.

There was a soft click, and Gabriel's companion rose. Gabriel opened the old wooden door ever so slowly, trying to anticipate any creaks. But there were none, his expert hand lifting up slightly on the handle so that the full weight of the door wasn't resting on the hinges.

The hardwoods inside were going to be more challenging, since it was impossible to assess visually where the loose boards would be. Gabriel and his backup entered on the balls of their feet, carefully testing each spot on the floor before committing their weight to it. Gabriel always felt more vulnerable inside, especially in a space as small as that one. Outdoors, it was easy to hide and blend. But if one of the family members exited a back bedroom right at that moment, Gabriel and his partner would be discovered instantly. He didn't want to think about the consequences if they ruined the General's grand plans.

The only light came from a flickering oil lamp in the kitchen. Gabriel extinguished it as quickly as he could, plunging the entire house into darkness. His companion stood near the front door, barely visible in the shadows unless one knew what to look for.

Gabriel moved into the back hallway, his heart racing. No matter how many times he had trained for such things, it was difficult for a mission like that to feel routine. It was still very possible that someone could get up in the middle of the night and bump right into him. The problem wasn't that he feared for his safety; he was confident that he and the other man could kill everyone in the house before any type of alarm could be raised. But the fear of a botched mission was very real – especially given the circumstances. He picked up his pace as much as he dared without throwing caution to the wind.

He slowly cracked the bedroom door and peeked in. The boy was still asleep, a gentle snore emanating from his nasal cavity. Gabriel stepped into the room, leaving the door slightly ajar. He knew that once the kid was is in his arms, he would need to reopen the door with only his foot.

Gabriel hovered like a shadow over the boy's mat, a thing of nightmares. He imagined being that age again, his parents telling him not to be afraid of ghosts or the monster in the closet, and then waking to what was about to happen.

Gabriel crouched down behind the boy's head, getting his arms into position. One slip up – one scream allowed to escape – and Gabriel's cover would be blown. Confident that he was positioned properly, he took a deep breath. Then, like a snake striking, he wrapped his arms around the boy's neck and head, one dark gloved hand covering the boy's mouth tightly.

The boy's eyes bulged out, and his whole body jerked reflexively. Muffled cries came from beneath Gabriel's hand, but they were weak, stifled by a crushing force. Small frightened eyes darted around, trying to ascertain what was happening. But the darkness in the room was profound, and Gabriel was behind his victim. The boy tried to hit his invisible assailant with an elbow, but the attempt was feeble. His eyes were already clouding over with the haze of unconsciousness.

A moment later he was limp in Gabriel's arms. After holding him for another fifteen seconds just to make sure it wasn't a ruse, Gabriel slipped a gag over the boy's mouth, then produced a syringe filled with tranquilizer to ensure that his captive wouldn't be waking up any time soon.

Gabriel stood up, flinging the boy over his shoulder like he was carrying a wounded soldier. It was harder to navigate the wooden floors with the dead weight, which was vexing since all Gabriel wanted was to get the hell out of there. Now that the deed was done, he desired to return to the comforting shroud of the jungle. Still, he took his time, slowly shutting the door behind him. It must be as though they were never there – it would be scarier that way.

Once he was back in the main living area, Gabriel handed the boy off to his companion, then crossed the room to relight the oil lamp. Its warm glow was comforting and would surely reassure anyone getting up before dawn that all was well in the house. Gabriel felt exposed again, and it took all he had to not just run for the front door. But no one emerged to discover him.

Finally he felt the cold night air on his face. The boy was laid out on the porch, and his teammate was on his knees, ready to lock the front door. As Gabriel hoisted the boy back over his shoulder, he heard another satisfying click that meant they were almost done.

As he stepped off of the front porch, Gabriel felt a huge weight lift off of his chest. The earth felt more comfortable beneath his feet, easier to manage. They were rejoined by the third runner, and moments later, the trio disappeared into the trees.

On that night, a boy, a son, disappeared forever.

054

Riker ushered them through the jungle towards an unknown destination, the General conspicuously absent. Gabriel was full of questions about where they were taking the boy and what they intended to do, but he was forced to march forward silently.

All the while, he could feel the rise and fall of a small chest against his shoulder. Occasionally the boy would move slightly, like the beginnings of thrashing from someone trapped in a nightmare. But he was too far under to actualize the movements that were being acted out in his mind. Eventually the small body began to shiver, and Gabriel suddenly remembered the cold. He adjusted the boy's position, cradling him instead of carrying him over the shoulder, hoping to cover more of his exposed skin from the chill air.

At some point Riker looked back and noticed Gabriel trying to warm the boy. The Lieutenant just shook his head, then turned and continued to lead the group deeper into the jungle. Gabriel looked down at the sleeping form in his arms, thinking of a son that he never had. He silently wished that whatever the General had planned, the boy would survive.

Soon they could hear the sound of water sluggishly lapping at a riverbank. Gabriel cringed at the sound, imagining the river's icy embrace as temperatures just seemed to keep dropping as the night wore on. All of a sudden, they emerged from the underbrush into a large clearing on the side of the river. The rest of the platoon stood there in the dark, gathered around Kurtz who waited near the water's edge. There was no need for fire since every man wore night vision visors – all except for the General who seemed perfectly capable of seeing in darkest night with his own eyes. Gabriel noticed a rope hanging over a sturdy branch that jutted out over the river.

"Finally," Kurtz said as he eyed the boy in Gabriel's arms. "I take it you were not detected?"

"No sir. It was like we were never there." Gabriel found himself clutching the boy more tightly.

Kurtz motioned at the riverbank. "Bring him here."

It took a couple of seconds before Gabriel's feet would obey him, but he knew that he didn't have a choice. He slowly approached, distrustful of what was about to happen.

"Hurry it up," Kurtz motioned more fervently. "This is just the second step of three." The elderly man pointed to the ground.

Gabriel crouched and gingerly laid the boy down, full of regret. He felt like an irresponsible father saying goodbye to a child. As soon as he rose, he moved to the back of the group, lest he be asked to participate even more in the scene unfolding before him.

"String him up like we talked about," Kurtz barked at a couple of nearby soldiers. Gabriel watched in horror as they tied one end of the dangling rope around the boy's feet, then grabbed the other end and hoisted him into the air until he dangled over the river. The boy's eyes were still shut. Gabriel was thankful that the tranquilizer was strong. He hoped that the boy was oblivious to what was happening.

"Now comes the gory details," Kurtz addressed the group. "When I was in the Philippines in fifty-three, the local rebels believed in a creature called the Aswang – part ghoul, part vampire. My unit pretended to be that creature and left a trail of victims until the enemy fled their underground stronghold."

The night suddenly seemed colder. Not a single soldier milled about or shifted his weight, as though breaking the terrible silence was a mortal sin.

"The locals here don't believe in the Aswang per se, but they do believe that a vampiric creature is responsible for the recent string of disappearances. Tonight we become that creature." Kurtz didn't seem human in the moonlight and looked even worse in night vision. "It had to be a child first, to show the locals just how terrible this monster is."

There was something strikingly odd about the General that Gabriel couldn't quite put his finger on until that moment. Peoples' eyes, when viewed in night vision, reflected infrared beams which made their irises glow. That wasn't the case with the General; both of his eyes were pitch black. And not just the iris, but the entire eye ball. Looking at him in night vision was like staring into the abyss.

Gabriel shuddered with this realization, fear suddenly gripping him. He wanted to turn and run, but his feet refused to move. He was paralyzed, held in the sway of the General's speech, forced to attend what was quickly becoming a black mass in the wilderness.

One of the Kurtz's bodyguards produced a wicked looking instrument that resembled a giant hook with two barbs. He positioned himself close enough to the boy to strike without falling into the river.

Gabriel breathed a sigh of relief that one of them had not been asked to perform the task. Finally the General's servants had to get their hands dirty. The bodyguard drew his arm back, then suddenly struck the boy in his jugular. The barbs bit into his neck like teeth, and blood instantly sprayed out from around the edges of the wound, released from the immense pressure of the boy hanging upside down.

As soon as the hook pierced his neck, the boy's eyes opened. The tranquilizer wasn't strong enough to save him from witnessing the moment of his own death. He tried to scream in sheer terror through the gag, his eyes searching the darkness for some answer to the single question burning in his mind.

The bodyguard pulled the hook out, and blood began to splash into the water below. The boy's heart must have been racing in panic, which only served to hasten his demise. Each contraction sent more blood to his head, which then never made back into his body.

The entire platoon was transfixed. Gabriel wanted to turn away but he just couldn't. None of them were strangers to death, but something about what was taking place crossed a line.

The fear in the boy's eyes faded into a profound sadness. Even though he couldn't see in the dark, it was suddenly as if he was staring into each and every man's eyes, boring into their souls. Finally that sadness disappeared as his eyes rolled back, then he was gone forever. Blood still dripped steadily into the river and was whisked away neatly by the sluggish current.

Kurtz leveled his soulless gaze right on Gabriel. "It will take about an hour for the blood to drain, then he must be left in the jungle close to his home. Pick a conspicuous location. We want the body to be found."

055

The body that used to be a boy had become just as cold as the night air, and Gabriel felt like he was carrying a block of ice. The boy's skin was impossibly pale and more resembled that of a mannequin than a person. Gabriel was thankful that he was covered from head to toe – he was already repulsed, and skin on skin contact just might have pushed him over the edge. He wondered how many more children he was going to have to kidnap in the night.

The worst part was that he felt like he was alone. There were eight other men all around him, some ahead and some trailing, but he was by himself in the middle like a pariah. He wasn't even sure why he was chosen for the job. With that many people, it was no longer a pure stealth run – especially since they weren't even going into the village. Only if Kurtz hadn't looked at Gabriel. But as soon as he had, every other man had an excuse not to volunteer to carry such a burden.

The group finally arrived at the jungle's edge, right outside of the village. The four men who had gone ahead were already waiting when Gabriel arrived with the body. As soon as he did, they all turned away and looked at the village.

Gabriel looked around for a good spot that wasn't choked with vegetation. He spotted an old, gnarled tree around which nothing seemed to grow. Unlike the surrounding trees, lush with green even in the chill weather, its twisted branches were barren and black. Gabriel wondered if the tree were actually dead.

He gently placed the body at its base and realized with a shudder that the boy's eyes were open – staring right at him. Startled, he fell backwards onto the barren earth. He thought that he distinctly remembered the eyes being closed.

Gabriel felt a little bit better as the four men bringing up the rear finally stepped into view. He was about to lean forward and close the boy's eyelids when he imagined the General's voice in his head. Surely the villagers would be more frightened if they saw the same thing he was looking at. So he didn't shut the boy's eyes, both relieved and filled with regret at the same time. But the more frightened the villagers were, the faster the platoon's grisly mission would be over. Hopefully before Gabriel lost his mind.

As he started to stand, something on the tree trunk caught his eye. There was an odd symbol carved into the bark. But the symbol itself wasn't the strangest part. Gabriel could have sworn that he had seen it somewhere before, but he couldn't remember where. Must have been in some former life, before the war.

He straightened up and looked over at his platoon mates, then nodded his head to the side to indicate that they should leave. As everyone else started moving out, Gabriel turned and looked one last time at the boy, wondering what his last evening had been like. The boy hadn't known a thing about the doom that had only been a few hours into his future. It reminded Gabriel that the same thing could happen to him at any time. He let his gaze linger for only a moment more then said a silent goodbye, sorry that the two of them had to experience the horror together.

As the group trudged several miles back to camp, Gabriel felt like it was worse to be the one who was still alive. He felt empty inside, like something essential had been removed from his being, and now he was just going through the motions of living.

The sky overhead was beginning to turn from a deep blue to a blood red as the sun began its slow ascent. When they arrived at camp, it was in total disarray as soldiers moved out in various directions. Riker stormed over to the newly returned group.

"You see anything out in the bush?" he asked of the Sergeant who had overseen their operation.

"No sir," the Sergeant shook his head, surveying the chaos in camp. "Should we have?"

"Schmidt is AWOL."

"What?"

Riker looked around again like he might find the man in question. "Yeah, got into an argument with the General about killing kids." He turned back to face the Sergeant. "He apologized when the General told him he was out of line, excused himself, and never came back."

Gabriel eyed Kurtz and his bodyguards who were across the camp, imposing as ever. He had questions that he didn't dare voice – like whether Schmidt actually went AWOL or if he just became a liability.

"I've already sent out two teams. Get some sleep," Riker said.

Gabriel made his way over to his pack, then crouched down and grabbed his bedroll. He noticed a sleek black boot in his peripheral vision and almost jumped up in terror.

Instead he stood up and turned to face Kurtz and his bodyguards. The older man placed a hand on Gabriel's shoulder, and it felt colder than the corpse had. Everything in Gabriel's being wanted to pull away, but after what might have happened to Schmidt, he didn't dare.

"I wanted to personally commend you for your work this evening," Kurtz said. "I know it wasn't easy, but trust me, the war will be easier for all of us because of it."

He finally pulled his hand away, and Gabriel just stared at him.

"Keep up the good work and you'll go far," Kurtz smiled. "One day you could be me."

Gabriel wanted to respond in some way, but he was speechless. All he could do was watch as Kurtz sauntered away.

056

Sleeping by day was always a fight. After freezing all night, Gabriel desperately wanted to bundle up. But when temperatures rose to the upper seventies by midday, he was drenched in sweat, ready to fling his clothes off. His sleep was fitful, a constant drifting in and out of dreams.

When he finally did wake up at dusk, he noticed that Vinh and the two other spies were sitting in camp. He scanned the area all around looking for Schmidt, but the missing man still wasn't there. Dusk was one of the rare opportunities when Gabriel saw the world in something other than night vision or moonlight. It was strange, but in the daylight everything seemed mysterious and surreal.

The sun had passed the horizon, and its last fading rays were barely visible when Kurtz finally made an appearance. It had never occurred to Gabriel before, but he had never actually seen the General in sunlight. Kurtz had been late to arrive on the night of their departure, and every morning he and his bodyguards left the main camp, only to return at sundown. It creeped Gabriel out.

Riker and Kurtz joined the spies, then Kurtz leaned over and said something to Riker. The Lieutenant signaled for Gabriel to join them. Gabriel reluctantly got up from his bedroll, an ache still in his soul. It was even more upsetting when Kurtz greeted him with a blood curdling smile, thin lips stretched over decaying teeth.

"I wanted you to hear the fruits of your labor," Kurtz told Gabriel as he took a seat.

"We spread out into the villages today," Vinh began. "The one you took the boy from found the body by mid-morning. When I left them two hours before dusk, they were creating a ring of torches around the village and planning for a night watch."

"Were they scared, or just reacting to a boy abducted in the night?' Kurtz asked.

Vinh paused for a moment, chewing on the mouthpiece of his unlit pipe since they weren't allowed to smoke in the bush. "They were more than scared." Vinh seemed to be pondering something. "I'm not from around here, and I don't understand the local superstitions, but there was something about the place where they found the body that scared them even more."

Gabriel's stomach lurched, but thankfully all eyes were on Vinh. That is until the General looked over at him with a questioning look. Gabriel just shrugged and shook his head, deciding to keep to himself the bit about the weird tree.

"Word spread to the neighboring villages by early afternoon, and we helped to spread it farther. But in the more distant villages, it was more of a rumor."

Kurtz nodded. "We need to strike far from the first village." He looked right at Gabriel again. "I need a grown man tonight." Then he shifted his attention to Riker. "Send a team back to the first village. They aren't to leave the tree line, and they aren't to be seen. But I want strange noises to come from the jungle."

Riker seemed like his mind was somewhere else, but after a moment he nodded to Kurtz. "We'll take care of it."

"I trust that you will," Kurtz said as he rose and left the camp, body-guards in tow.

Gabriel wondered where the hell they went when they left. What could they possibly be doing out in the bush for hours on end?

"Did they ever find Schmidt?" Gabriel asked Riker.

The other man just shook his head. "Get the map and pick a village. I'll tell Sarge to get a group together." Riker rose and started giving orders.

Even though the sun was long gone, their day was just starting.

057

The man was a lot heavier than the boy had been. Gabriel slowly worked his way through the bush carrying the feet while another runner had the upper end. Initially, Gabriel had doubts about their ability to abduct a grown man from his own bedroom. Most men would have been lying next to their wives. But they got lucky and spotted the village drunk half passed out on a porch. The rest was child's play.

Gabriel's arms were hurting. He and the other runner had been taking turns with the head, but they had also been walking for miles. Even though their victim wasn't an enemy soldier, Gabriel didn't feel nearly as guilty about this one. Especially not after the man pissed himself during their trek.

A familiar sight greeted them as they arrived at the river. Only this time a portion of the platoon was missing – presumably at the village they had hit the first night. The General stood on the riverbank waiting like a preacher before his congregation. The men of the platoon were silent, and Gabriel wondered why they were even there. Why did they want to watch? Or why had they been required to attend?

He and the other runner set the body down at the General's feet, then backed away slowly. Gabriel wanted to retreat altogether and not give Kurtz another opportunity to saddle him with the return trip, even though he knew it was coming.

Other men stepped forward to tie the rope around the man's legs. This time it took a few of them to hoist the body into the air using a primitive pulley. The man swayed from side to side over the brackish river water, dangling like a pendulum.

All too anxious, one of the bodyguards produced the giant hook and waited for the back and forth movement to slow to a halt. Gabriel had taken extra tranquilizer with him and had just administered a second dose right before they arrived in camp in the hopes that this one wouldn't wake up.

The bodyguard punctured the man's jugular neatly, then removed the hook to let him bleed out like a pig at slaughter. Gabriel breathed a sigh of relief when the man's eyes didn't open on impact. None of their victims deserved to die, especially not that way. The man's pulse was weaker than the boy's, probably deadened by the tranquilizer and alcohol coursing through his veins. The blood ran out slowly, making a splashing sound that was like a gentle waterfall or a garden fountain.

The man slowly opened his eyes and blinked a couple of times. Gabriel frowned. Enough of the tranquilizer must have run out into the river for the man's pain threshold and survival instinct to finally kick in. That notwithstanding, the man's reaction was a far cry from the boy's. He appeared groggy and disoriented, like a patient waking in the middle of surgery. A couple of times, his eyes widened briefly before heavy lids relaxed again. It was like he was trying to grasp what was happening and even realized it on some level, but couldn't gather his consciousness enough to panic. Eventually the blood loss overcame him, and the light faded from his eyes, leaving only a cold dead stare. Even though the man had woken up, Gabriel supposed that was still a better way to go.

Everyone was so transfixed by the transcendence of death that none of them noticed the ripples in the water below. A massive reptilian form leapt up and grabbed the body in its jaws. The noise of the beast erupting from below the surface of the water was so loud that several men staggered back and fell. Gabriel watched in awe as the huge crocodile – well over twenty feet in length – crashed back into the water, pulling the body with it. It began to roll round and round, oblivious to the soldiers still on the bank.

The General hadn't even flinched when it attacked, even though he had been the closest. He now glared angrily at the river. Unbidden, his bodyguards raised their strange guns and opened fire into the churning water. The shots were so quiet that Gabriel couldn't hear them over the thrashing of the beast. Only when it ceased to move could he hear the subdued crack of concussive force filtered through silencers. Each time the guns fired, it sounded like someone was snapping a finger. It was impossible to tell through night vision, but Gabriel imagined that the water was bloodier than ever.

Kurtz turned quickly to face the group. "Recover the body," he said in a stern tone. Every man in the platoon looked at everyone else, eyes wide. "Quickly! Before it floats down river!"

Riker sprang into action barking orders. Gabriel was glad that he wasn't selected for the task, but he suspected that one far worse was about to fall on his shoulders.

The men were reluctant to enter the water and tried to snag the body with ropes. But it didn't work, and soon four men waded into the bloody water. The dead crocodile floated, the man still held tightly in its jaws. Gabriel half expected one of his fellows to go under any second, fallen prey to some other river predator. Surprisingly nothing happened – perhaps because all the commotion had scared everything else away. Once they got a hold of the man's feet, two of the soldiers had to pry the reptile's jaws open until the others could yank the corpse out of its mouth.

They all swam back to shore and threw the body on the bank. The sight was gruesome. His upper body was horribly lacerated in jagged lines, and he was barely recognizable amidst the tattered clothes that clung to his unmoving frame.

The General smiled. "This isn't what I was thinking, but this will add a new element to the killings." Gabriel knew what was coming next as Kurtz turned in his direction. "You know what to do."

058

Gabriel cursed silently as he carried the mauled corpse back through the jungle with another runner. It was probably the single worst job he ever had to do. The torso looked like chewed up hamburger meat, and Gabriel knew that he was going to have figure out a way to clean his gloves in order to remove the stench of death.

The most infuriating part of the ordeal was that it wouldn't actually become a stealth run until they neared the village and had to sneak the body back in. En route, it was two runners with a shitty job and an eight man escort. Gabriel kept wondering how they got stuck with the body. He resolved to have some words with Riker when he returned to camp.

The group slowed as they came within a quarter mile of the village. In hopes of accelerating the process, Gabriel had decided to actually dump the body in the village proper instead of the jungle. The rest of the group had instructions to stay behind. Since the guy was drunk on the front porch when they found him, it was possible that someone had been out to look for him. The worst case scenario was that search parties would already be out in the bush. But Gabriel doubted it.

He and his partner drew closer with their macabre cargo, only encountering the silence of the night. Nothing stirred in the village except for the occasional oil lamp casting dancing shadows along the ground. It was so cold that condensation hung in the air and formed a mist.

They arrived at the front porch without incident, and Gabriel looked around. He hadn't put much thought into where exactly to leave the body, but now that they stood in front of the shanty, it seemed ridiculous to leave it right where they had found it. Gabriel almost chuckled to himself at the idea of a man so severely mauled just sitting in his rocking chair. But then again, that would make the story all the stranger, wouldn't it?

He tilted his head towards the porch, then he and his partner began a creeping advance that got even slower once their boots met the wood of the structure. It was challenging to haul the dead weight and coordinate the steps of two people without making any noise. Soon they were trying to sit the man upright in his rocking chair – only the body kept slouching. So they gave up and let it settle into an unnatural position. The other runner stepped off of the porch while Gabriel still fussed over a few details. Satisfied, he turned to leave when the front door opened.

"Bao?" A female voice called softly into the night. Gabriel spun around to see a woman who must have been the deceased's wife standing in the doorway. She didn't carry any kind of light, so it took her a moment to realize what she was looking at. Gabriel tried to picture what he looked like to her – a strange black form standing on her porch. There was a moment in time when both of their hearts skipped a beat.

In the second that she was paralyzed by fear, unable to scream, Gabriel was upon her. He ripped her out of the doorway, cupping a gloved hand over her mouth that was covered in her dead husband's blood and muscle tissue. She kicked, so he lifted her slightly off of the ground to lessen the noise.

Gabriel looked right at his partner with grim resignation – he knew what he had to do. He made it quick and snapped her neck. After a few random muscle spasms, her body went limp in his arms. He looked around in confusion for a moment, unsure of what to do with the body.

She needs to disappear, his partner signed. Gabriel nodded, then drug her off of the porch. The other runner grabbed her feet, and they headed back to the tree line.

Gabriel knew that his partner was right. If the man's wife were found nearby, killed in a much more banal manner, it would make the creature seem less terrible. But if she were flat out missing, the front door still ajar, there would be a real mystery in the morning. Gabriel could hear Kurtz commending him. The very thought made him cringe. He never signed up to kill civilians, but he didn't have a choice but to be a pawn in the General's games.

Once they were back in the bush, Gabriel began to ponder exactly what they should do with the body. He imagined what would happen if they took it all the way back to camp. The General would complain that congealed blood wouldn't drain. Then on further consideration he would hatch a new scheme to the tune of letting the body sit for three days to rot before dumping it next to a completely different village.

Gabriel decided that he would spare the poor woman such a fate – not to mention himself. Once they were about three miles from the village, they dug a shallow grave, buried her, and covered up the disturbed earth. It was very unlikely that anyone would ever find her, and even if they did and somehow connected the dots back to her dead husband, it would be even creepier.

They barely made it back to camp before dawn with dirt streaked faces. The first rays of the sun marked their mandatory curfew. Even though the camp was quiet since only essential verbal communication was allowed, Gabriel could still tell that something wasn't right. The men seemed on edge. Instead of tending to bedrolls and personal effects, they all faced outward to the bush, weapons easily within reach.

"I was starting to think you weren't coming back either," Riker said as he rushed up to them.

"What do you mean?" the Sergeant asked.

"The team we sent back to the first village," Riker glanced around nervously, "they never came back."

"How many?"

"Five," Riker said.

The Sergeant looked around. "You sure? It's not quite sun up yet."

Riker nodded. "They were just supposed to go for an hour or two and scare the shit out of the night watch. After they were gone for four, I sent out another team to find them."

"And?"

"Nothing. No signs of a firefight. No signs of a struggle. They just disappeared."

Everyone shifted their weight around uncomfortably.

"So first Schmidt and now this," Gabriel said as he scanned the camp. "Where's the General?"

"Fuck if I know," Riker said. "I only see him when he rolls through here giving orders before he disappears back into the jungle to jerk off."

"So we're down six?" the Sergeant asked.

"Yeah," Riker said. "Of the original forty-two."

"What do you think happened to them?" Gabriel asked.

"Most likely enemy soldiers," Riker said. "Maybe they were responding to what happened last night."

Gabriel considered the ramifications of that. If the enemy realized that they were the cause of the deaths, the mission would be futile. "Then maybe the next victim should be a soldier," he said.

059

When Gabriel awoke at sunset, he was glad to see that no one else was missing. The three spies were nearby, huddled close as though they were sitting around an imaginary fire. Gabriel had questions for them before the General arrived. He stood up and crossed the camp, then sat on a fallen log next to Vinh.

"The second one was better," Vinh smiled at Gabriel before wedging the end of his unlit pipe between his thin lips. "The locals are afraid to leave the villages. They didn't even send out a search party for the missing woman."

"You think this might be over soon?" Gabriel asked.

Vinh sucked non-existent smoke through his pipe and seemed to ponder the question. "Your job is about to get a lot harder."

"What do you mean?"

"Now that all the villages are taking the threat seriously, they will all have night watches. It won't be as easy to sneak in," Vinh said.

"I'm not worried about that," Gabriel said. "We're talking about villagers. It'll be easy enough to snatch someone from the fringes of their perimeter."

"There's one other thing," Vinh said. "The second village also sent a messenger to the enemy base. The locals have decided to cease their normal supply runs. I would think the enemy will dispatch soldiers to quell the fears and restore their supply lines."

"Do you think that's what happened our men last night?" Gabriel asked just as he noticed Kurtz and Riker approaching from across the camp.

Vinh shook his head. "The villages didn't reach that decision until today."

Gabriel had more questions, but was cut short by the arrival of the commanding officers. The General eyed him and Riker seemed on edge.

"I'm ready for my debriefing," Kurtz announced.

Vinh nodded in greeting. "Your plan is working. The villagers are already refusing to make their regular night time deliveries to the base. From what I could gather today, this is critical because it will only allow deliveries at night."

Kurtz smiled and slapped Gabriel on the shoulder. "Well done soldier! I like the extra touch you added last night."

"The missing woman?"

Kurtz nodded. Gabriel didn't mention that it was an accident necessitated by damage control.

"Do we know if they are deploying kill teams?" Riker asked.

Vinh shook his head. "I only know what I have overheard. The villagers won't even speak to me directly about the base. The whole region is in on the secret."

"If they send out kill teams, we're the ones at a disadvantage," Riker addressed Kurtz. "They don't have to worry about stealth."

"Oh but they do," Kurtz replied. "They might not have to worry about making noise as they move through the bush, but they are on strict radio silence too since they aren't supposed to be out here either. That means they can't coordinate their efforts or radio for help. Each kill team is on its own. The way I see it, they are the sitting ducks." A crooked smile crossed his face as he shifted his gaze from Riker to Gabriel. "I say that we take the Private's advice and start killing soldiers. We've already scared the shit out of the villagers. It's time to spread the fear."

Kurtz seemed as excited as a boy on Christmas morning. "Pair your runners up with trackers and tail one of the kill teams. Snag a scout or someone off the back end. If you can't find a patrol, you'll have to get a guard from the actual base. Am I understood?"

"Yes sir," Riker said, a little less than excited. Gabriel was happy to finally get to stalk the enemy rather than helpless villagers.

"Tonight, a soldier must die or we're going to have problems," Kurtz stated, all vestiges of a smile gone from his face.

060

Gabriel's feet glided silently across the jungle floor. Since that was his specialty, he had to continuously force himself to slow down to match the crawling pace of his companions who could barely achieve the same quietude.

A tracker and two scouts were somewhere up ahead, looking for prey. They had already been at it for two hours. The environs of the base and its surrounding villages covered well over a hundred square miles. Looking for a random kill team wandering the jungle was like looking for a needle in a haystack. To increase the likelihood of success, they had limited their search to the vicinity of the second village – which also happened to be the closest to the hidden base. If time started to run short, they intended to approach the base for guaranteed results. The General's orders had been clear.

The jungle was strangely quiet that night. Gabriel attributed it to the plunging temperatures which likely had an adverse effect on the usually noisy insects. The cold had also created a sense of isolation. Each man withdrew deep into himself to find some semblance of warmth. But there was some part of Gabriel's mind that screamed out that it was more than just the cold – something was just wrong.

He almost laughed at that thought – like something was actually right about men creeping through the night in hopes of killing other men. Yet sadly, that was normal. It left Gabriel wondering what could possibly be abnormal and frightening in such a context.

It was in that instant that one of the scouts came back to relay a message: the tracker had found something. There were at least a dozen men ahead of them, not taking any care to hide their passage. Gabriel felt a sudden jolt of adrenaline. When they got close enough to this group, he would have to go ahead alone, isolate a target, and quietly remove him from the group without detection. It gave him a certain joy because that was exactly what he had trained for – not to kill low hanging fruit like the boy and the village drunk. He relished the challenge of hunting down an equal, or at least someone who had a fighting chance.

The Sergeant looked back at him and made a hand signal. It was time for Gabriel to go ahead with the scout and join the tracker. Everyone else would stay back just in case damage control was required.

It seemed even colder as Gabriel left the cluster of men. He followed the scout so silently that the other man turned around several times during their trek to see if Gabriel was still there. When they finally joined the tracker, he barely noticed them, his gaze affixed to the ground. He was a different kind of hunter than Gabriel. He could locate their prey, but couldn't take it down without a fight. Not like Gabriel could.

The more Gabriel thought about it, the more he realized that their platoon had been specifically tailored for this mission. The only anomaly in the well-oiled unit was the General and his bodyguards. Gabriel suspected that Kurtz's companions would make any man in the platoon look like an amateur, which made him wonder why they weren't the ones picking soldiers off. They were the most silent, the most mysterious. Where were they now, while lesser men were tasked to execute the General's wishes? Gabriel realized that he shouldn't worry about things that he had no power to change. There was only the mission right in front of him, in the cold of night.

The tracker continued ahead of them, moving forward until what sounded like a muffled scream broke the silence. Everyone froze in their tracks and listened, but they were only greeted by the occasional sounds of the jungle. The tracker looked back at Gabriel, but all he could do was shrug. They had all heard it, and it was probably what they thought it was – but that didn't make it any clearer as to how they should proceed.

As each man stood there deliberating within himself, there was another sound in the night. It was the distant sound of twigs snapping and dried out foliage cracking underfoot. The sounds of someone running with reckless abandon. And it was getting closer. Each of the men took up a defensive position with their backs up against trees, guns at the ready.

For a split second, Gabriel's imagination ran wild as he tried to picture what was crashing through the jungle. Being used to a pervasive and persistent silence, such a ruckus caused him to panic. He jumped to conclusions and guessed that whatever it was, it couldn't possibly be any smaller than full grown grizzly bear. But as it got closer, it became clear that it was bipedal and much smaller.

An enemy soldier came crashing through the underbrush unarmed. The tracker extended the barrel of his gun and held it a couple of inches above the ground, tripping the running soldier who toppled face first and slid along the ground. Then Gabriel and the two scouts were standing above him, guns aimed downward. The enemy soldier still wore a night vision headpiece and could obviously see what was happening.

He began babbling madly in Vietnamese, and despite the fact that he had three guns aimed right at him, he tried to scramble to his feet. It didn't like look he was trying to attack the men; he was just trying to get the hell out of there as fast as possible. It was hard to make out over all the commotion, but he kept repeating one word, sometimes by itself, other times in a sentence. *Pontianak.*

As the enemy soldier tried to stand, one of the scouts slammed the butt of his gun across the man's face with a loud crack. The man fell back to the ground, silent.

061

The rest of the platoon was already gathered at the riverbank by the time they arrived with the enemy soldier. A sleepy eyed Vinh also stood among them. Gabriel had sent word ahead that this one needed to be questioned before they killed him. They needed to know what had befallen the rest of the kill team and why he was running like madman through the jungle.

Gabriel had only lightly tranquilized him, and he woke easily when injected with uppers. As he came to, he blinked his naked eyes weakly and tried to jerk away from those who held him. Vinh began speaking to him immediately in Vietnamese before he could scream. The enemy soldier answered, and they spoke for about a minute. Gabriel noticed the same word as earlier.

Vinh turned to the General who waited steps away. "He was bringing up the rear of his group at a distance of about a hundred yards. They were on patrol for some sign of whatever was killing the villagers. Then he saw two figures with white faces jump out of the trees and attack his team. He took off screaming then he ran into our unit." Vinh paused for a moment, and just as the General's lips began to curl into a question, he continued. "He's new. He thinks the other soldiers were playing a trick on him. He says you should let him go before they find you."

Kurtz glared at the enemy soldier, and Gabriel thought the older man was going to spit on him for a second. Then a sinister laugh erupted from his gaunt form. "He's in no position to threaten me. Who the hell does he think he is?" The General shifted his gaze to the tracker. "Did your group find any sign of the rest of the enemy unit?"

The tracker shook his head. "No sir. After we saw the look on his face, we figured it best to return to base."

"We already had our target," the Sergeant interjected. "Why risk the rest of the kill team finding us?"

Kurtz nodded. "Understood." He looked at the enemy soldier who tried to follow the foreign conversation in pitch black darkness. "Let's get on with it. Someone put a gag on him. I don't see any reason to put this one back to sleep." He smiled.

A reluctant soldier walked up with a bit of cloth and shoved it into the man's mouth, then wrapped the loose ends around his head and tied it tight. Gabriel resigned himself to watch a familiar horror unfold as the rope was secured around the man's feet. There was a violent tug on the other end that ripped his feet out from under him. He fell face first, then the lower half of his body was hoisted off of the ground until eventually he dangled over the river.

"Lift this one nice and high. I don't want to share," Kurtz said. One of the bodyguards stepped forward, iron claw in hand, and in one swift motion not only punctured the man's neck, but ripped flesh away. As blood began to pour into the river, his feet were pulled almost all the way up to the overhead branch.

In that moment, Gabriel decided that he hated Kurtz for subjecting them all to this. The whole affair could have been carried out with dignity and respect. Not only did the bastard insist on starting with civilians, but once a soldier was rightfully in the hot seat, the General still found a way to pervert the act and make them all witness to it. To watch that man's eyes was truly horrifying – maybe even more so than the child. This one knew exactly what was happening.

Gabriel wondered if the dying man cherished the seconds as they flew by, trying to grab onto one of them for just a little more time. The only consolation, Gabriel thought, was that it only got easier as more blood poured out. A victim of exsanguination increasingly became drowsy and disoriented, the brain unable to function properly without fresh oxygenated blood. Gabriel hoped that it was like drifting off to sleep forever.

Once the man's body hung limply from the rope, Kurtz decided it was time to make his exit. "Make sure he's bled properly," he said to no one in particular. "Then I want this one dumped right on the enemy's doorstep." As the General left them to do the dirty work, Gabriel hated him even more.

062

The infrared lights of the base burned brightly in Gabriel's second generation night vision. Since the enemy only had first generation, they were blind beyond the fringes of the pools of artificial light. If Gabriel's unit had wanted to, they could have simply opened fire on one of the pillboxes from a safe distance. But instead they were going to carry a corpse to the very edge of the enemy's field of vision and leave a present.

The Sergeant signaled to Gabriel that the rest of the group wasn't going any farther. Gabriel nodded and waited as the body was brought up from the back of the formation. He had insisted that if they wanted him to actually be capable of sneaking up right next to an enemy encampment, he'd need his strength. He wasn't expecting it, but the Sergeant had agreed with him and ordered other men to carry their cargo – at least until it was time for Gabriel to shoulder the burden.

He and another runner each grabbed a side of the body and set off at a snail's pace towards one of the pillboxes. The base itself wasn't visible from their position since it was apparently located down in a ravine beyond the guard posts. Gabriel scanned the nearby area for any signs of roving enemy soldiers, but he didn't see anything other than foliage waving in the chill wind.

He and the other runner watched each other's feet and gauged the movement of the body as it swung back and forth, carefully timing their footfalls to work in tandem. All of the stealth runners had been trained to walk silently on various types of terrain and in various situations – including while carrying a body. The context though, had been different. Their instructor had told them that one day they might have to carry a wounded or dead companion out of the bush.

The monotony of their crawl had Gabriel thinking back to his time at the Academy. There had been a battery of assessments early on to determine what each boy's specialty would be. Some talents were obviously linked to measurable physical traits. Snipers, for example, had to have above average vision and a steady hand. Trackers had to have the ability to perceive and process their surroundings faster than a normal man. Gabriel wasn't quite sure what had singled him out to be a runner, but he suddenly wanted to know what innate trait had delivered him into the hell that he was living.

The pillbox was getting closer, its ambient green glow almost blinding. Gabriel could see the ends of heavy machine gun barrels poking out in every direction, including towards the inside of the ravine. He wondered if that was standard operating procedure or if they were scared of the creature that Kurtz had conjured up.

They got so close to the pillbox that Gabriel could see movement through the narrow slits. It would have possible to take a clear head shot without a gun scope at that distance. He came to a stop, not wanting to risk getting too close. If there were even a hint of movement at the edge of what the enemy could see from inside the pillbox, Gabriel and the other runner would be cut to ribbons.

Surely the body would be spotted instantly once the sun started to rise. Just to make sure, Gabriel sat it up against the trunk of a tree staring right at the pillbox. Then he rose, and they were on their way again, creeping through the bush back towards their companions.

They didn't make it very far before Gabriel heard someone coming towards them. The other runner apparently heard the same thing, and they readied their pistols, even though it wouldn't be prudent to shoot in such close proximity to the pillboxes. They listened as whoever it was drew closer, obviously trying to mask the sounds of his approach, but lacking the proper skill set to be whisper quiet.

A soldier, Gabriel signed to his partner who just nodded in response.

Finally they spotted the figure approaching. He was waving his arms slowly through the air, wanting to be seen by them. Gabriel recognized the gear – the other man was one of their own. They moved towards him, signaling from afar so as to not startle him. The other soldier stopped and waited for them to arrive, glancing behind himself repeatedly.

Once they were closer, Gabriel recognized the tracker from earlier that night. The other man's face was stark white like he had just seen a ghost. The first thing he did was hold his gloved index finger up to his lips, signaling quiet, which struck Gabriel as ironic since he sounded like a bear crashing through the underbrush compared to them.

The tracker looked around warily again. Gabriel tried to see or hear what his fellow soldier was so concerned about, but it seemed like they were completely alone. Gabriel shrugged at the tracker. He really wanted to know what had compelled the other man to come out and meet them. The tracker looked at Gabriel and gave a simple sign. *Dead.*

Everyone? Gabriel signed back.

The tracker nodded, then held his palm out and placed two fingers in the center, then moved them like legs until they had walked off of his palm. *Or Gone.*

What?

Later, the tracker signed. Then he pointed in a totally different direction – away from where they had all come from. The tracker led the way back towards the ravine, then skirted around the edges, careful to not get too close. Eventually they looped back around to the general direction of their camp, completely avoiding the route that they had previously taken.

During their long trek back, Gabriel tried to piece together what could have possibly happened. His first thought was that the others had run afoul of a kill team. But that shouldn't have been possible considering that the kill teams were using the antiquated night vision that would have given them away from quite a distance. And even if they had somehow managed to get within firing range, there would have been gunshots. Most puzzling of all was how the tracker had somehow managed to escape. It was absurd that Gabriel couldn't just ask this of the man who stood five feet away. But it would have to wait until they arrived in camp.

He thought about the other five men who had disappeared the night before, and also Schmidt. Now they were down thirteen men. A shiver rocked his frame as he wondered who or what was responsible. Did the enemy have some kind of new super soldier that none of them knew about? And what about the General and his bodyguards? Gabriel shook his head. That wouldn't make any sense. Maybe with Schmidt, but not the others. At the same time he couldn't shake the feeling that the war had driven Kurtz into a profound madness. It was like the man was no longer human. Outside of the context of war, he would be considered a criminal at best – a monster at worst. But weren't they all monsters?

After hours of constantly being on edge, feeling that they could be attacked at any moment by an unknown enemy, Gabriel finally relaxed as he saw the first signs of dawn overhead. When they arrived in camp, everything seemed normal – at least as normal as it could be. Men were getting ready for bed, others for first watch. The three spies were just waking up, eating a cold breakfast, and preparing to leave for the villages. The General was nowhere in sight.

"Where's the rest of your team?" Riker asked as soon as they were within earshot. Others in the camp looked up warily at the conspicuous absence.

"We were hoping they were here," Gabriel said before turning to the tracker. "What the hell happened back there?"

The tracker leaned in and whispered. "Just after you left to dump the body, the Sergeant sent me out alone to check the surrounding area for signs of kill teams." His eyes were wide, his face still just as pale as it had been hours earlier. "I circled back, and when I was several hundred yards behind the main group, I did find something. Very recent, headed right towards everyone else. Whatever it was, it was light footed. A broken twig here and there, a slight indentation. I wasn't even sure if I had found anything concrete." His voice cracked.

Gabriel noticed that the tracker's hands were trembling.

He swallowed hard before continuing. "When I got back," his voice cracked again, and he paused, almost in tears. "They were gone."

"Define gone," Riker said incredulously.

"Just gone. No signs of struggle or even any signs that they had left. It was like they were standing there one second, and then gone the next."

"Are you sure?" Riker asked.

The tracker nodded. "I checked the area as quickly as I could. But... I just felt like I had to get out of there." He looked at Gabriel. "That's when I left and met up with you."

"Seven soldiers can't just disappear," Riker said. "There were no gunshots?"

Gabriel shook his head. "I can also attest to that sir."

"The General isn't going to like this," Riker said.

"Neither do we," Gabriel responded, wondering how narrowly he had missed his own death. The four men stood in silence for a long time, staring at nothing.

"Have you ever considered, Lieutenant," Gabriel finally broke their disquietude, "that just as we are here to fuck with them, they are fucking with us?"

Riker looked up at him, seeming to consider the possibility.

"If they spook us, but leave some to tell the tale, maybe they think Command will have trouble sending in more troops. Or least future offensives would be at a psychological disadvantage," Gabriel offered.

"Perhaps," Riker gave a single nod. "I'll have to see what the General thinks. Try to get some sleep."

As Gabriel returned to his bedroll, all the other men cast nervous glances his way. They all wanted to know what happened, but didn't want to know at the same time. The only person who dared to look him right in the eyes was Vinh, who was preparing to leave for the day with his fellows.

Gabriel had the overwhelming urge to flee while the sun was out. The latest development meant that they were in for trouble later that night, and Gabriel wasn't confident that the General was going to make decisions that preserved life – including their own. How many more men would disappear? And what would they do when there were only a handful left?

Gabriel looked around the camp as the other men got back to whatever nervous distraction they had chosen to help them ignore reality. It would have been easy enough for him to leave. Everyone would have just thought that he was going to take a piss. Then he would slip away and distance himself as much as possible in the first few hours. Once night fell, they would never find him.

It's not that he wanted to be disloyal, or to go AWOL. He also didn't want to die because he was under the command of a madman. Gabriel noticed the three spies as they grabbed their satchels and started to depart. Two of them took the shortest route out of the camp. But Vinh headed straight for him.

"If I were you, I would get out of here," Vinh whispered so low that Gabriel could barely hear him. "I lied about what the soldier told me last night."

"What did he say?"

Vinh seemed to ponder his response. "There is something out there, and it's angered by what the General is doing. The kill team wasn't looking for it – they were trying to stop us from continuing. Leave if you can." With that, Vinh departed before anyone could notice their exchange.

Gabriel knew that he wouldn't be seeing him again.

063

Gabriel found it harder than usual to sleep that day. As he drifted in and out of unconsciousness, he dreamed about slipping out of the camp. It was pitch black, and he was able to slink away one tedious step at a time. It was a dream in which a simple action seemed to take forever and couldn't ever be completed. When he awoke towards dusk, he was already exhausted.

His heartbeat was faster than normal. He knew that exact moment in time was another opportunity to escape before complete darkness fell and the General emerged from his hiding place. An inner battle raged in him. He had not been trained to run; he had been trained to obey – and to kill. It was all that he had known since his teens, and these new feelings were completely foreign to him.

As soon as Kurtz finally did enter the camp, right on cue as the last rays of the sun disappeared, Gabriel knew that he had hesitated too long. Now he was locked in, at least for one more night. Everyone seemed despondent as their true commanding officer strode past them towards Riker. They all secretly watched the exchange between the two ranking officers in their peripheral vision, pretending to be indifferent.

Finally the two broke from their huddle, and Riker called for everyone's attention. "We're going to operate a little differently tonight," he said as the last of his men gathered around. "Because we are not sure what happened to some of our deployed units the past two nights, we are all going to move together in tight formation. If someone wants to attack us, they are going to have attack all of us." Riker looked at Gabriel. "At least until we need to split off for the stealth run."

Of course, Gabriel thought. But he quickly remembered that it was that very thing that had saved his life the previous night. It was all a roll of the dice.

"We're going to target enemy soldiers again for the nightly kill. Only take essential items with you. We head out in ten."

Everyone slowly dispersed, their motion slurred by a lack of desire. Gabriel walked over to Riker. "What exactly is the plan?"

"What do you mean? I just told you," Riker said.

"I don't think we can all just sneak up on a kill team. And good luck snatching someone out of one of the pillboxes."

"The General seems to think we can ambush a regular patrol outside of the base."

Gabriel bit his lip as Kurtz approached. "Based on what I saw last night, there weren't any regular patrols, just the kill teams. The guards were scared, holed up inside the pillboxes."

"There is another option," Kurtz interjected. "I know a thing or two about this base. Once you get down into the ravine, there are a couple of places where you could quietly detain one of the guards."

"Inside of the ravine?" Gabriel raised an eyebrow.

Kurtz nodded. "There are a couple of blind spots between pillboxes." He motioned his head towards his bodyguards. "We've found them. A man of your skills should have no problem, but we'll keep this one simple. You'll take the hook down with you, strike a guard and wait for him to bleed out in the ravine. It will look like our creature of the night had its meal interrupted." The General smiled. "It will scare the shit out of them."

And me, Gabriel thought.

064

The platoon moved in a cluster, every man in sight of another. Because someone had to bring up the rear of the group, those men were tied to the soldiers in front of them with bits of string. If something or someone snagged them from behind, the weak string would tug at the wrist of the person ahead and then break. It might not save the rear guards, but it could save the platoon once they became aware of a threat. It was a technique they commonly used when traversing open areas where snipers were a concern.

The General marched at the center of the formation along with Riker. Gabriel had been spared guard duty on the fringes only because he had much dirtier work to do once they arrived. He actually wasn't afraid of trying to slip past the pillboxes. What he was not looking forward to was wielding the sinister hook to claim another victim. Up to that point he had just been the messenger, transporting portents of doom. But now he was also about to become the executioner as well – an angel of death. He wished that it could just be a simple firefight instead, a fair exchange of bullets in place of the wicked barbs. In spite of his wishes, the teeth of a monster were about to become an extension of his being.

Gabriel was baffled by his reaction to it all. Back in training they had always joked about being tough. Not afraid to kill. Not afraid to do what needed to be done. But back then the enemy had been faceless. And killing was just a game. Something on their mission had stripped away the veneer of ignorance and exposed some raw response to the terror around him. It made him feel weak.

A spike of adrenaline hit him as soon as the infrared lights of the base shone through the foliage ahead. They were still distant, yet all too close.

The time was nigh when Gabriel would be forced to become a monster. He considered descending into the ravine and hiding, then pretending to have done the deed once he returned. He would be alone down there, and no one would know any better. But he knew that would only prolong their mission.

The group slowed to a crawl as the men in the front of the formation peered through the edge of the tree line. The General drew close to Gabriel and shoved something into his hand. Gabriel opened his palm and peered down at a small white capsule.

"If you get caught, bite down on it," the General whispered. Gabriel looked up at the older man, a hint of shock in his eyes. "Trust me, you'll want to."

Just then, one of the recon specialists in the front signaled back. He looked at Riker, pointed at his own eyes, and then indicated the tree line. Riker started walking, signaling for Gabriel to follow. The General invited himself.

Something was clearly amiss. The infrared spotlights that had been perched above one of the pillboxes were toppled over. Four heavy machine gun barrels protruded like stingers from the slits, but the other, smaller gun barrels from the extra occupants were absent. One infrared spotlight lay on its side, shooting rays of invisible light through one of the slits. Gabriel strained to see, but there didn't appear to be any movement inside.

Looks like a trap, Gabriel signed.

Could have happened while we were still miles away, Riker responded.

Gabriel knew that he didn't have a choice when the General shoved the hook into his hand. He could feel the icy steel through the layers of his gloves, despite the fact that Kurtz had been holding it for some time. The General didn't know how to sign, but he looked at the edge of the Ravine, then looked at Gabriel.

After a moment, Gabriel nodded in resignation then slipped his rifle off of his shoulder. If he had understood correctly, there was no coming back if he found himself in a situation where he would have to use it. He also removed the troublesome pistol that had always bothered him.

As he stepped out from the tree line, he could feel the others watching him – probably glad that they weren't in his shoes. Even he wondered if perhaps this might be his final journey. After all, the other thing they had all been trained to do was die.

Gabriel noticed that since the lights had been toppled over, there was actually a huge blind spot between the disturbed pillbox and one of its neighbors. An ominous valley of shadow separated the illuminated patches of green. He entered it, anxious to see what was beyond the lip of the ravine. He felt like he had been there before, but knew that was foolishness. He found himself searching the ground for signs of... he didn't know what. Couldn't remember.

Even though the ravine was the main attraction, Gabriel made sure to constantly check his surroundings. In the pillbox to his right, which was still manned, he could see hints of nervous movement through the narrow slits. The one on his left remained still.

He froze in place when he noticed a detail that was impossible to see from afar. From his particular vantage point he had a clear view inside of the left pillbox. It was brightly illuminated by a fallen IR light that beamed through the slit and bounced off the ceiling inside. The forms of several men lay belly down on the floor, guns in hand.

At first he couldn't tell if they were alive or dead, but he suspected the former. They were too neatly laid out, all in the same position, just waiting to spring up at a moment's notice. He watched for a long time until finally one of the men shifted his position slightly as one might do if he were uncomfortable. Gabriel realized that he had been right – it was indeed a trap of some sort.

If it were a game of psychological warfare, he knew that he had the advantage – at least at that point. How damaging would it be for them to lay a trap and still fail to detect an intruder? Of course Gabriel wasn't even sure if he was the intended target. But what else would creep into their base?

He neared the lip of the ravine and caught his first glimpse down into the deep gash in the earth. Foliage choked most of it, stray tendrils encroaching on carefully maintained pathways. A large doorway of sorts was at one end where the various paths converged, but it was closed. Gabriel couldn't be sure, but he thought he saw the same strange symbols that were carved into the gnarled tree. He still couldn't figure out where he had seen them before – but he knew that he had.

As he continued his inspection of the ravine, he made out several snipers at the bottom who were carefully hidden in the flora. Since the entire inner lip of the ravine was lit by IR lights, anyone who attempted to descend would easily be spotted and terminated. Gabriel imagined the entire platoon taking the same pathway he had taken between the pillboxes, then all heading downward. That's what the enemy wanted. As soon as the last man was over the edge and they were all sitting ducks, target practice would begin.

He stood there for a long time, taking pleasure in trying to find all the hidden snipers, but more so trying to decide what he should do. If he tried to enter the ravine, he would die. If he went back, who knew what the General would say or have him do next.

Gunshots erupted in the jungle behind him, followed by screams. When Gabriel turned around, he could see the men inside the left pillbox sitting up and peering out. Whatever was happening, it wasn't something they were expecting.

Gabriel started heading back the way he came. If the enemy was no longer trying to maintain the ruse, the shaft of darkness he had traversed to arrive at the edge of the ravine might quickly disappear. Or he might find himself in the midst of abruptly deployed kill teams. With the cover of the gunfire, he didn't bother to mask the sound of his footsteps, which allowed him to move at much brisker pace. He felt relief as he put the pillboxes behind him, but a new sense of dread crept over him as the gunshots beyond the tree line ceased.

He froze again, unsure if he should proceed to his presumably fallen comrades or if he should just run and never look back. Then he thought he heard a voice speaking in familiar, confident tones. He knew that he should flee, but curiosity gnawed at him, and the voice drew him closer to the tree line. If anything, his presence would be unexpected, and he could still turn back.

The voice became clearer. It was the General's.

"Don't go! I have a message directly from the United States Joint Chiefs of Staff," he said. "A proposal to make."

Gabriel suddenly felt deflated when he realized that their mission had not been what it seemed. They were merely pawns in a bigger game. But one of the bishops was just ahead on the board, and Gabriel had just decided that he was now of the opposing color.

Gabriel could see them through the tree line. The General stood in the center of a sea of corpses that had been flung around like rag dolls – bones broken and necks twisted at horribly unnatural angles. In front of him were the two bodyguards, aiming their slender rifles at something up in the trees that Gabriel couldn't quite see. He wondered how Kurtz had been spared in the brutal attack, but guessed that the two imposing figures clad in body armor probably had something to do with it.

"If your kind were on our side, there would be more sacrifices," Kurtz continued. "The people here are frightened and reluctant to volunteer themselves, but in my country there is a ready supply of those who need to die. An endless supply of blood."

Just like the platoon, Gabriel thought. His fellows had unknowingly been sacrificed for the perceived greater good. Gabriel strained to see what was up in the tree. Whatever Kurtz was talking to, his voice never wavered nor was there any trace of fear. Gabriel wondered what kind of man could have over two dozen people slaughtered around him and still talk like it was just another day at boot camp.

"No!" the General screamed as the leaves overhead rustled. "Take it down, but don't kill it," he barked. The two bodyguards opened fire. Their guns were so silent that Gabriel could hear the bullets whizzing past leaves and branches in the dark.

The two soldiers sprang into action, impossibly fast. They gave chase to whatever was fleeing and disappeared into the night. There were more gunshots and the sound of branches breaking. A muffled yell came from behind a face mask followed by a sick gurgling sound.

Then there was silence.

Gabriel watched Kurtz for a full minute. The other man drew a pistol from his waist, hand shaking, but refused to move forward to investigate.

"Hello?" Kurtz called out as Gabriel approached him from behind. "Thank God you're here soldier," he said without turning around, confidence seeping back into his voice.

Gabriel staggered, wondering how Kurtz knew that he was there.

"We can finish this, you and I." Kurtz turned around and seemed to size him up for a moment. "I'm not quite sure how they missed your talents, but you should have been in the Specter program. Help me and you will be."

"That didn't save them," Gabriel looked beyond Kurtz into the now silent jungle.

"Actually we don't know what happened. That's what I want you to find out."

"I'm pretty sure they're dead," Gabriel said, no humor in his voice.

"Perhaps, but they might have killed or wounded it. I'd rather a live specimen, but I'll gladly take a dead one back to Command at this point. You have no idea how important this is."

Gabriel noticed a fire in the General's eyes. It could have been sheer madness, or a man at the end of his life desperately grasping at straws.

"Why is this so important to you? Did Command really pull you from retirement?"

"You don't know what it's like. You're young, just starting the war. I was in it for over thirty years." The glint in his eyes intensified. "I've seen tank battalions level villages. Entire fields of dying men cradling their innards in their own hands. After that, sitting at a goddamned desk at home in the suburbs pretending like I have a purpose isn't living. You'll see. It'll happen to you too. You'll take less and less leave because home isn't home anymore."

Gabriel knew that it was true. Already, he craved the rush of prowling the night. As he stood across from Kurtz, he knew that he was staring into his own future. The General was a pathetic shell of a man who had never lived, or perhaps had lived too much. Now that shell was animated by some unholy power. Kurtz was no longer just a man.

"What are you waiting for Private? I gave you an order."

Gabriel felt the call of duty which had been ingrained into his being. But as he stood there in the cold jungle, face to face with a monster, something finally broke in him. Something that wasn't supposed to break.

Gabriel and the General just stared at each other for a long time. Then with a single swipe, the hook went behind Kurtz's jugular and ripped it out in an explosion of blood. The General never wavered or even looked surprised. He just stood there watching Gabriel. In night vision, his blood was black as night as it flowed down his body and into the thirsty earth. In a single motion, he finally collapsed onto his back and stared at the canopy. Even in death, Kurtz's eyes were alive with a dark energy.

Gabriel found himself staring into those eyes – into the abyss. He saw a father and a past he had yet to live. Amidst the darkness, there was a profound emptiness. Gabriel felt that emptiness within himself.

He glanced into the jungle where the two Specters had met their demise and decided it was best to head in a different direction. Before he left, he took one last look at his fallen companions. He considered grabbing a gun, but realized that he had never actually used one on the entire mission. His gift was stealth; if he needed a gun, he was probably already dead.

So he slipped into the night, the hook his only weapon. The future was uncertain, but he figured that sooner or later he would encounter more U.S. soldiers in the area and could rejoin a different platoon on a different mission. Or not.

Gabriel didn't know it, but even at that moment he was being watched by another man who had become one with the jungle. Shapes flitted in the night. Eyes playing tricks on someone.

CHILD OF WAR

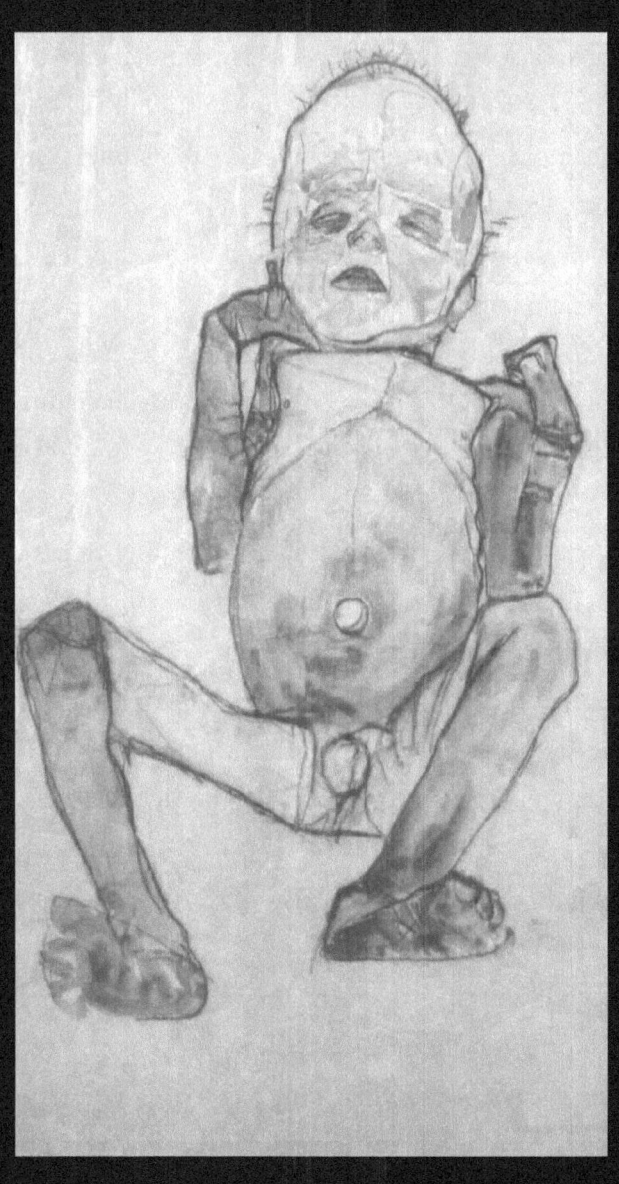

065

2118.

Prelude

After being a dark secret for over a century, the war came back into the light when the U.S. found an excuse to openly assault their enemy for first time since the original Vietnam War. It wasn't about one country anymore; all of Southeast Asia now belonged to a single communist empire. Even though the war wasn't about communism and never had been, politics provided a lovely excuse to kill.

If the war had not been a secret for so long, the West could have won many times over. By 2050, guided missiles and unmanned drones had come to rule the skies. Entire wars were waged from the safety of control rooms by teenagers who thought they were playing video games. But those had been other wars, ones fought in the open. Instead of raining death down from the sky, the U.S. still had to do things the old fashioned way in its secret war, which meant sending elite ground troops into the jungle.

Once South East Asia was under the strangle hold of one iron fist, communist leaders knew they were just waiting for the day when western powers would swoop down from above with deadly force. Instead of trying to play catch up, they opted for a different tactic and developed the most sophisticated anti-air grid to ever exist, effectively blanketing the entire region under a no fly zone.

To further solidify their defenses, they turned to what had been their greatest ally throughout the entire war. The general population was herded into sprawling megalopolises, and the countryside was terraformed into a dense, nearly impenetrable jungle. Scientists toyed with the DNA of native plant and animal species, purposely creating monstrosities to naturally guard against land incursions. The harsh environment was designed to wear against mechanical creations, making the use of land based drones next to impossible – at least not without the presence of human handlers to keep them in working order.

And so the war came full circle. Just as they were over a century and a half before, ground troops are forced to enter a garden of evil in hopes of victory, falling prey to guerrillas, traps, genetically modified predators and most of all, the jungle itself.

066

Outer Base Camp

Mouth of the Red River

19:35

The sky had slowly shifted in color from bright orange to a deep crimson as the day faded into night. It was the wet season, and a steady drizzle fell over the massively sprawling encampment that marked the U.S. entry point into enemy territory.

Thousands of soldiers lazed in the setting sun, some having just arrived for deployment, others about to be on their way home. Outer Base Camp was a city of tents and mobile buildings under the watchful gaze of six giant tank fortresses. The Goliaths would never have made it through the rough landscape and thick vegetation of the jungle, but they stood as towering bastions of raw power at the coastline to ward off would be attackers. And if that weren't enough, three battleships were ready to bombard the surrounding area from sea. Perhaps this was why, unlike in the rest of the war zone, the soldiers of the Outer Base Camp had fallen under a false sense of security.

When the men under one pavilion near the edge of the base first heard the sounds of a baby crying, it didn't even register. Several of them dozed in the late afternoon heat, swatting away huge mosquitoes that could drain half a syringe of blood at a time. Another stared at his face in a cracked mirror, running a straight razor over his face, the steel grinding against invisible stubble.

The cries grew louder, and a few men finally sat up and looked around. Then the others quickly realized that something was out of place. A soldier in full gear emerged from the nearby tree line, cradling a small bundle in one of his arms. The dirty cloth writhed and screeched. As he neared the pavilion, the off-duty men crowded around.

"Where the hell did you get that?" one of them asked.

"Not too far from here," the soldier replied as he brushed the edge of the cloth away from a baby's face. It couldn't have been more than three months old.

"You on patrol?"

The soldier nodded. One man patrols were allowed during the day, but they traveled in groups of three at night.

One man in particular leaned in for a closer look. "Wait a second," he said. "Is that baby white?" Others drew in closer for a better look.

"I hadn't realized that," the soldier said. "That's weird."

"Yeah, what the hell is it doing here? I could see a chink baby, but," another shrugged. "I dunno."

The baby's crying intensified as it wiggled around.

"What's that," someone else said, pointing towards the baby's belly. The soldier holding it unwrapped the cloth some more, revealing a small bloodstain that was spreading across the front of the baby's shirt.

"What the fuck?" he said as he lifted the shirt and revealed a bad stitch job along its torso. And suddenly it made sense why the baby was white. If it hadn't been, he might not have taken it back to camp so easily.

A glowing dome of light engulfed all of the Outer Base Camp, incinerating flesh and melting steel in an instant. The explosion sent roiling waves crashing towards the distant battleships in the bay. And just like that, thousands of lives were extinguished in seconds, and the United States' grip on the war zone slipped.

067

Inner Base Camp

Red River Delta

21:05

A hundred miles upriver, closer to the front lines, the Inner Base Camp shone like a beacon in the night. It was just as massive and sprawling as the Outer Base Camp, but far more disorganized. Fortifications had been built up around its perimeter, and huge artillery canons bristled against the night sky like angry spines. There was no false sense of security there; the base was on the edge of insanity.

Anxiety was in the air. Armed guards and huge mechanized walkers lined the perimeter. Soldiers even patrolled the interior of the base like ants swarming over a pile that had been stepped on. Sweat streaked faces looked side to side nervously through eyes that bulged with fright.

At the center of activity was a mobile fortress, the last bastion of civilization for hundreds of miles. Its clean halls and bright lights were a sharp contrast to the gritty, moist world outside. But even there it was hard to keep nature out. Colonel White watched as a mosquito stupidly bumped into a florescent light repeatedly in the central command chamber. The walls were lined with men at oversized computer terminals who monitored all communications and action in the field. White and the senior officers under his command sat around a dais in the center of the room. His nostrils twitched at the artificial smell of the conditioned air being cycled through the room.

A glass lens in the center of the dais flared to life with pristine light. A moment later, a bluish hologram hovered in the air above it, dust swirling in its translucent center. The officers found themselves face to face with a

General who was stationed offshore with the Pacific fleet. They all stood and saluted the illusion of a man.

"At ease," he said, his voice hollow and processed – a byproduct of the encoding and decoding of the cyphered channel. Everyone sat as he continued. "As you all know, we lost Outer Base Camp in its entirely a couple of hours ago."

"So there were no survivors?" White asked.

"Only a handful of men on patrol," the General shook his head. "We've been reviewing surveillance, and we believe we've isolated the cause."

The image of the General flickered and was replaced with a square viewing area that showed grainy footage of the soldier carrying the baby into camp. Then the view switched to another camera that was closer to the pavilion where men clustered around the child. Light blossomed from its writhing form and spread in slow motion until the view was replaced with static.

The hologram stuttered back into existence. "We believe that a high grade explosive device was actually implanted into the infant's body. Otherwise the soldier presumably would have noticed something secured to it externally." The General paused, letting his point sink in. The men seated around shifted uncomfortably in their seats, realizing just how much more vulnerable they were.

"Your orders, sir?" White asked.

"From here on out, no one – and I mean no one – enters your camp without a body scan. I'm not just talking about prisoners and babies you find in the bush. Your own men need to be checked too."

"Yes sir," White nodded.

"We also need an immediate sweep of the surrounding area. Kill or destroy anything that looks even remotely suspicious." The signal feeding the hologram faltered, sending flashing blue light across the faces of the General's audience.

"When the battleships contacted us, we sent out teams immediately," White said.

"How many men?" the General asked.

"Eight platoons."

"Triple it."

White nodded in deference again.

"The sweeps should continue for the next forty-eight hours. We can't afford to lose both principle camps – especially not yours. You need to establish a firm outer perimeter that surrounds your base in a three mile radius."

A couple of jaws dropped. "You know how many men that will take? The whole camp will be on active rotation."

"We don't have a choice," the General said gravely. "The baby was an ingenious way to get the bomb into the camp, but what's to stop a single runner from dropping a bomb half a mile away? Your outer perimeter needs to be impenetrable."

"Will we be getting reinforcements sir?"

"As soon as I can get them to you, but we just lost twenty thousand men. There's a huge vacuum to fill. Make do with what you have."

"Copy that," White said without enthusiasm. "I'll relay those orders right away."

"There's one more thing," the General said. "Although it would be less devastating, I'm not really interested in losing any of forward camps either. I know they won't be able to manage a three mile perimeter, but they need to observe the same orders to the best of their ability. Until we get this under control, all camps are to recall men from field operations except for those deemed critical."

"I'll relay the message sir," White said in the same flat tone. A single drop of sweat trickled down his temple despite the air conditioning. The General didn't bother to say goodbye. The hologram flickered and disappeared, leaving the room darker in its absence.

O68

Edge of No Man's Land
Undisclosed Location
22:00

Another seventy-five miles beyond Inner Base Camp lay one of several smaller camps, the last points of depart for any man deployed deep in the bush. The camp was a far cry from its two larger counter parts. It barely held three hundred men, their commander a mere Major. The only some-what permanent emplacements were a medical tent, a shabby HQ tent worn by the elements, and a dozen pillboxes backed by heavy artillery. Getting a tank fortress or mobile HQ that deep in the jungle was just out of the question without air transport.

A general malaise hung over the camp in normal times, its occupants potentially steps or seconds away from death at any given time. So it came as no surprise that under the circumstances, an epic sense of doom had settled over the camp. If Outer Base Camp wasn't safe – their days were numbered.

The Major had just received orders from Inner Base Camp, and at that very moment two full platoons prepared for departure. He didn't like sending almost a third of his men into the bush, especially not at night. While the camp did serve as a way point for teams that practiced nocturnal operations in the deep bush, the camp regulars understandably preferred the day.

As the Major watched his men pass from the pool of light at the edge of camp and into the darkness beyond, he was just happy that it wasn't him.

069

The Bush

01:13

Private Eiger didn't see what the big deal was, even if her comrades' fear was visible in every measured step that they took. She figured that her indifference had something to do with her implants. As one of the platoon's snipers, she could see clear as day even though not a single ray of moonlight managed to penetrate the overgrown canopy. She also figured that their little base out in Podunk wasn't worth the kind of bombing that had obliterated Outer Base Camp.

She considered that most of the others had become too comfortable in camp, spending night after night playing cards and lazing around fires – luxuries that units in the bush didn't have. So for them to be sent out at night was like a slap in the face to their false sense of reality. Now they were scared shitless.

Eiger, on the other hand, found it exciting. At the Academy she had so wanted pass the assessments for more elite units like Delta Force or the Specters, but it didn't happen. And in an unfortunate roll of the dice, she had found herself on guard duty at Inner Base Camp. She had finally managed to talk her way closer to the action, and now things were just starting heat up.

She paid close attention to every nook and cranny that came into view, following their mission to the letter. The others seemed more concerned about lesser dangers like the giant panthers or fifty foot snakes that the enemy had engineered to make things more difficult for them. While scary, those threats weren't capable of wiping out the entire base.

They had been following a zigzag path north from the camp and were just reaching the most distant point of their intended sweep. The Lieutenant held up a black gloved hand, signaling them to stop. He then turned and pointed both index fingers back the way they had come. The group quickly turned around, anxious to begin their return journey.

Eiger's gaze lingered a second longer than the rest – just long enough for her to witness an unidentifiable blur darting from a nearby tree and hauling the Lieutenant away without a sound. Eiger blinked, distrusting her own eyes. The rest of the platoon continued forward, bumping into her as she stared behind them in disbelief. She raised her gun and pointed it in the direction of their aggressor. The others suddenly perceived that something wasn't right and began to turn around, readying their weapons.

Gunfire erupted at the opposite side of the group, and they all turned again just in time to see the muzzle flashes from a soldier's gun as he was drug into the darkness at a speed that defied reason. After that, every remaining gun in the platoon lit up the night. Plasma charges felled entire trees. If anything was alive within several hundred feet – it wasn't anymore.

But the din of constant fire from multiple weapons covered the sound of more disappearances. When the group stopped shooting, another ten were gone. It was precisely at that moment that Eiger realized that if she were part of the group, she was painting a huge target on herself.

It's not that she wasn't loyal to the platoon, but the fact of the matter was that she was a sniper and stood the best chance of salvaging lives if she distanced herself from the action. If she died with the lot of them, she wasn't going to accomplish anything. She ran perpendicular to the latest set of abductions, then dropped to the ground and rolled into a natural shelter formed by dead wood and vegetation.

From a distance, it was easier to see their attacker's pattern of movement. But it moved so damned fast. She tried to anticipate its arrival and took blind shots, her abnormally long rifle barely making any noise. It reminded her of playing a video game, trying to figure out the patterns exhibited by an AI. The only problem was that she was running out of chances as the remaining soldiers dwindled. And when it was over, it was over. She didn't have another life.

The eeriest part of the attack was that each time someone was carried away, there was no screaming. It was incomprehensible to her how that was possible, but it elevated the attack to a nightmarish horror. Trained killers were being picked off like they were insects, and they couldn't even cry out for help.

When there were only three left, she felt guilty. She wanted to scream at them to hide like she had, but at that point it wouldn't have done any good. She watched helplessly as the last of her platoon was snatched from view.

In the silence that followed, she dwelt on her decision. What had seemed like a good idea at the time now felt like a selfish bid for survival. She hadn't managed to kill their attacker, and now she had she had live with that failure.

But she didn't feel guilty enough to stand up and scream out for the murderous something to return. Instead, she remained right where she was, not daring to move until the sun came up hours later.

070

Red River
07:40

No one spoke as the small boat made its way upriver towards Inner Base Camp. Even though Specters were no longer a secret branch as they had once been, Azrael was always amazed at how reverent everyone was to him. The other three men only spoke when spoken to, unless they absolutely had to say something critical to their mission.

Azrael took the opportunity to enjoy watching the sunrise, which was a rare luxury. To his eyes, it wasn't just a deep blue blossoming into pink. He could see things no one else could – like ultraviolet light and the traces of radiation that lingered in the air even though the explosion had been forty miles downriver. The sunrise looked even more beautiful when he switched to thermal imaging with a thought. Birds appeared as hot spots gliding in front of a deep blue backdrop.

When he had arrived from the bay, there had been much discussion about the proper way to transport him upriver. Normally he would have been hidden inside of a larger transport barge, but those were all tied up. In the end, the General had decided there was no issue with ferrying him out in the open. They still controlled the river, and if anyone was stupid enough to attack a Specter... well then God help them.

Azrael noticed one of his companions sneaking a glance at him. The other man quickly averted his eyes like he had been caught in a sin. Azrael reasoned that since there were only a handful of his kind in existence and the average soldier had only ever seen basic body modifications, he was probably remarkable to behold.

His muscles had been genetically modified and further augmented by hardware implants, making his physique perfect as if he had been molded by the hands of God. His most striking feature though, was the dermal coating that was perfectly form fitting and as flexible as his own skin. It was also black as darkest night, and with the exception of the armored plates covering his genitals and rear end, it looked like he was naked. His second skin could easily deflect normal bullets and plasma charges, or even withstand direct impact from a heavy artillery shell. He was impervious to extreme heat or cold, and the coating regulated its temperature to blend in with surroundings if viewed through thermal imaging.

Even set against the tableau of the rest of his body, his mouth and eyes were his most freakish qualities by far. His creators didn't want to leave any vulnerable soft spots, so the black dermal coating also ran inside his mouth and nose, then down into his throat, making him look like a demonic apparition. He no longer had the eyes that he was born with. They had been removed and replaced with solid black artificial orbs, making blinking unnecessary. It had taken Azrael awhile to get used to sleeping with his eyes open, but in his profession it was probably for the best.

His outward appearance was just the tip of the iceberg. His lungs were entirely mechanical, making him impervious to airborne agents and even thick smoke. Microsurgery had augmented his nerve endings, rendering his reflexes superhuman. But maybe the scariest part – at least to him – was the kill switch hidden deep within his body that would freeze his heart instantly if Command deemed it necessary. To ordinary soldiers he might appear to be a dark and vengeful God, but he was actually a slave to darker wills.

As they slowly made their way upriver, he pondered what could possibly require his immediate attention in that theater. Yes, the utter destruction of the Outer Base Camp was a big deal, but one born of stupidity and lax protocol – nothing they couldn't handle without him. And so what if an entire platoon had been wiped out in the bush except for one soldier – it happened all the time in ambushes. Clearly there was some detail that Command was withholding. His only instructions were to investigate the attack and subsequent disappearances at one of the last camps along the northern front.

A readout in his right eye displayed their estimated arrival time. All he could do in the meantime was sit and wait for answers.

071

The woman named Eiger sat across from Azrael. The Private's face was pale and her eyes wide after recounting the events of the previous evening.

"This is the approximate location of the attack," the Major showed Azrael a view of a map.

"It was right at the end of our run," Eiger said, her voice small.

Azrael wanted to be incredulous, but it didn't seem as though the woman were lying. In fact, he knew she wasn't. Her voice and vitals were being continuously analyzed by his CPU and even if her story wasn't accurate, she truly believed it. As he pondered his own incredible aptitude for doling out death and the fact that even he could not replicate the attack as described, he wondered what exactly he was up against.

"Am I –" Eiger started to speak before her voice caught in her throat. She looked up into Azrael's unreadable eyes. "Am I going to have go back out there... sir?"

Her confusion over how to address him was understandable as the Specters actually didn't hold any official rank. Azrael shook his head. "I will survey the area alone." His voice came out as filtered and processed, a necessary evil of having his vocal chords replaced.

Eiger looked visibly relieved. "Thank you."

"No one's going out after what happened," the Major interjected. "We don't have that many here to begin with, and Command has made it clear that there won't be reinforcements."

"Was the attacker humanoid in form?" Azrael asked. An enemy super soldier was at the forefront of his theories, followed by a horribly mutated beast.

"I couldn't see it. There was a just a blur, but..." Eiger just started shaking her head. "I don't know what it was."

Azrael had permanent adjustments to his brain chemistry that made it impossible for him to feel fear, but he that knew that whatever was out there was very dangerous – maybe an equal to him. When he considered everything in his life that he had killed with ease, that thought should have been scary.

He stood up, towering over Eiger and the Major who were still seated. "Talking more about it won't accomplish anything. I've noted the coordinates." He turned and headed for the door. "I'll be back."

072

The Bush
19:30

Azrael always felt more comfortable alone. Since he had been transformed into a Specter, he had become a pariah – feared and respected, but mostly feared. Rank and file soldiers – people who were still human – didn't interact with him in the same way that they treated each other. It reminded him of the story of Frankenstein's monster. It too was an aberration of nature doomed to a life of profound isolation. The thought just made Azrael want to kill things more.

He sat perched on a thick branch twenty feet above the ground, perfectly silent. Just below him was where the grisly scene had transpired on the previous evening. Broken branches, fallen trees, and vegetal detritus covered the ground, which made it difficult to piece together what exactly had happened. He had managed to find places where heads had hit tree trunks and splattered blood all around, and other places where heavy combat boots had been drug over the soil. But outside of a certain radius, all signs of struggle or movement just disappeared, right along with the bodies.

Azrael just waited patiently to see if perhaps whatever it was would return or pass by. Without anything to track, he was blind. His next step was to start roaming the jungle, hoping to stumble across it, but that was horribly inefficient. Perhaps he should have brought the young woman with him as bait. Even though she probably would not have survived, her death would have saved countless others – which was the whole point of being a soldier after all.

As he leapt from the tree to the ground with little more than the sound of a few disturbed leaves to mark his passage, he resolved to take

Eiger back with him if his search didn't yield results that night. As he started moving, he could feel the jungle floor on the soles of his feet, which made it a lot easier to gauge pressure and when things were about to snap underfoot. In hindsight, he didn't know how he used to do it with shoes on.

The jungle seemed strangely empty like it could sense that something was out of place – which wasn't something that Azrael was used to. Animals were either oblivious to his presence or merely wary of him, keeping a respectful distance. But this was odd. There was simply no other life around him.

A split second before it happened, he sensed that it would.

He twisted his frame into a combat stance just he felt something trying to grab him from behind. Whatever it was firmly gripped his arm as he felt a sharp claw drawn across his throat right over his vocal chords. However, it failed to penetrate his dermal coating.

For a millisecond, predator and predator shared an ironic sense of mutual surprise. Azrael was shocked that it had managed to sneak up on him. And whatever attacked him was clearly surprised that he hadn't succumbed.

Since he was already in motion when the attack came, he continued to spin around, probably three times faster than a normal human. Even though not even a second could have passed, it was already gone. Azrael was fast, but not that fast. He quickly decided to stay in motion, expecting to get hit from different direction. The slight instant of hesitation cost him.

Something slammed into his back, sending him down to the ground. He tried to lift himself up and roll over, but a hand pushed him back down. It wasn't impossibly strong, but strong enough to challenge Azrael. As he tried to lift his upper torso off of the ground again, his assailant grabbed his shoulder and flipped him over.

More shock.

A slender hand with long nails pushed his chest down, and he let it happen. It was totally against his training, but he didn't know how to react to what he was seeing. A naked woman with ghostly pale skin, a slight frame, and long black hair was straddling him. She seemed to be sizing him up just as much as he was her – trying to figure out what the hell he was.

Her hands and arms became a blur, and he felt his wrists being grabbed and placed in front of his neck. Then a single, strong hand pressed down on both wrists, holding them crossed right over his throat. Her other hand moved to the area just below his belly, and he panicked as she began tearing at the dermal coating there. It was the one place that was made to come off. While that section was incredibly resilient to external pressure, it wasn't expected that something might try to remove it. After all, nothing was supposed to be able to get close enough to him to even be able to attempt doing what she was doing.

He tried pushing away from his neck with both hands and rocking his body back forth – anything to shake her hold. If she were able to able to remove the armor plate over his crotch, she would be able to eviscerate him from below, doing more than enough damage for him to bleed out. She might even be able to sever a femoral artery from the inside.

But how the hell did she know his one Achilles heel?

He tried kicking his legs violently, but she squeezed him firmly between her own thighs so he couldn't get any leverage. It was like wrestling in the Academy – strength mattered, but only to a certain degree. And given that they seemed to be equal in that department, the fact that she was faster was a problem. He was pinned and couldn't get out.

A draft of fresh air brushed against his real skin as she finally figured out how to part the coating. He felt even more air as she removed the small plate that sat over his genitals. He braced himself for impact, expecting a sharp nail to neatly open his lower abdominal cavity. He knew that he wouldn't feel pain for long because his built in medical pumps would dispense powerful pain killers within seconds of damage.

But instead of a sharp pain, he felt something else. Something he hadn't felt in a long time. Moist warmth brushed against his penis – something soft and inviting. Despite the fact that his mind knew that he was engaged in a life or death struggle, his body had a very primal reaction to what she was doing. His penis stiffened, and she maneuvered it inside of herself.

So many conflicting thoughts battled in his mind – utter confusion, a logical thought to try to fight free of the situation, and pleasure. Being an aberration of nature, he had not enjoyed the sexual company of another living creature since he had fully become a Specter. As he slid inside of her, he felt guilty pleasure. It wasn't something he should have been enjoying. Discipline and patience ruled his life – which is exactly why he found it difficult to ignore what was happening.

He was battling his own sympathetic nervous system as she undulated her hips. It wasn't helping that he had been optimized for lightning fast response times. Very quickly he realized that he wasn't going to be able to stop what was about to happen. But he knew that what was more important was what happened immediately after. It was possible that she would try to kill him then, or try to flee. Either way he had to be ready.

Even as he ejaculated inside of her, he continued to struggle, feigning continued resistance while he monitored her movements carefully. As soon as he felt a slight reduction of the pressure on his wrists, he sprang into action.

As she arched her back away from him, it was obvious that she was opting to flee. Otherwise she would have already sliced him open. She was probably expecting him to try and get out from under her, but instead he followed her up as soon as she let go of his hands. He grabbed her neck and used the element of surprise to position himself behind her.

He pinned her arms to her sides by wrapping his arms completely around her, just above the elbows. Once he had her in that position, his broader frame worked to his advantage. She tried raking his stomach with her nails, tried kicking at him, and even tried to head butt him. But his dermal coating was impenetrable. It was like a flea biting a giant – it was nothing more than an annoyance.

She seemed to settle down, but Azrael suspected that it was a trick. He let his body relax ever so slightly, sending the false message that he thought she had given up. Her head spun around, and she tried to bite him. As he tilted his head back to dodge the attack, he noticed that she had prominent fangs.

He couldn't help but wonder what she was, but brushed the thought aside. There would be plenty of time for interrogation if he could figure out how to get her back to the camp and confine her. At that particular moment, he knew that if he adjusted his grasp at all, she'd be gone in an instant.

He still felt air against his bare skin just below his belly. There wasn't going to be an opportunity to seal it back, or to recover the plate of armor that lay thirty feet away on the ground. He had a replacement at camp if he could survive long enough to make it back. He was keenly aware of his vulnerability were she to slip out of his hold.

One foot in front of the other, he began a slow advance back in the direction of the base. She writhed and kicked with every step, but he managed to keep hold.

He had already decided that he wasn't going to mention the fact that he had been raped to Command. His creators were already toying with the idea of removing genitalia altogether and installing a hormone pump so that more permanent dermal coating could be applied in that area. He didn't want to add any fuel to their line of thought.

As he crept through the jungle at what felt like a glacial pace, mental exhaustion began to set in. The constant need to anticipate her every move while holding her in an awkward position was tedious. The idea of traveling five miles that way was daunting, but there was no one other way to do it. One foot after the other.

073

The closest thing the camp had to a prison was the medical pod. It was constructed from carbon and steel, designed to hold up to two patients who required treatments in a regulated environment. The conversion to containment unit had been easy. There was even a small glass panel where one could look in, as well as a two way intercom system that could be operated from the exterior of the pod.

When Azrael had arrived in camp carrying his strange cargo, soldiers had actually emerged from the pillboxes to get a closer look. He yelled at them stand clear, and once he was able to confer with the Major, he dumped her into her makeshift cell. The satisfying thud of the lock meant that he was free again.

She had initially tried to escape by ramming the door repeatedly, then by trying to break the reinforced glass panel when the door wouldn't budge. The walls were next. But the pod held firmly, even though she managed to shift its position. Azrael had the soldiers pile crates of ammo up against the outer walls to prevent even that from happening. Now she just sat, brooding in silence. Azrael hadn't thought about it before, but she actually hadn't said a single word since he encountered her.

"No one is to attempt communication but me," Azrael told the Major who stood nearby.

"Is that really what attacked us?" Eiger asked. She had followed them to the pod in spite of Azrael's orders.

"Yes," Azrael said. "Don't let her appearance fool you." He shifted his attention back to the Major. "I want three machine gun batteries set up immediately and pointed at the door, manned twenty-four hours a day. Before dark, you need to set up batteries between each of the pillboxes facing outward. There's too many gaps in your perimeter."

"Are you expecting company?" the Major asked.

"I don't know what to expect," Azrael said truthfully. "I just know that we have something special here." He moved towards the HQ tent, intent on summoning a full detachment of Delta Force.

074

Edge of No Man's Land
Undisclosed Location
15:30

When Azrael rose in the afternoon, all was quiet. As he strode across the camp, he was pleased to see that the Major had executed his orders perfectly. A quick stop in HQ confirmed that Delta Force had been deployed and at that very moment was headed upriver. Azrael's plan was to ensure that their prisoner was well guarded overnight until a transport barge could arrive in the morning.

"How come when I request reinforcements they tell me to fuck off, but when you do it we have Delta Force here within eight hours?" the Major asked, the traces of a smile on his face. It was the most human way that anyone had addressed Azrael in a long time.

"Command generally takes me seriously," Azrael said, attempting to sound funny. He wasn't so sure that it worked.

"You speak directly to Command?"

"To the very top. I keep the General apprised as a courtesy."

The Major followed him out to the pod. When Azrael looked through the glass panel, he took a step back in surprise. The woman was still inside, just as she had been, but her belly bulged out slightly when she stood.

Impossible. As Azrael stared at her as she stared at him, he switched views to display her vitals. As expected, her body seemed to operate by a totally different set of rules. Her heart rate and temperature didn't make any sense. Azrael concluded that it was very possible that her metabolism and cellular reproduction rate also defied the rules of logic. And if that were the case, it was possible that a new life was developing in her belly at record speed.

His child.

He was speechless at first, then almost let the cat out of the bag before he realized that no one knew what had happened out in the jungle except for him. Everyone else would just assume that she was pregnant – if that were even the case. He kept telling himself that maybe she was already that way, and he had failed to notice.

"There's been no change in behavior sir," the Sergeant assigned to the guard detail reported.

"No communication?" Azrael asked.

"Not a word."

"Good," Azrael looked at all the others who crowded around out of curiosity. "Leave us," he said, and they all scattered. The Major stood behind the machine gun battery.

Azrael depressed the intercom button and spoke. "Who are you?" There was no response, but the woman inched slowly towards the door until she was inches away from Azrael through the bullet proof Plexiglas. "Who are you?" he repeated.

The woman had perfect features – not a single wrinkle on her face. Her stark white skin was as smooth as porcelain, which struck Azrael as odd considering she lived in the bush. But the most bizarre thing was her eyes. Even though daylight filtered through the glass panel, her pupils were dilated and flecks of crimson shone in her brown iris.

"Say something – anything," he said. Her thin, perfect lips didn't even part. That's when it occurred to him to turn to the Major and request a translator. He didn't really expect results given that even if she couldn't understand him, she could theoretically have at least made an effort to communicate in whatever language she did speak. Her silence indicated a blatant unwillingness to make contact.

As Azrael suspected, she was also unresponsive when two different translators tried a variety of Asiatic languages. Her expression remained indifferent the entire time. If she heard something that she recognized, her face didn't reveal it.

Azrael gave up and started checking the perimeter of the camp, making minor adjustments to the defensive positions. He hoped that all the measures wouldn't be necessary because he wasn't sure that they would be enough.

When Delta Force finally arrived in the late afternoon, it seemed like overkill considering how quiet everything had been. The black clad men and women took up positions all around the edges of the camp. At Azrael's behest, they had brought special equipment from the fleet and immediately got to work setting up a ring of motion sensors all along the inside of the tree line.

Azrael had restricted access to the pod to only himself and then made it a point to not look inside. He knew that if something was constantly watched, changes would seem more gradual and potentially go unnoticed. But shortly before dusk, he permitted himself to peer in. What he saw was definitely cause for alarm.

Her belly had grown noticeably. There was no mistaking the physical form of an expecting mother.

075

Edge of No Man's Land
Undisclosed Location
18:00

Azrael found himself watching the sunset from above the medical pod. He had opted to stand there where he could watch the entire perimeter and respond to potential breaches where needed. The dark red sky over the dense canopy was an eerie reminder of the way in which the enemy had chosen to respond to superior technology. It was remarkable how well that strategy had worked. No matter how incredible the engineering in Azrael's own body, the thing beneath his feet was even more awesome.

As he waited for darkness to fall, Azrael was finally able to ponder his strange prisoner. The foremost question on his mind was whether or not she was a creation of the enemy, and if so, he needed to know if she was controlled by them. He would have assumed that she was, but there was a problem with that supposition. The tech required to engineer such a thing would undoubtedly have to be recent. But Azrael remembered a story – really more of a myth – from the early days of the war.

Not only had there been tales of soldiers encountering strange women in the jungle, but the U.S. Government had allegedly acknowledged their existence at one point in the distant past. It seemed more like rumor though since there was nothing on the official record. It was a story often told in hushed whispers around a campfire on the edge of camp, part ghost story and part creepy conspiracy. For some reason Azrael had always found it interesting even though it was only one of many strange tales of war.

But nothing that he had heard mentioned rape. Azrael figured that this was most likely because the victims were always killed after their seed was collected. He wished that the strange woman would just talk and reveal her secrets. Besides the sheer mystery of who or what she really was, there were a slew of other questions that Azrael had for her.

He still had not decided how he was going to address the baby situation, and quite frankly it was causing him more angst than he had experienced in a very long time. If he were just a rank and file soldier, it wouldn't have been a big deal – just another trauma to add to a long list. But not only did he not want to appear weak, he was now genuinely concerned about the future of the Specter program and what natural body part they might want to do away with next. Azrael also feared that if the child had his DNA, he or she might somehow get sucked into a series of dark experiments in the name of war. Azrael was no stranger to the military labs, and it was a fate that he didn't wish on anyone, much less his own offspring.

The transport barge would be there in the morning, only a mile away at the river. What if she were still pregnant when it arrived? Or worse, what if she had already given birth?

As the sun finally disappeared behind the trees, Azrael realized that the time for reflection had passed. He had no idea what, if anything, was going to happen, but he decided to spend his energies monitoring the perimeter for any signs of approach. The alien metal of his special issue weapon felt reassuring in his hands. The extra-long barrel spun the charges into a high velocity, propelling them to penetrate almost any kind of armor plating. He had already been a damn good shot with his real eyes, but the artificial ones only elevated his sniping skills to an otherworldly state.

The motion sensors that Delta Force had installed would give everyone else the necessary edge. The moment anything set them off, a signal would be delivered to every headset indicating the location of the potential attacker. Azrael had given strict orders that as soon as an alert came, the pillboxes and batteries in that zone were to simply open fire.

They didn't have to wait long.

Once darkness had truly settled in, a red warning flashed in front of everyone's eyes. Gunfire erupted a second later, finally breaking the nervous tension that gripped the entire camp. The night was suddenly ablaze in the orange glow of muzzle flashes.

Another warning came from the other side of the camp. Either it was the same assailant trying to sidestep the first volley of death or there were more than one of them. Soon the entire perimeter was a ring of fire. Azrael spun in circles, trying to spot one of their attackers. That's when the screams started.

He watched as the occasional blur would zip away from the edge of the jungle and grab a soldier or two. Clearly stealth was not an objective as they weren't bothering to sever the vocal chords. In fact, their behavior was totally different from what Eiger had described. Instead of disappearing into trees, men and women fell to the ground in agony, gripping bloody stumps – or sometimes headless. But as soon as one of the shapes flitted into camp, Delta force stepped forward to deal with it. Or at least to fill the air with so many bullets that the attacker had no choice but to flee.

An unearthly shriek rang out – at least one bullet had found its mark. It was incredible that it took thousands of shots fired to get to that point. Azrael swung his rifle into position, ready to add to the number of hits. Up to that point he had been collecting valuable visual data that he hoped to review as soon as possible.

His superior vantage point, cybered reflexes, and enhanced vision made it a little easier for him to hit the mark. There were more screams in the night as he correctly anticipated the movements of their near to invisible enemies. He felt the pod below his feet rock slightly – his prisoner anxious to join her would be rescuers.

Through the roar of gunfire, it took the soldiers a moment to realize that they were no longer being attacked. As the last shots echoed in the darkness, a bone chilling silence descended over the camp. The surrounding jungle was nearly decimated. Gigantic trees lay in piles of splinters, and sap ran like blood.

For a full fifteen minutes everyone stood on edge, waiting for the next wave. But it never came.

076

Edge of No Man's Land
Undisclosed Location
19:10

Azrael hopped down from on top of the pod to check on his captive. She stared out of her window to the world, her expression a mix of anger and sadness. Her belly had become ridiculously large considering the amount of time that had elapsed. Azrael knew that he had to time his next move carefully or risk missing the birth.

When he turned around, everyone except for the men tasked to watch the door of the pod still faced outward as he had ordered. He activated a comm link and spoke: "I'll be back, I'm going in after them. Maintain current orders."

He ran and jumped over one of the pillboxes, sprinting into the jungle. During the attack, he had observed that most of the activity seemed to come from one particular direction. He set out that way and searched the jungle for any signs of passage. Cool blue hues filled his vision as he switched his view over to thermal. Distinct yellow spots formed a trail that lead off into the distance. He pressed a fingertip against one of them, then rolled it against his thumb. It had the texture of blood congealing in the absence of a warm body.

Following the trail was easy enough. As he sped through the jungle, he was able to start reviewing the data that he had captured. Even though it had clearly cost lives, he had spent the first moments of the assault recording video for Command. It had required special attention so that he could magnify the view and increase the frame rate of the recording so that he might actually see more than just a blur.

In one eye he followed the trail of blood and in the other reviewed the recordings. He was able to take advantage of the faster frame rate to slow the footage down and give definition to the mysterious blurs. As the first came into view, he noted that it was very similar to the prisoner. Female, pale skin, dark hair. As the recording spun around, following the sequence of attacks, he was able to confirm that there were indeed multiple attackers and that they were all female.

Which could explain why Azrael had been raped.

If these were the same strange women mentioned in the old campfire stories, then there were yet more questions to be answered. Considering the fact that Azrael had only seen them as blurs of motion with one notable exception, and considering the technology he had to use to get a clear view, he wondered how men in the mid to late nineteen hundreds could have possibly seen the creatures and lived to tell the tale. Then he remembered the whispers of conspiracy. In all probability, he just wasn't going to get anywhere because the answers to his questions were sitting in some old data-store under lock and key.

He switched off the recordings so he could focus his full attention on what lay ahead. As he drew closer to wherever they had fled to, he presumed that he would most likely be attacked unless he could remain unobserved. His goal was not capture or kill them, but to learn more about them.

He assumed a different stance, adjusted his gait, and began a series of movements that made it seem like he was gliding through the shadows instead of walking. Even though his dermal coating doubled as a cloaking device that deflected infrared light and made him look like an amorphous mass in night vision, he suspected that these women of the jungle could sense him using other methods. It forced him to proceed more slowly than he would have liked.

After a long time, he came to a natural break in the trees and found himself standing before a wide ravine. Something about the place felt incredibly old, like it might have been there at the time of the primeval jungle. Through dense foliage he could see stone columns and the remnants of what looked like a doorway. Strange symbols were carved into the rock on either side of the opening.

The same unsettling silence that pervaded the jungle right before Azrael had been attacked was present in the ravine, and he knew that he had found their home. As he continued to examine the location, he noticed plants growing in square blocks at regular intervals around the lip of the ravine. Then he spotted steel peeking through parted leaves and realized the box-shaped growths were actually abandoned pillboxes – another mystery left from a bygone era, albeit a more recent one.

Something abruptly broke the silence – something that a normal man would not have heard. The artificial ossicles in Azrael's ear picked up subtle vibrations coming from beneath the earth under the ravine. It was the sound of a baby crying. That at least explained the attack on Eiger's platoon. Azrael wanted to descend to the floor of the ravine and enter the ancient door. He wondered what he would find in their subterranean world. Would there be a platoon's worth of cadavers, or were the men still alive, kept as breeding stock?

As another newborn joined the cries of the first, Azrael tried to guess how many of the women were down there. Surely there were enough to overpower him if he dared to trespass – or even enough to overwhelm the entire handful of Specters in existence. He came to the realization that there was no elite team that would ever be able to handle the nest of creatures. He wasn't sure what role, if any, they played in the war or if they posed any threat. But he did see a neat solution to two messy problems.

He crept back into the relative safety of the surrounding jungle, then broke into a sprint all the way back to camp.

077

Edge of No Man's Land
Undisclosed Location
Dawn

The strange woman sat on the floor of the medical pod, legs spread. As Azrael watched her through the glass panel, he considered the irony of what was about to happen. He didn't have a wife, nor would he ever. Sadly, his fleeting encounter might very well be the last time he would touch a woman in that way. Among the general populace, there were surely fetishist who would love the fact that he was what he was, but to the general public, he didn't exist. And in the military he was freak. While there were female Specters, he rarely saw any others of his kind.

Yet there before him, his only child was about to be born of two abominations. He made sure that no one was around to witness it. The woman's legs were splayed open, her cervix dilated. Sweat beaded on her brow, and her breathing was quick. As the crown of a head appeared at her vulva, Azrael felt like he should want to cry. But even if the desire were there, he had no tear ducts in his mechanical eyes.

Once enough of the baby protruded, the woman grabbed it and pulled it out, severing the umbilical cord with one of her claws. A shrill wail filled the air as the child took its first breath.

It was then or never, while she was still weak from childbirth. Azrael had already given orders that no one should approach once he entered. He gripped a blanket tightly in one hand as he opened the pod with the other.

The woman glared at him with hatred as he advanced towards her. She sprung onto her feet, cradling the baby close to her body. As soon as he reached out for it, she swatted his hand away – still strong, but not as much as she had been the previous evening. He used his broad frame to back her into the corner, then pinned her as he removed the slick newborn from her grasp.

Azrael wrapped his daughter in the blanket and turned around. He didn't want to see the woman's face when he walked away. As a soldier, he had killed civilians in the name of war and even his own countrymen. But there was something about taking away a child from its mother that felt horribly wrong. He just couldn't bring himself to stare in the face of absolute loss.

He shut and locked the door behind him and never looked back. By that time, the transport would be making its way from the river along the dirt path that had been cut through the jungle. It would lift the entire pod up and take it back to the barge. There were strict instructions to not open the door under any circumstances until the pod was inside of a secured facility back in the States. Azrael had advised the presence of at least two Specters when that moment came.

He had no intention of seeing his daughter's mother before she was whisked away to what would undoubtedly be unspeakable horrors. He just kept moving towards the HQ tent carrying his only child.

078

Edge of No Man's Land
Undisclosed Location
Morning

Even though Azrael had already prepared everything, he felt compelled to sit and watch the child. She had stopped crying and stared through luminous blue eyes that bore into him. He wondered how she saw him through superhuman eyes. Holding her felt awkward, like it was a thing that he was supposed to do in his life, but never had. He had a cold feeling of detachment, yet something foreign stirred inside of him.

He saw a different life that he could have lived. Suburban home. White picket fence. A wife and two-point-five kids. There would have been an inane job and sleepless nights as he questioned the point of existence.

War had given him a purpose – one that he had never felt as a young boy in middle school. As soon as he had been whisked away to the Academy at thirteen, he had instantly felt more at home. Before Azrael's departure, his mother had settled into a reality numbing pattern of manageable alcoholism coupled with the occasional pain pill, while his father worked a corporate job and dreamed of a life he would never have.

Azrael – who had a different name at that time – was the child they were 'supposed' to have. Yet his mother had been so happy the day he left for the Academy. Azrael had never factored into his father's grand plans either. They were glad to get him out of their hair. And he was glad to go.

Azrael often thought about the fact that while civilization was supposedly a better alternative to the epic struggles of hunter-gatherers, it burdened people with too much time to do nothing. They became lost in the malaise of empty existences. Once upon a time, one needed children in order to survive. Now people wanted children as accessories. Perhaps if he had been born into a different age, Azrael would have been too busy to desire what he had become.

Not only did war give him a purpose, it had bestowed him with power that he could have never imagined. Unlike a rank and file soldier, he was a solo operative with an incredible amount of oversight. He did receive general orders, but in the thick of it, he was judge, jury, and executioner – no questions asked. That same power brought him to the unfortunate task that was before him.

He unwrapped the blanket from his daughter's form and lay her bare skin on a cold metal tabletop which elicited renewed cries. As he picked up a scalpel, he hoped that the child was not yet as resilient as her mother. He wanted a clean, quick incision – not a hack saw operation. He had been wondering about the dilution of DNA from generation to generation. If each daughter were only a half-breed, how much weaker were they from previous generations? Azrael supposed that since the women defied so many other expectations, it was wholly possible that there was no dilution.

He winced as the pitch of his daughter's crying changed when the scalpel sliced through her belly. He was just thankful that it was fast. The camp doctor could have performed the operation, but he felt a strange obligation to do it himself.

He grabbed the slender fusion bomb from the table and placed it inside of her. Just as her mother had been pregnant only hours before, the infant now bore her own gift. Only this one would bring death.

In that particular age, there was no need for hand stitching. The doctor had a machine capable of fusing skin back together, but Azrael didn't want to deal with the knowledge that others would be aware of the horrible sin that he was committing. Only Command would know what he had done, but even then he would omit that fact that the infant was his own.

He ran thread through the eye of a needle and secured it in a knot. Then he closed the open wound on his daughter's belly. The crying never ceased after that point. It was a sound that would echo in Azrael's mind for the rest of his days.

079

The Ravine

Dusk.

Blood red light spilled over the canopy and trickled down to the jungle floor. An unusual sound filled the air – a baby crying.

As soon as the sun was gone, lithe forms slipped through the stone entryway and ascended from the ravine in search of its source. Soon one of them found the child swaddled in a plain brown blanket. Even though it was pitch black, the baby could see a face that she recognized as one of her own kind. Motherly instinct trumped suspicion, and the woman rushed the bundle of joy back into their subterranean lair.

She never noticed the thin red line spreading from the baby's belly.

Azrael watched from a distant mountain top as a white dome of light spread from a single point and engulfed the surrounding terrain. The charge wasn't strong enough to reach the camp, but Azrael had ordered them to evacuate anyway.

He hoped that the explosion was sufficient to eliminate what he had found in the jungle. He also hoped that it was strong enough to erase all traces of what he had done.

He turned his back on the crater that was left behind in the wake of the explosion and wondered if he had any remorse over killing his own child. Command had done some pretty dastardly things to his brain to regulate his emotional response without the use of medications. In a way, it was like an amputated limb – or so they said. He couldn't actually feel anything, but occasionally there was a dull ache where the feeling should have been.

He wondered if his alcoholic mother or self-important father felt any remorse in his absence. He shook his head slowly, all to himself. If only they knew what he had become. When he first entered the Specter program, he had assumed they would be proud if they knew. But as he became less and less human, that thought had slowly transformed into hatred – one of the two emotions he was allowed to feel.

There had been times when he felt an overpowering desire to return home and end his parents' lives. They would have been like insects to him as he exited the night and invaded their home like a God of war. He would have crushed them and watched their steaming insides spill out over the pristine floors of their home, their false sense of reality shattered. But what would that accomplish? It was better that he was dead to them.

The war had become his father and mother. It molded him and thousands of others, if not millions. But war was a wicked parent, twisting its children into monstrosities. Or was it that war allowed them to be who they always were?

Azrael had been turned into a weapon, and in turn he used his own child as one. For that, he resolved to not have any regrets. If anything, his child had the easy way out. Azrael often wondered if he was still alive. There was no normalcy or relaxation to look forward too. Only more death.

The moon rose over the jungle, casting the same bluish light over the entire war zone. Azrael put one foot in front of the other as he marched towards his next mission.

REVENANT

OOO

An unknown time.

Cold darkness suddenly gave way to dim light. A man opened his eyes from a deep sleep and blinked slowly, not fully registering what was right in front of his face. He shivered uncontrollably and realized that he was wet and naked.

He was inside of something that enclosed him like a tomb. Bright light trickled in through a small crack at a seam in the container. He felt something attached to his left arm as he lifted it and gave a feeble push against the smooth surface that was only inches from his face. It gave a little when he pushed, but something on the outside seemed to be holding the lid shut. Condensation formed inside, occasionally dropping onto the man's face.

He had no idea where he was or who he was, but his primal survival instincts didn't let him dwell on that for too long. All he knew was the immediacy of feeling trapped. It was so cold, and he was so weak. He knew if he didn't get out soon, he never would.

Whatever was attached to his arm slapped against the side of the container when he lifted his hand again. He positioned his other hand against the inside of the lid and after a count of three pushed against it with all the force that he could muster. It still held fast, but gave a little. There was a rustling on the outside, like leaves shaking violently. He shoved again, getting the impression that a series of short thrusts would work better than a long sustained one.

After several tries, he let his arms fall onto his bare chest in exhaustion. As he tried to breathe in fresh air, he felt like there wasn't nearly enough in the enclosed space. The lid was just above his face, and the sides weren't much wider than his body. A sudden jolt of panic hit him hard. What if he couldn't get out? The space seemed to be getting smaller by the second with each unfulfilled breath.

He lifted his arms into place again and pushed. His desperation must have helped, because after three or four shoves it was like something snapped, and the lid opened up half an inch. He gasped for air as soon as he felt it rushing in, then took a moment to calm down before resuming his efforts. The extra space gave him more leverage, and soon something else snapped. The lid opened another inch, and he could see that vines were wrapped around the outside of the container. It took another couple of minutes before he was finally able to escape.

He sat up and looked around. The room was dark except for a couple of places where daylight spilled in, and the ceiling and walls were covered by thick vegetation. Dozens of containers just like his were spaced evenly throughout the room. He looked down at his naked body and shivered again. It was impossibly cold, despite the heat that he felt in the room. It was like the chill was coming from inside of him.

An IV dangled from his arm and ran back into the container. He gingerly removed the needle and tossed it to the side. When he tried to stand, he realized just how weak he really was. After a false start, he fell back into the wet container. The room spun, and a steady pounding afflicted his temples. He gripped the side and vomited onto the leaf covered floor below. There wasn't much more than yellow bile, and most of his body's efforts were wasted on dry heaves.

After a long moment of feeling like he was going to pass out, he regained his composure. He held onto the sides of the container and pushed himself back into an upright position, then swung both legs over the edge.

The dead light fixtures overhead indicated that the facility was supposed to have power – yet it didn't. All of the containers in the room looked like coffins on raised pedestals. Each had a built-in touch screen on the lid

– also dead. Some of the lids were slightly ajar, pried open by predatory vines that wound into the darkness inside.

He approached one and severed the vines that were wrapped around it – a much easier task from the outside. As soon as he opened the lid, he panicked again. Slender white bones in the perfect form of a human lay inside. Everything in him wanted to back away and let the lid shut, but something caught his eye – scratch marks on the underside of the lid.

He noticed for the first time how quiet it was in the room. There was definitely life present, but it seemed like he was the only human left. He counted forty-two of the containers in the room. Many were open, having been penetrated by one form of invasive plant life or another. He didn't bother to repeat what he had just seen.

The ones that were still closed had no obvious way of being opened. He ran his fingers along the edges, trying to find a seam that would give. Based on what he could remember, the mechanism to release the lid was controlled from the touchscreen. It was probably a safe bet that if someone were still inside, he or she was just as dead as the screen.

He began to ponder what perfect storm of circumstance had led to his miraculous survival when so many others had died. His own container must have recently been cracked open, just in time to coincide with what he supposed must have been the end of backup power.

A set of letters peeked out from behind clusters of leaves – a sign mounted on the wall. It took a moment to decipher what it said since some of the letters were hidden. Finally he made out the words "Emergency Personnel." A sinking feeling tugged at him as he looked around the room again. He wasn't sure what disaster they were supposed to avert, but the room meant to house saviors had become a mass grave. He made his way towards the only door and exited the room.

The rest of the small complex was in a similar state. At one time, perhaps it had been manned by support personnel, but those days were long past. Desks and other furniture crumbled, vestiges of some other time now lost to the hungry advances of nature.

He wished that he could remember why he was there. Or what the point of the facility had been. His body was well-muscled, and he had vague memories of some kind of training. As he went from room to room along the lone corridor, he noticed that he was walking in a strange way that wasn't intuitive. And he constantly stopped and listened, especially as he neared a new room. He couldn't help but think that he was executing a learned behavior that had been deeply ingrained.

A sign above one of the doors read "Armory." Inside, he found clothing and began to drape his cold form. Then he found boots and black plates of body armor. His hands seemed to follow some long rehearsed drill as he laced the boots up and prepared for some long forgotten purpose.

His name could have been any name, and he could have been any man. He couldn't shake the feeling that there had been many before him, executing the same carefully sequenced pattern of dress. Even though he was utterly alone, he was one of many.

He found a wicked rifle in the same room and shouldered it. Somehow he remembered how to use it – and knew that he had used it before. In another set of compartments were neatly prepared packs filled with rations, water, and basic survival gear.

As he continued down the empty hall towards what he supposed was the main entrance, he had no idea where he was going. He only knew that there was nothing but death where he stood, and that eventually the food and water would run out. He had no interest in being surrounded by his dead comrades, haunted by ghosts of the past.

The shade of the interior had masked the true heat that awaited outside. As he swung the metal door open, it hit him like a wave and sweat instantly formed on his brow – a welcome change to the ice he still felt in his bones. The sight of the jungle conjured up a vague feeling of déjà vu. But the feeling was more than that. It was like he was home.

The smells of rotting vegetation and mud filled his nostrils, and he struggled to remember. There was no direct link – only memories of memories. The only thing that he could recall from before waking was that he had been dreaming, even though he couldn't remember the actual dream – only that it was important.

He took his first step away from the facility, feeling the earth give a little beneath his weight. The sun was setting, and he knew that he didn't have much time to figure out what he intended to do. As he admired the rich red tones on the treetops, he spotted something in the distance – a lone tower. He remembered it from somewhere. At least he thought he did. It was mysterious, its purpose veiled by the past.

It seemed just as good a place to head as any. The man with no name took another step, then another, heading into an unknown world that was terribly familiar.

THE END

To see more of Britt Pitre's books and films, please visit:
www.deviantpixel.com